4/20

A CEILING MADE OF EGGSHELLS

Also by GAIL CARSON LEVINE

NOVELS
Dave at Night
Ella Enchanted
Ever
Fairest
The Lost Kingdom of Bamarre
Ogre Enchanted
Stolen Magic
A Tale of Two Castles
The Two Princesses of Bamarre
The Wish

THE PRINCESS TALES
The Fairy's Return and Other Princess Tales
The Fairy's Mistake
The Princess Test
Princess Sonora and the Long Sleep
Cinderellis and the Glass Hill
For Biddle's Sake
The Fairy's Return

PICTURE BOOKS
Betsy Red Hoodie
Betsy Who Cried Wolf!

NONFICTION
Writing Magic: Creating Stories That Fly
Writer to Writer: From Think to Ink

POETRY
Forgive Me, I Meant to Do It: False Apology Poems

A CEILING MADE OF EGGSHELLS

GAIL CARSON LEVINE

HARPER

An Imprint of HarperCollinsPublishers

Library of Congress Cataloging-in-Publication Data

Names: Levine, Gail Carson, author.
Title: A ceiling made of eggshells / Gail Carson Levine.
Description: First edition. | New York : HarperCollins, [2020] | Audience:
   Ages 8–11. | Audience: Grades 4–6. | Summary: From age seven, Loma relishes
   traveling with her beloved grandfather across fifteenth-century Spain, working to
   keep the Jews safe, but soon realizes she must also make sacrifices to help her
   people. Includes historical notes, recipe, glossary, and a link to a bibliography.
Identifiers: LCCN 2019040581 | ISBN 978-0-06-287819-9 (hardcover) |
   ISBN 978-0-06-287820-5 (library binding)
Subjects: LCSH: Jews—Persecutions—Spain—Juvenile fiction. | CYAC:
   Jews—Persecutions—Spain—Fiction. | Grandfathers—Fiction. | Family life—
   Spain—Fiction. | Spain—History—Ferdinand and Isabella, 1479–1516—Fiction.
Classification: LCC PZ7.L578345 Cei 2020 | DDC [Fic]—dc23
LC record available at https://lccn.loc.gov/2019040581

Typography by Catherine San Juan
20 21 22 23 24   PC/LSCH   10 9 8 7 6 5 4 3 2 1
❖
First Edition

To my sister, Rani, and to my cousins Joe and Lucienne

A CEILING MADE OF EGGSHELLS

1

Columbus sailed the ocean blue
in fourteen hundred and ninety two,
and in the self-same year, it's true,
Spain's king and queen expelled the Jews.

1483 CE, JEWISH YEAR 5243

My younger brother, two-year-old Haim, sat on the carpet, watching the kittens with me. I was in charge of him while Mamá, who had baby Soli with her, worked in the kitchen and bossed around our cook, Aljohar. I loved being Haim's little mamá, as my older sisters were my little mamás.

Abruptly, the biggest kitten, the one I had named Goliath, curled himself into a ball in the middle of play with the others. I wasn't alarmed. Kittens often slept suddenly.

Haim reached his hand out to Goliath, but, fearing he'd be too rough, I guided the hand to my mouth and kissed his fingers. When I had my own babies someday, I would cover their hands with my kisses, too.

Haim said, as if it were two words, "Kit-tens!"

Mamá, with the baby on her hip, came to take him to bed. She was in one of her silent bad moods, not a yelling one—it was always one or the other. Haim jumped up and raised his hand for her to clasp. They left me.

I continued to watch the kittens as I had done by the hour since they were born. Now two of them were suckling, but three were curled up, sleeping, including Goliath. None had ever missed a meal before. It was another warning, though, at seven, I was too young to realize.

Soon, Mamá came for me, too. I followed her flickering oil lamp to the courtyard balcony, which led to all the upstairs rooms, including the bedroom I shared with my older sisters Vellida and Rica. Even Haim wouldn't get lost, because the balcony made a big square, and no matter which way you went, you'd always come back to where you started. In the dimness, I couldn't make out the tapestries on the walls or the floor tiles—412 green and 412 brown, which had taken me hours to count, because I kept having to start over. I loved to count.

At intervals, Mamá burst out, "No one listens!" and

"What I put up with!" and "Why!"

Mamá's *Why* was never really a question.

In my bedroom, she said the nightly prayers with me, clipping every word, reminding me of the *pop! pop!* when grease spills on a fire.

I climbed into bed, wondering if the Almighty minded her angry prayers. I didn't want Him to punish her. Since He knew everything, He should know she was angry at everyone, not just Him and me.

When Mamá left, she didn't snuff out the pole lamp, knowing others would come soon.

I prayed, as I did every night, for forgiveness for hating my brother Yuda. I hated him secretly, in my heart, and God utterly condemned heart-hatred. Yuda's hatred for me, which was on his tongue, was a lesser offense.

His tongue was bad enough. Rather than my name— Paloma, or my nickname, Loma—he called me Unblinking Lizard, based, he said, on my way of staring. In my mind, I called him Ugly Camel Head, because of his long eyelashes, full lips, smooth tan skin, and not much chin.

To distract myself from thoughts of him, I counted by sevens while I waited for my *abuela*, my grandmother, whom we called Bela. She was soft-footed, and I strained to hear her in the corridor.

The door creaked.

I had failed again. When I was younger, I thought

she could float in air, despite her plumpness. She was the shortest in our family, her head barely topping Belo's chin. Belo was what we called our grandfather, our *abuelo*. To sit on my bed, Bela had to rise on tiptoe.

I breathed ten times before she spoke. She always paused, seeming to know I liked a moment to get used to anyone's presence.

"Shall I tell you a story, little fritter?"

"Yes, please." I slid toward the middle of the bed to make room for her.

She heaved up her legs, wriggled to me, and lifted her arm to let me snuggle. "This story is—"

"—about a girl named Paloma who lived a long time ago in the kingdom of Naples." I inhaled Bela's cinnamon-and-rose perfume.

"How do you know?" she said with mock surprise.

I giggled. All her tales started the same way. Bela's sister lived in Naples, and every story took place there.

"Was she Jewish?" I said, though I knew.

"Of course she was. She—"

The door creaked again, and Belo filled the doorway— or seemed to fill it. He always appeared larger than he was.

Bela slipped off the bed, and they met halfway between the bed and the door.

I stood, too, to show respect—and, with my feet planted, I felt less afraid.

They were hugging! He had just returned from a trip somewhere. I knew only that he'd had an audience with the king and queen. He and Bela lived with us—or we lived with them, because he owned our house. He kissed the top of her head.

Then he loomed over me, his smile for Bela lingering.

No one in our family was tall, but he seemed to be and seemed heavyset though he was slender. The deception lay in his pulled-back shoulders and in the flow of his robe, which he let hang open, revealing his silk doublet and heavy gold chain necklace. His beard, which he kept combed and trimmed to two inches below his chin, was brown and gray. He was only fifty-one, though he seemed ancient. His wisdom was renowned. Even I knew he'd written two biblical commentaries and three books of philosophy.

"What did you learn today, Loma?"

I hadn't learned anything! "The kittens sleep a lot." But I'd known that since the day after they were born.

He frowned. "What else?"

My stomach knotted.

"Don't grill her, Joseph!"

They were arguing! I had created discord, which I hated.

But Belo's face relaxed. "I'll be in my study, Esther. Come soon." He patted my shoulder and left.

Esther was Bela's name, after the queen in the Bible.

She and I returned to our spots on the bed.

"He didn't mean to frighten you, fritter." She stroked my forehead. "Your abuelo is a great thinker who doesn't always think. He frightened your papá, too, when he was your age."

This astonished me.

She added, "He'll be nicer when he knows you better."

He'd known me my whole life!

"You're still a new arrival, and you're different every day. You're growing almost as fast as the kittens"—she tapped my scalp—"and you're changing in here." She returned to stroking. "Even I'm not sure who my fritter will be tomorrow."

I moved away from her hand and sat up. "Will Vellida's husband be nice?" My older sister was eleven. Soon Papá would find a husband for her. My oldest sister, Ledicia, who was eighteen, had been married for years and had two children: my niece, Beatriz, and my nephew, baby Todros.

"What does *nice* mean, fritter?"

Not like Yuda. "Kind."

"Kind, certainly. And *your* husband will be kind and gentle. God willing, I'll see to that."

I settled against her again. "Will we have a good life?"

"You'll have many happy, healthy children. Fritter, you'll be a mother beyond compare."

That's what I wanted most: to be a mother. Yes, beyond compare.

"I see that in you. You'll live in a house like this one, and when you're my age, you'll tell your own fritters stories every night."

"Will we be safe?"

"My sweet plum, Jews have lived in Spain for over a thousand years. We're in Spain, and Spain is in us. Sometimes the gentiles behave badly. We wait, and times get better." She chucked my chin affectionately. "Are you ready for the story?"

I said I was.

"King Solomon, who was visiting Naples, wanted to marry the beautiful Paloma, but she would consent only if he first made her a ceiling of eggshells . . ."

I laughed at the silliness, imagining egg white dripping on King Solomon. My eyes closed themselves. How many eggs would be needed to make a ceiling? I began counting and slipped into sleep.

But I woke briefly when Bela moved on the bed as she prepared to leave. "Did she get her ceiling, Bela? Was there a happy ending?"

"The eggshell ceiling was painted in many colors. It was as beautiful and surprising"—she shook her head, smiling—"and even as improbable as we Jews are in Spain.

The ceiling never fell down. After her troubles, that long-ago Paloma had such a good life—many healthy children, who were her reward for doing her best."

Satisfied, I slept. As usual, I neither heard nor felt Vellida and Rica slide in next to me.

The next morning, when I entered the dining room with my sisters, there were no kittens. The benches that had penned them in were stacked in the corner.

I arrived at the conclusion I wanted: The kittens had grown too big to be confined. They were now roaming free, hunting rats.

I went to the trestle table, on which rested barley bread and farmer cheese. When I'd put a big slice of bread and an even bigger chunk of cheese into a pewter bowl, I joined my brother Samuel, who sat on a bench. He moved to make room for me, although there already was room. Pleased, I smiled at him as I sat. He didn't smile back.

Yuda came in and did smile at me. My breath became shallow. A smile from him didn't bode well. After he cut his own bread and cheese, he ambled over.

"Lizard, I threw a *reale* on the kittens of blessed memory."

A reale was a silver coin, and "blessed memory" was what you said about the dead, but I didn't let the words sink in. "Why would you throw anything at them?

Did you hurt them?"

Samuel's hand found mine.

"They are past pain," Yuda said piously.

Meaning broke on me. A lump rose in my throat. I might have created discord then—even kicked him—but fear of him stopped me. My sin of heart-hatred grew.

2

Samuel had let my hand go, but I seized his and squeezed. I held the tears in, and, I believe, kept my face serene. That night, however, I sobbed in Bela's arms.

"They were good kittens," she said.

I hiccupped. "I wish they could have lived long enough to kill a rat. Just one." I wasn't greedy on their behalf.

She kissed my forehead. "Their mother lived. She'll have other kittens."

She wouldn't have another Goliath, not exactly.

After Bela left, I was still awake. A few weeks earlier, an old woman in the *aljama*—our Jewish community in Alcalá de Henares, where we lived—had died. Belo had talked at dinner about what happens to dead people. He said no one knew for sure, except that they were with God, but that, according to legend, they couldn't bend their elbows and so couldn't feed themselves. If they were good, they fed each other. If they were bad, they starved.

Smiling, I pictured the kittens feeding each other.

The next morning, I woke up shivering under my sheet, with what seemed like spikes drilling into my skull. The bed was empty. My sisters had risen before me, which had never happened before.

Mamá came in, carrying blankets, which she tucked around me. "Now God does this to me. Your abuela will bring you broth." She left, saying over her shoulder, "Your worthless brother is sick, too."

She meant Yuda, who got the worst of her, more than I did, more than any of us.

Bela came in. "Drink, little fritter." She propped me up in bed.

The broth had no flavor. I drank anyway, hoping to please her and make her look less stern.

"Good. Lift your arm for me, please."

I did, even though it hurt. She breathed in sharply.

"What?" I said.

"A pimple. That's all." She removed her pendant and hung its velvet string around my neck.

I'd never seen her without the pendant, a triangle made

of red stone set in silver, which now rested on my belly. Etched into the stone were four Hebrew letters that stood for God. She always wore another necklace, too—the Cantala family dressed well. Today, her other necklace was a string of pearls from which hung a sapphire set in a gold circle.

"The amulet gives the evil eye something to look at other than you." She lay next to me, curling herself around me and spreading her arm across my chest. "Warm up, fritter. Pretend you're in a frying pan, gently simmering, gently simmering, gently simmering." The repetition took on the cadence of a prayer.

The frying pan failed to warm me. I passed into delirium.

It never snowed where we lived, but in my fevered dream, I stood in a shallow cave while a blizzard raged outside. At my feet, a weak fire wavered and kept me from freezing. Against the cave wall the kittens sat on their haunches and waved their front legs.

Brush grew at the mouth of the cave. I knew what I had to do and hurried back and forth, carrying twigs to feed the fire, certain that if it died I would, too. When I threw on the wood, I was aware of my elbows bending and straightening, meaning I still lived.

On my tenth trip, I glimpsed a figure beyond the cave—

Belo!

Snow mounded on his round cap and collected on his shoulders. He stood still, like a boulder, with only his eyes moving, searching. When they found me, they glared. I backed away.

But I didn't want to die! So, despite my fear, I returned to the fire and continued my task. Eleven trips, twelve. Counting tied me to life, too.

A flame ignited in my chest, which I fed from glowing embers at the edge of the fire. Gradually, I warmed. And slept.

Fatima, our maid of all work, stood over our bed, bearing a tray.

"You're awake?" she asked.

I was staring at her. Didn't that mean I was awake? I swallowed. "Where's Bela?" Probably busy. I tried to sit up but collapsed back. Bela's amulet, which had been nestling in the hollow of my throat, slid lower on my chest.

Fatima's eyes swam, as if she were close to tears. "Are you hungry?"

I discovered that I was and nodded.

She put the tray next to me on the bed and came around to the other side, where she raised me up, turned my pillow to vertical, and leaned it and me against the headboard.

She touched my cheek. "I'll say you're awake."

"You'll tell Bela?"

But she exited without answering, leaving the door open behind her.

My stomach grumbled. I turned to the tray, on which rested a shallow pewter bowl containing lentils, three hard-boiled eggs, and olives. We ate round food after someone died, but we also ate these foods when no one had died, so I didn't think of death.

I poked the lentils with my fork and estimated forty-two. Then I counted them. Forty-two.

They were half burned, and I wondered why, since Aljohar was the best cook in the *judería*, the neighborhood where we Jews had to live. Bitter as the lentils were, I ate them all and everything else. I could have eaten as much again. With food in me, I was able to lean away from the pillow. I decided not to wait for someone to come and slid off the bed—

—onto the floor, because my legs wouldn't support me. Though I tried to use the bed hangings to pull myself back up, I was too weak. I didn't call out. No troubling anyone. No discord.

I heard birdsong from the myrtle bush outside our window and smelled its flowers. How long had I slept? Had Don Israel, the physician, been called for me? Would Yuda punish me for getting special attention?

The door opened, and Belo stood on the threshold. His eyes were always intent, but now they bored into me. What had I done? His beard was uncombed and his robe, a faded green one, had been torn on the right side of his chest. We Jews ripped our clothing when someone close to us died, to express our sadness. Was he mourning the kittens?

I didn't ask. I couldn't question Belo.

He shuffled to me like an old man, though he usually walked briskly. To my astonishment, he joined me on the floor, put an arm around my shoulders, and pulled me close. Ordinarily, he smelled of the almond oil Bela gave him for his beard, but now he smelled sour.

"Don Israel said no one could be as sick as you were and live." He let go of my shoulders and cupped my cheeks in both his hands, forcing me to meet his eyes. "I watched you. You hardened your face, as if you had work to do. Your hands and feet never stopped moving. Do you remember?"

I nodded, hoping I wouldn't have to speak.

"What do you remember?"

I swallowed and told him about my dream. "I think I went back and forth to get twigs twenty-three times."

"Ah. That's what your hands and feet were doing. You were stubborn." He kissed the top of my head. "Stubbornness in a Jew is a virtue. A necessity." He let go of me, then tipped up my chin. "Your bela once said that she was just like you when she was your age."

Really? That gave me the courage to say, "You were in my dream."

"No wonder, since I was with you often. I sat with everyone."

Who else was sick? But I didn't ask, protecting myself. Instead, I said, "Thank you for mourning for the kittens." It sounded silly, thanking someone for mourning.

"What kittens?"

It was rude not to answer, especially to Belo, but I couldn't. My mind had stopped.

Belo didn't speak, either. I heard the birds in the myrtle again.

"Oh. Kittens." A strangled sound came from him. A moment later he was sobbing, his shoulders shaking.

I patted his hand. "Why are you sad, Belo?" I wished Bela would come in. She'd comfort him for being sad and me for being frightened by his grief.

Ledicia, my oldest sister, opened the door a crack and slipped in. She wasn't weeping, but her eyes were red. I started to cry, though I wasn't sure why. She knelt in front of me and Belo.

"Sh . . . sh . . ." Ledicia thought I knew about all the deaths. She stroked my arms. "Bela of blessed—"

"Hush," Belo said.

But she'd said enough. Sobs shook me.

3

The plague had killed my next oldest sister, Rica; my brother Haim, whose fists I'd kissed while we watched the kittens; Soli, the baby; and Bela. Both Papá and Belo were untouched, because they'd survived an earlier outbreak, and no one could suffer it twice. Mamá, Yuda, Vellida, Samuel, and I lived through it and would now be safe from it, too.

The capricious plague, which hopped from certain houses to others, had skipped Ledicia's home. She, her husband, and my niece and nephew were never sick at all.

Of our household, a maid of all work and one of our menservants died. Aljohar, our cook, survived.

I'd been told that death would last until the end of days, but, even so, I kept expecting to hear Haim's chortle and to see him charge into my bedroom. I listened constantly for baby Soli's wail or her happy cry, when she seemed bent on showing how much noise she could make. At night, I lay awake, waiting for Rica to thrash about and throw an arm across my chest in sleep as she often used to. Vellida was a quiet sleeper. I was glad to have her next to me, but two seemed almost as lonesome as one.

The funerals took place while I was still delirious. Now, I had to stay in bed for two days. The plague had exhausted me, but it wasn't only that. All of me felt heavy.

I often had company. My family came, except for Yuda, who stayed away, perhaps because he didn't want to be cruel and didn't know how to be anything else.

They meant well; probably even Mamá did. I heard her before she came in, often yelling at Yuda, because she always blamed someone for whatever trouble befell her, and he was the one to get the brunt of it.

In my room, she sat on the green velvet settle across from the bed. A settle was a bench with arms and a back. This one was hinged between the back and the seat, and I used to open and close it and make creaking noises, which had delighted Haim.

She sat quietly, except when she exploded with "Jupiter and Mars! Gemini!" and then fell silent again. She wasn't weeping, but her eyes were red. After a few minutes, she kissed my forehead, pressing harder than I liked, and left.

Papá came frequently, though I wished he'd stay away. Usually, I loved to be with him, because he was full of good humor. But now, he just sat on the bed with me, stroked my arm, and dripped tears.

Best were my sisters and my brother Samuel, because, even though I was now the youngest, our losses were identical: grandmother, sisters, brother. They talked about who had come to pay their respects, what Belo or Papá or Mamá had said, what Yuda was doing with himself—and I listened, absorbed by their words and feeling a little less sad.

My most frequent visitor was Belo, who always left when anyone else arrived. I imagined he came because of what he'd told me, that Bela thought I was like her. Gradually, I became less afraid of him.

Sometimes he sat on the settle, never on the bed; sometimes he stood and looked at the street through my window. Our house faced north, which was supposed to discourage the plague from entering, though the protection had failed this time.

Often, Belo prayed or just talked to God, and when he talked, he praised Bela, telling the Almighty what a good wife and mother she'd been and how beautiful she was. "She never stopped being beautiful. Age didn't tarnish her."

That comforted me, even though she had looked old to me. I'd loved her face: the soft pouches under her eyes, her round cheeks, the wrinkles above her eyebrows.

Once, Belo said, "She put herself aside for me, knowing that the Jews need me. Who will do that now?"

She'd put herself aside for me, too, but I didn't tell him or anyone else. It was my terrible secret. If Bela hadn't given me her pendant, the evil eye would have seen me and not her. I would have been stubborn without its protection, but she had needed it.

Or she might have given it to Soli or Haim or Rica, and they would have lived. Someone's death was my fault.

I'd taken the pendant off and pushed it under my pillow. As soon as I was strong enough to get out of bed and walk across the room, I hid it. Ferns grew in urns under the windows. I buried the pendant deep in the dirt around the biggest one.

An hour later, I dug it out again. I may have caused Bela's death, and now I was doubly guilty for getting her gift dirty. I wiped as much of the soil as I could off the velvet and put it back on, hiding it under the loose neck of my shift. The amulet came down almost to my belly button.

On the third day after Bela's funeral, I was allowed to leave the bedroom. Jews sit shiva after a death, which means we mourn at home for a week. Our house was worse hit than most, and Belo and Papá were prominent in the aljama and beyond, so we had a steady stream of visitors.

I joined the rest of the family in the dining room, where people stood, or sat on benches or settles or in one of our two armchairs or on pillows on the floor. I stood in the doorway and watched. Through the open windows I heard the *clip-clop* of hooves, and the rumble of iron wagon wheels.

Servants had put platters and tureens of food—bread, goat stew, lettuce-and-radish salad, and stuffed eggplant—out on the long trestle table covered with embroidered linen. Mealtimes weren't observed during shiva. We ate whenever we were hungry.

Along the wall between the archway to the stairs and one of the two windows that overlooked the street was a dark wood cabinet wonderfully carved with flowers, leaves, and berries. The cabinet stood on long legs that rested on sculpted lion's feet with curling toes. When I was in a happy mood, I imagined the feet dancing in place.

Yuda leaned against this cabinet, spearing stew meat from his bowl with a knife. Bowl to mouth; bowl to mouth, with never a pause. Glutton!

But he had loved Bela, too. She was the only one he never smirked at.

A knot of men stood in the middle of the room, reciting the morning prayers. Samuel was in front of Papá. Belo's deep intonations rose from the center of the knot.

No one noticed me. Bela would have. Haim would have come running. Rica, for all I loved her and she loved me, probably wouldn't have.

Mamá stood at the other window, looking out at the street, her bony shoulders raised, her hands making fists at her side. Vellida sat on a bench near the trestle table, balancing a bowl on her lap. I put a slice of bread and a helping of goat stew in a bowl and ate near her, standing up. Vellida reached out to squeeze my wrist, since both my hands were occupied.

When prayers ended, Samuel, whose nose was red from crying, sat on a bench against the wall across from the table. I joined him. Of all my family, he and Papá reminded me most of Bela. After a minute of sitting in silence, Samuel put his arm around my shoulder, and we leaned into each other. The room was warm from the heat of August and from the crowd, but we didn't move apart. I heard his breath and synchronized mine to go along.

Ledicia and her husband arrived with their two little ones. As soon as the greetings were over, two-year-old Beatriz made towers of the wooden blocks her mamá spilled from a sack for her. When her tower collapsed, she wailed. I hurried to help her start building again, which quieted her.

Ledicia patted my shoulder. "Thank you."

Baby Todros, at eight months, crawled everywhere and

put every small thing in his mouth. I trailed after him, extracting one of Samuel's marbles and the sole of a shoe that must have come from one of our visitors. Once, I caught him before he slammed into the pole lantern and brought glass and brass crashing down on us.

I picked him up.

He crowed, "Lolo," his baby name for me.

Tired from my illness, I set him down and resumed following him.

After an hour or so, Ledicia crouched and scooped him up. "Loma, do you mind watching him again when I come back?"

"I like it."

"What a good mamá you'll be, God willing."

I'll be perfect, I thought.

When she returned, I resumed my vigilance, confining him to the dining room, although I could have followed him all over the house. But I wanted to stay. Bad things seemed to happen when I wasn't watching out. And I was wearing the amulet, which might protect the people near me.

Early in the afternoon, several Christians stopped by, men and their wives who had business with our family. Some, I knew, had once been Jews themselves.

When they left, Belo asked Don Ziza, the goldsmith, "How is it with the gentiles?"

"More dead than we have, may they all rest in peace."
Don Ziza had Christian customers and often visited them
in their houses, as Belo and Papá did, too, when our family
wasn't grieving.

"Woe!" Mamá cried, at that news or out of her own
sorrow.

When evening came, Ledicia and her husband left with
Beatriz and Todros. Unless the grown-ups forgot about
me, someone would soon put me to bed, where I didn't
want to go.

Maybe I could help them forget by becoming less visi-
ble. I scooted under the cabinet and sat there, cross-legged,
hunched to keep from bumping my head. People continued
to come, stay awhile, and leave. Samuel was sent to bed. He
left, his head turned my way, probably envious.

If Samuel had been aware of me, Yuda had to be, too,
and he'd give me away as soon as he was sent to bed. My
time in hiding was limited unless I could find a better
place. The tablecloths over the trestle table, which hung
almost to the floor, would hide me completely, but how
would I get there without Yuda seeing?

I watched him, hoping something would capture his
attention, but he just continued to look bored, sitting
between Papá and Mamá on the bench.

Then a distraction came: shouts from the street and
pounding feet on the cobblestones.

Belo said, "Stay here, everyone. I'll go." He ran down the stairs.

I had to go, too. I reasoned that I had to be nearby if my pendant was going to protect him.

Mamá began a wail, which was cut off, probably by Papá. I slipped out of the room after Belo.

At the bottom of the stairs, he flung open the door. I crept almost all the way down. Outside, torchlight flickered on the brick walls across the street and haloed Belo's blocky shape.

People—Christians!—shouted, "Hellfire or eternal life!" Most of the voices belonged to men, but a few higher-pitched notes mixed in.

Someone cried, "Death to the Jews who poisoned the wells!" This sounded like a chant and was picked up by other voices.

Belo didn't move. I pulled Bela's pendant out from under my gown so the evil eye would see it and not him or me.

"Here!" a man yelled.

The mob came to a noisy stop. A friar faced Belo, his features obscured by his hood. Only his jutting, clean-shaven chin caught the torchlight.

For a moment, neither man spoke. Then Belo asked, "Do you believe it wise to murder me and my family?"

I gripped Bela's velvet string so hard my hand hurt.

"Not murder, Don Joseph. Salvation! We'd rather save you."

"But if not . . ." Belo's voice was dry and calm in all the uproar. "We'll never convert. Do you think you'll be honored for my death?"

"God will reward me!" But he hesitated, then cried to the throng, "Follow me!" and ran down the street.

Belo would see me when he turned!

But he didn't move. I saw Yuda and Samuel's teacher, Señor Osua, and one of the aljama's butchers pulled along with the mob. The teacher's mouth was open in a scream that was lost in the clamor.

Several minutes went by for the crowd to pass, three or four abreast through the narrow street, eighty-six people, according to my rough count. When they'd all gone, Belo ran the other way.

If he got too far away, the evil eye would see him! I followed.

4

I hoped that the noise of the receding mob would cover the slap of my sandals. Bela's amulet swung annoyingly from side to side with my steps.

Belo was fast! His shape diminished ahead, but, luckily, the street was straight and the night bright. I counted steps as I ran. My breath came in gasps, and my legs burned. Illness had weakened me. I sweated in the warm night air.

The houses looked taller in the dark, the slice of sky narrower. I wasn't often in the street, except on holidays and celebrations. Jewish girls spent their days at home.

Someone passed Belo, coming my way. I moved closer to the houses and kept running, hoping he'd go by.

But the someone—a man—stopped. "What's this?" His arm snaked out and pulled me in. He crouched, holding my shoulders. His breath smelled of wine and something else—pork, I supposed. I'd smelled the same scent on the breath of a few of our Christian guests.

"A little Jewess. What's your name, girl?"

I couldn't speak. My heart thudded against my ribs.

Belo was getting away from the amulet's protection.

He softened his voice. "I won't hurt you."

I calmed a little. "Loma."

He picked me up and tucked me under his arm. My terror rose again. I began a wail, which he muffled with his free hand. He started walking after Belo, much too slowly to catch up to him.

I wriggled and kicked, but his gait didn't change, and he didn't drop me. Out of habit, despite my fright, I counted his steps.

I recited the Shema in my mind: Hear, O Israel. The Lord is our God; the Lord is One.

My captor passed through the gate of the judería, which the mob had left open, and turned right. Which way had Belo gone?

The man turned again, and again. My mind ran on three tracks: counting steps, memorizing turns, and repeating the Shema.

No. Four tracks, the fourth a channel of terror.

After several minutes, he stopped at a door, just two wide boards, not carved or set with iron bands and studs like ours. He lifted the latch and pushed. "María! Light a lantern!" He carried me up a narrow flight of eighteen wooden steps.

As we rose, a glow grew above us. In a moment, we entered a low-ceilinged room, where an oil lamp flared on a low table. I tried not to gag at the smell of rancid fat. A woman stood in her shift in the middle of the room.

Her gaze flicked from her husband to me. "What's this?"

He set me down.

Sobbing, I started to run, but he grabbed me—not trying to hurt me—and held me by my shoulders. "I found her running in the judería. We can save her and raise her. We'll take her to the church at dawn."

The church! Only Christians went inside the church.

Raise me? Keep me?

My sobs threatened to choke me.

"It would be a blessing for her." The woman took my hand. "Come here, child."

She drew me close to the lantern. "Look, Mateo!" She fingered my sleeve. "Silk."

To me, she said, "Where's your badge?"

Jews had to wear a red badge on their right shoulder, but I'd never had to, and no one in our family wore one. I didn't know why we didn't, so I was silent.

"She's rich," María said. "We can't keep her. What's

this?" She raised Bela's amulet to the light. "Silver, and the stone must be worth something, too."

Though I fought her, she lifted the ribbon over my head, then moved on to my hands and pulled off my two silver rings and one gold.

"Leave her in the streets but not near us. It's up to God what happens to her."

Señor Mateo didn't argue. Outside, I kept track of steps and turns again. After perhaps ten minutes, he set me down on a street that looked just like his—winding, punctuated by simple doors.

He patted my cheek. "I would have saved you from hell." He hurried back down the street.

Weeping, I retraced his steps. I had to go all the way to his street to know how to get home.

How many of my steps would equal one of his? I made mine big but decided that even my longest steps were shorter than his, so I adjusted my counting.

Belo would be furious that I'd lost the rings and Bela's amulet—especially the amulet.

I missed the pendant's protection, which had kept me alive and saved me from being permanently stolen and having to enter a church. Now, I was at risk with every step. Would a different Christian door open? Would someone else snatch me, and would this person decide I could be kept?

When I reached the judería at last, the gate was locked. I sat on the cobblestones in front of it, knees to my chest, drawn up as small as I could be. The night was quiet. Whatever had happened with the mob seemed to have ended.

I fell asleep and woke when the gate groaned open, rolling me on my back. It was still night.

"Loma!" Papá scooped me up in his arms.

Belo was with him, so he was safe. Relief set off my tears as I was borne along, sobbing into Papá's chest.

When we got home, candles and oil lamps were bright in every room, and the whole family was assembled in the living room.

Papá set me down. "She's all right, Violanta." Violanta was Mamá's name.

She whirled on Yuda, who stood next to Ledicia. "God will punish you for doing this to me."

His face reddened. "I'm sorry, Mamá, Papá, Belo. Please forgive me, Loma."

"I forgive you." If he'd gotten in trouble because of me, I was in danger.

"Good." Papá picked me up again. "That's settled."

But it wasn't, because Mamá added, "A bad child is a viper in the nest."

Silence followed this until Vellida asked, "Where did you go, Loma?"

I didn't want to say in front of everyone, and now it seemed silly to tell them I'd left to protect Belo. And I'd lost Bela's pendant. My tears started again.

Papá said, "We'll sort it out in the morning." He carried me to bed. For once, I had the same bedtime as Vellida, who followed us down the corridor.

When he left, she sat up. "Yuda will take his revenge on you."

I said, "What did he do?"

"They didn't realize you were gone until I went to bed and you weren't there. They looked all over the house." She giggled. "Even in places that were too small for a cat!"

I laughed, too, imagining my head sticking out of a pitcher. This was nice, the two of us talking at night, as if I were Vellida's age, as if I were important. I watched her black shape against the lighter window behind her.

"When Belo came back," Vellida said, "Papá told him you were missing, and Yuda said he'd seen you follow him out. I could tell he expected them to thank him, but they were furious that he didn't say anything right away. Even Papá was angry."

Yuda always hugged his secrets close and waited for the most dramatic moment to reveal them. This time, he'd gotten it wrong.

"Where did you go?"

I wanted to tell her, but I would have had to reveal that

I had Bela's amulet, so I didn't answer.

"Stupid baby! I knew you wouldn't tell." She dropped down with a thud.

I dreaded the interrogation that would come in the morning, but Yuda's vengeance arrived first.

5

Yuda waved me to the bench where he sat with his breakfast. I went because I had to, or he'd make my punishment worse. No one had come yet to sit shiva with us.

"The stars made Bela die, Lizard."

Ugly Camel Head, she died because I had the amulet.

"I remember when you were born."

He'd been five.

"Papá and Mamá had your chart done."

My horoscope. They'd had charts made for all of us, including the girls, but they never told us what the stars predicted.

"Mamá was angry when they came home."

As always.

"Do you want to know what she said?"

"No." But I did.

"She told Bela the stars predicted you wouldn't have children. I heard her. She said, 'Cursed! Just a baby, and Paloma is cursed.'"

I wouldn't cry. "You're lying." Bela said I'd have many children.

"Ask Mamá or Papá."

I'd never caught Yuda in a lie. He sought out terrible truths and squirreled them away. He'd held this one for seven years.

I wanted a husband and children more than anything, just as Vellida did. Samuel wanted a wife and children most. Family was paramount. Because of Mamá's bad example, a happy future family was everything to me.

As soon as I'd eaten my breakfast, swallowing tears with my bread and cheese, Fatima came for me and delivered me to Belo's study.

My heart galloped. Belo sat in his folding leather armchair, facing away from his desk, which was piled with books. His elbows rested on the chair's arms; his hands supported his chin, making a sharp triangle above which he peered at me.

Papá and Mamá stood next to him, on the other side of the desk from the door. Fatima left.

Papá came to me and crouched to my level. "Little bug, we've wondered where you went when we couldn't find you."

A corner of me was confused by being called an insect. I didn't answer.

Mamá broke out. "We spent hours looking for you!"

Papá interpreted. "Your mamá was very worried."

Belo said, "Loma, Señor Rodrigo needs to know what happened, so he can protect you."

The chief constable of the *hermandad*—the police! A Christian! I started to cry.

"She won't tell us anything." Mamá circled around me and stalked out of the room.

I sniffled. No one spoke.

After a few moments, Papá took my hand and led me out, too. I hoped that was the end of it, but he went downstairs with me to our courtyard and lifted me onto a wooden bench, though I could have sat on it without aid. A decorative nailhead pressed into my thigh.

A parrot squawked in the myrtle bush. The parrot is Mamá, I thought. More melodious birds lilted in the lemon tree. Both bush and tree grew out of big stone tubs.

Papá sat next to me. "When I was your age, my belo fell off a ladder. I was afraid he'd die, so I hid. As long as I didn't know, I reasoned he could still be alive." He grinned. "I hid really well."

"Where?"

"You know the chest in Mamá's and my bedroom? In there!" He sounded triumphant. "It was your belo's and bela's before your bela gave it to me. Nobody looked in it, because it was kept full of linens, which I artfully stowed elsewhere."

"Had your belo died?"

"No. He broke his ankle, which I learned a day later when I came out."

A whole day!

"I would have stayed longer if I hadn't been hungry. Your belo snores. I counted eighty-five snores before I fell asleep."

"I do that, too," I said.

"Do what?"

"Count."

"Ah." Papá proved his cleverness with his next question. "Did you count anything last night when you were outside?"

"Steps."

"In a staircase?"

I shook my head.

"Footsteps, little bug?"

I gathered my courage for a bit of discord. "Loma."

Papá frowned. "Yes, I asked you, Loma."

"A bug can't talk."

"You're right. Footsteps, Loma?"

"Yes."

He kneeled in front of me. "Li— Loma, please tell me about last night. No one will be angry."

Belo would be.

"Not even Belo. I'll talk to him. Tell me your adventure."

Adventure was a good word. I began. He returned to the bench. I watched his face to make sure he wasn't angry. He didn't seem to be until I mentioned the Christian man, and I knew he wasn't mad at me. When I said the man wanted to take me to the church, I feared he was going to explode.

At the part when Señora María said they couldn't keep me, he said, "At least someone could think."

I started crying again, and finally the worst came out: that they'd taken the amulet, that I shouldn't have had it in the first place, that Bela would still be alive if she'd kept it. Or Haim or Soli or Rica, if she'd given it to one of them.

Papá lifted me onto his lap and murmured over and over into my hair, "Not your fault. You aren't to blame." He held me until I'd cried myself out.

"Better?" He wiped away his own tears.

I nodded.

"Loma, I'll never stop missing my mamá, but the amulet didn't save you. It doesn't have that power. Your abuelo says it was your stubbornness that made you get well." He put me back on the bench. "I have one more question: How did you find your way back to the judería?"

I told him about counting steps and keeping track of turns. "I knew my steps weren't as big as Señor Mateo's even though I made mine as long as I could." I wondered why Papá's eyebrows were climbing up his forehead. "I decided three of my steps made two of his."

"Do you like numbers, little— one?"

I smiled. "I love them." I paused. "Papá, last night, why were Christians running down the street? Why were they angry?"

"They think we poison their wells and that's why they get the plague worse than we do."

"Why *do* they?"

Papá shrugged. "We're not even sure they do. Who counts?"

I would count!

He went on. "The Almighty may protect us, or the air may be better in our juderías."

"Did the Christians hurt anyone? Are Señor Osua and the butcher all right?"

"They are. Just a few bruises. Your abuelo ran to the hermandad, and the constables came before any real harm was done."

"Why did they help the Jews?"

"Your abuelo and I donate to the hermandad, so they like us and protect the judería."

Oh.

Papá added, "And the king and queen don't want anything bad to happen to us."

That was good, and surprising. "Does the amulet protect anyone, really?"

"I don't think so, but your bela believed in its power. She could list a hundred disasters it had averted, which may not have happened anyway."

I had to think about that.

"Would you be able to show me the house of Señor Mateo and Señora María?"

"Yes." I took a deep breath. "What would have happened if they took me to church?"

He hesitated. "A priest would have baptized you and made you a Christian. Once a Christian, a Christian forever, even if you were forced."

A peep of fear erupted out of me.

He put his arm around my shoulder. "This is a lesson for you: You're safer at home. Don't run away again, if you please."

Safer but not safe, since the mob had come to our door. Jews weren't safe anywhere. A ceiling made of eggshells could fall down, even if it hadn't so far.

6

After the noon meal, I led Papá and Belo to Señor Mateo's house. I worried that the señor would hurt us, but he just stared when he opened the door.

"Señor Mateo?" Belo's voice sounded like velvet. He opened his hands, palms up.

My kidnapper nodded.

Belo waved us away, so we waited across the street while he spoke to Señor Mateo. After a minute or two, Belo opened the purse on his belt and took out some coins. Señor Mateo disappeared back into his house but returned quickly with Bela's amulet and my rings.

Belo gave me the rings but not the amulet. "I'll keep it until you're older."

I decided Papá was wrong. It did have power, or Belo would have let me have it.

On the day after we finished sitting shiva, Mamá let me help in the kitchen, an unexpected kindness.

I followed her, hurrying to keep up, because she was always in a rush. We flew down the fourteen wooden steps to the vestibule and then behind the stairs to the door to the courtyard. Thirty-one of my quicksteps took us to the kitchen, which was behind the house.

Inside, Vellida sat on a stool, slicing onions, with a tear hesitating on the tip of her chin. Two eggplants and a bunch of parsley lay on the worktable beyond her cutting board. Aljohar, on another stool perhaps four paces away, was mashing garlic and basil, according to my nose. Both of them smiled at me.

"Teach her!" Mamá told Vellida, and left.

My sister fetched another stool from the pair under one of the two windows that looked out on our back garden. She set it down between her stool and Aljohar's, right up against her own. "Sit."

We both did.

She took my right hand in hers and folded my fingers around the handle of her knife. "It's sharp. The goal is to have ten fingers at the end." Her voice was smiling, so I smiled and felt unafraid.

Vellida held the onion in her left hand. Our right hands rose and fell.

"Mamá likes the slices to be even." Vellida whispered, "The casserole doesn't care."

I giggled, but for once I agreed with Mamá. They should be regular. I foresaw many opportunities for counting in cooking. Vellida and I finished the onion, and she let me transfer the slices into a bowl, which I did without losing any.

Our new servant, Hamdun, entered from the back door to the garden, bearing two wooden buckets of water. Thin as he was, I wondered if he could manage them, but from the steady way he set them down in front of the fireplace, I saw he was strong. When he straightened, he blazed a smile at Vellida and me. I couldn't help smiling back. I was happy to be cooking, anyway.

Then I remembered our dead and felt guilty.

When it was noon and time for dinner, Aljohar told me I'd done well. She said there would be more to do after we ate.

But when we'd finished and Belo had intoned the prayer, he said I should come to his study.

I sent a look of appeal to Mamá, who didn't see, because she was glaring at Yuda (the only expression she ever had for him). She couldn't have helped me anyway, even if she wanted to. Belo was the patriarch.

I followed him out of the dining room. From the court-yard balcony, we passed the living room and turned the corner to the next door, which led to his study.

Inside, filtered light came from the windows above the desk and the door we'd just come through. Bright sunlight poured in from the two windows that faced the street and lit the book on his desk that was open to Hebrew letters bordered by gold-and-brown flowers.

Belo turned his chair away from his desk. Holding me by my shoulders, he positioned me and sat so that I faced him, which made me feel like a thief or a gambler brought before the aljama council.

"Your papá says you love numbers."

I nodded cautiously.

"You're seven now. How old will you be in two years?"

He knew. Why was he asking me? "Nine."

"If you had twenty-five grapes to divide between Yuda, Samuel, and Vellida, how many would you give to each one?"

I didn't have to think. "Twenty-three to Yuda, one apiece to Samuel and Vellida."

His mouth hung slack for a moment, and then he erupted in shoulder-shaking laughter.

I smiled uneasily.

When he stopped, he said, "Twenty-five *evenly* among the three of them."

Ugly Camel Head would be mad. "Eight to each, with one left over."

"What would you do with that one?"

Eat it? "Belo, a grape is small and squishy."

"True. Imagine they're oranges."

"I'd peel the last orange and count the parts." *Parts* didn't seem like the right word. "Most have ten. Three and a third parts to each, but the thirds would be squishy."

"Excellent." He leaned over and tipped up my chin. "Your bela used to say you were a cabinet with hidden drawers."

I felt uneasy at his scrutiny, and the mention of Bela brought me close to tears.

"There's the stubbornness drawer. You saved yourself twice—once from the plague, and once from baptism. And there's the drawer full of numbers. What else?"

I couldn't answer. Bela had known me best, so if she said I was full of drawers, then I was. I understood they weren't real drawers, but, still, my urge to count made me wonder how many. Six drawers? A hundred?

Belo stroked his beard and asked me if I could read yet. "Yuda teaches you, like a good boy, yes?"

"Samuel." He was the good boy. I didn't mention that I helped him with his math problems.

Belo took a prayer book from the books on his desk and

waved me close. He opened it and pointed at a passage in Hebrew. "Read this to me."

I liked to read, though I felt more comfortable with numbers. I'd been reading for only two years, but I'd been counting for as long as I could remember.

"Good."

Not excellent.

"Can you read Castilian, too?"

Castilian, the language we spoke. Samuel had started reading it just a month ago. "A little. I'm better at Hebrew."

He gave me a letter written in Castilian. In the first sentence, I could make out only three words.

"Mmm. You'll learn." He went to the shelf on the wall across from his desk. "Ah. There it is." He handed a book to me. "Poems in Hebrew. If you see a word you don't know, memorize it to ask your brother later. Don't ask me. You can sit there." He indicated a red leather floor cushion. "Your bela used to sit here with me sometimes." He returned to his chair and began to read.

Belo's book weighed as much as a pitcher full of milk. I wondered what Vellida was doing in the kitchen. Still, I was excited—books held secrets. I opened it to the middle.

Traps in my mouth, on my tongue,
waiting; on my lips, spiders' venom;

the important lords and honored dons,
my elders, refusing to repent, have clung
to deceit. They sing their wicked song.

I wasn't sure what *deceit* meant. This poem wasn't for children. I turned pages and saw that none were. Even more exciting. My sisters were educated, as Jewish girls in wealthy families were. All the girls in poor families could read Hebrew at least. But I doubted that any of them— rich or poor—had read these poems. I memorized words I didn't know and continued to read about kings, gardens, God, men's feelings, women's beauty.

But after half an hour, I grew drowsy. I snuggled into the cushion and fell into a dream of stirring a stewpot and counting the times my spoon went around.

A pattern began. In the morning—and much of the day if Belo was away—I helped in the kitchen. Out of kindness, at other times when she could, Vellida took it on herself to teach me to spin, weave, and embroider. I loved the care that each task called for. What I didn't like was choosing colors. I couldn't tell which was pleasing and which ugly.

"What's your favorite color?" Vellida asked.

People had a favorite? "What's yours?"

"Green. Yours?"

I frowned. "Orange?"

Vellida told me not to worry. "The fate of the Jews does not depend on the hues in a cushion cover."

The fate of my marriage might, if my creations disgusted all my suitors. The handiwork of girls was on display on pillows and wall hangings.

"I like spinning best," I said. Whatever I spun would go next to the dyer, who, as far as I was concerned, could pick whatever color he liked best.

When Ledicia came with her children, my task—my beloved task—was to watch and play with them, while she helped in the kitchen in my place. Todros delighted in making things fall, so I had to take care that he dropped objects that wouldn't shatter. I always kept a bowl of walnuts on hand for him to play with. I gave Beatriz my first doll. She named it Tusa and played with it and talked to it by the hour, though sometimes she interrupted herself to say, "Tía Loma, guess what happened to Tusa."

"She grew fins and swam to Egypt."

"No, Tía Loma!" she shouted with laughter. "She'd drown!"

After supper, I studied with Samuel. At bedtime, Mamá planted a hard kiss on my forehead, and Papá, if he was home, sat with me and kissed my cheek softly.

In the afternoons when he was home, Belo called me to his study, and I had to go, even if the little ones—the littles, as I thought of them—were visiting. Occasionally,

I'd find Fatima there, kneeling and massaging a salve into Belo's feet while he read a book or wrote in a folio on his lap. While he was reading or writing, he ignored me. I dipped into his books, which I could understand only in glimmers. I was often bored. But sometimes he read to me or had me read to him.

I liked best when he talked about his ideas, almost as if I were grown-up. He'd tell me he was trying out a thought, and when he finished, he'd tell me if he was pleased or if he had to think more. He didn't ask my opinion, so I didn't have to reveal my confusion, because I was often confused. But I'd think later about whatever he'd said and work out my own understanding.

I grew less afraid of him, and I came to love him much more than when he just loomed over our family like an eagle over a field, regal and remote. By wanting my company, he let me know that I was important to him. He was more interested in me than everyone else was combined. His attention became precious.

Two months passed. One afternoon, Belo put down his book, turned his chair, and asked me what Bela used to say when she came to me at night.

She said different things every night. And I was starting to forget. I didn't know how to answer.

The air seemed to harden. I had to say something. "One night, she said Vellida's husband would be kind and mine would be kind and gentle. She said I'd have many children. Do you think I will?"

Belo frowned. "You will if God wants you to."

Was he remembering my star chart? Did he believe God wanted me to be childless? "Belo, do you believe in astrology?"

The air softened. He clasped his hands in front of his chest as he often did when expounding a theory. "The Almighty put the stars in the heavens. He directs His purpose toward us. Thus, yes, I believe the position of the stars influences the life of every man—Christian, Muslim, or Jew—and every nation."

"Mamá had a chart done for each of us when we were born." I wanted to ask him about my chart, but I didn't feel brave enough.

"Daughters, too? I didn't know." He went on. "The stars' effect on a man is less than their influence on a nation. That makes sense, doesn't it, Loma?"

I nodded.

"If the stars predict famine in a kingdom, a particular man may die even if his chart augured a long life for him. Just so, the stars' sway over a wife isn't as strong as it is over her husband."

I smiled so widely my cheeks hurt. "Really?"

He frowned in mock displeasure. "You doubt your abuelo?"

Then if I married a man who was destined to have many children, his fate would win over mine, and I would be a mother. Hooray!

Ha, Ugly Camel Head!

How could I make sure my future husband had a good chart?

"What else did your abuela say?"

"Um . . . She said that Jews are safe in Spain."

"Were you thinking the Jews were safe when you ran after me?"

The night of the mob. I shook my head.

"We're not safe if we do nothing, so we do something."

"What do we do, Belo?" I hoped the question wasn't bold.

He didn't seem to mind. "Your papá and I make ourselves useful."

"How?"

"With donations. We buy the church an altarpiece, and we pay for armor and swords for some of the king's knights to help them win wars. The constables and the bishops and the king and queen don't forget when the Jews need them. That's how our family keeps us and all the Jews safe."

When we went to synagogue, Bela had always stayed outside in the street with me for a quarter hour or so, until a priest, or more than one, left the building. Then we'd go in. I never asked why we waited, because priests frightened me, and my mind shied away from them.

But after she became Bela of blessed memory, the next time we went to the synagogue, which was for Rosh Hashanah—the Jewish New Year—no one kept me outside. Feeling grown-up, I followed Mamá in with everyone else and up the stairs to the front of the women's gallery, where I could see the *tevah* downstairs by peering through gaps in the lattices of the low balcony wall. The tevah was where the Torah was read and where the rabbi and other men addressed the congregation.

When everyone had come in and the rustling of clothing had stopped, a priest mounted to the tevah. Sunlight from a leaded-glass window made an X on the bald center of his uncovered head.

He raised his hands, palms up, and screamed, *"Woe* to the Jews! *Stinking* in sin, sinking in *sin*. God curses you! Jesus Christ curses you!"

This was discord beyond anything Mamá produced. I could barely breathe.

Next, in a normal voice, he urged us to convert. If we did, he said, we'd no longer be devils.

We were devils? A *chirp* of alarm escaped me.

His voice rose again. "You are evil. You are *sin*! You are abominations!"

Tears blinded me.

"You will burn forever. Demons will torment you."

I wailed and drowned out his voice—

—and the sound of his feet on the stairs.

Hands girdled my waist. The priest raised me over his head and carried me downstairs.

I became rigid. Terror, even greater than I'd felt a moment before, silenced me. I squeezed my eyes shut. My breath came in gasps.

In seven steps, he returned to the tevah and climbed the three stairs. "This blessed child"—I felt him rotate me so that everyone saw my frozen face—"doesn't want to burn. You heard her. She longs for salvation, longs for eternal life among the angels of the Lord."

7

The priest lowered me in his arms, descended, and passed me to someone else, who passed me to a third person, while my stomach lurched. This third person carried me out of the synagogue, set me down in the street, and turned out to be Ledicia.

The priest could decide he still wanted me. Sobbing, I ran to the end of the street, turned, turned again, and sank to the ground in front of our door.

Though she was no longer a girl, Ledicia lowered herself to the cobblestones, too, and hugged me. "The priest won't get you." She held me at arm's length. "Did you see Belo glare at him?"

I hadn't.

"That's what made him stop." She chuckled and let me

go. "That and the weight of you. His arms shook when he put you down."

I was plump.

"He was just saying those words. He does it whenever there are services, him or some other priest. Don't worry."

I'd have to hear it again?

But my need to not cause discord had returned, so I pretended to be comforted. A servant let us in, and Ledicia stayed with me until, exhausted by emotion, I fell asleep on the bed I shared with Vellida.

In the dining room, first thing in the morning, Papá waved to me to join him at the window. "Loma, the Christians believe we'll be punished after we die for being Jews. The priests want to save us from that."

Were they right? I nodded and didn't ask.

Papá added, "The priest shouldn't have touched you. I'm still angry about that."

In the afternoon in his study, Belo said, "We don't believe what the Christians do. It's all death with them."

I ventured, "But everybody dies."

"We don't believe in their hell." Belo moved a book on his desk toward him.

Did we have a different hell? I didn't ask that, in case ours was worse.

"That priest won't touch you again. No priest will. I'm

going to speak with the bishop tomorrow."

I nodded.

But by now, Belo knew me. He sighed. "Your abuela would have known the right words to say to you. I don't. Forgive me."

I forgave him.

At night, I asked Mamá, who, I was sure, would tell me the truth, even if the truth was awful. "Will demons torment us when we die?"

"Jews don't believe that, but I haven't died yet."

That brought comfort, actually. The priest hadn't died, so he didn't know yet, either. "Why did he shout like that when nobody knows for certain?"

She drew the sheet up to my chin. "Be glad when they just shout." She pecked my forehead and left.

Ai! What else would they do?

I developed a terrible habit. In bed, after the last person had kissed me good night, usually Papá when he was home, I counted my worries:

A priest picking me up again.

Dying and burning and being tormented by demons with pointy teeth and bright red skin.

Marrying a man whose horoscope also predicted childlessness.

Falling out of Belo's favor.

Plague returning and sickening Ledicia and her family.

Sometimes I fell asleep after only one or two, but sometimes I stayed awake for hours, adding items to my list.

A week later, Yuda disgraced himself. He was discovered to have been dicing. Vellida and I learned the details from Aljohar, who wasn't fond of Ugly Camel Head, either.

Gambling was considered by both Christians and Jews as a terrible vice, even a crime. Yuda had won twenty-five reales from fifteen-year-old Astruc, the son of Yuda and Samuel's teacher. After he lost, Astruc had complained to the rabbi, who had gone to Belo, and Belo had made Yuda return his winnings. My brother spent an hour in Belo's study with Belo, Papá, and Mamá, whose cries rang through the house, blaming both Papá and Yuda: "You failed to instruct your son! Better if I'd given birth to a fox!"

At dinner, Yuda apologized for shaming the family. His eyes traveled to each of us, even Samuel, Vellida, and me. "I won't disappoint you again."

"After next month," Papá said, "we won't be able to protect you."

On November 19, he became our family's first bar mitzvah. At dinner, Belo and Papá, but not Mamá, kept smiling at him. Aljohar cooked his favorite: beef stew with garlic and onions.

He was next to me. For a change, when he filled our

bowl—because two people always shared a bowl at meals—
he said, "I'm a man now, and Papá is my example. The meat
is more for you than for me." He beamed at me the smile he
once reserved for Bela.

I smiled back, as I felt I had to. I expected a trap, but
he actually ate little.

The transformation lasted only a few days, and then
he was his gluttonous self again. I saw no benefit in his
rise to adulthood until, two weeks later, he was apprenticed
to Don Ziza, the goldsmith. He left home to live with his
master, returning only for Sabbath dinners and holidays.
Soon after, Papá negotiated for him to marry Dueyna, a
merchant's daughter, the prettiest girl in the aljama.

The engagement was to be celebrated in December, on
the day after Hanukkah ended. I was thrilled, because it
was the first engagement in our close family that I would
remember. I had been only two when Ledicia had her party.

The day came. I woke up wishing I were the betrothed—
but not to an ugly camel head!

Vellida still slept. The winter sun hadn't risen yet, so
I dressed by feel, putting on my tan silk gown with the
green velvet border around the neckline and pulling over
my head the heavy silver chain that had been a gift from
Papá. I wished for Bela's pendant, but Belo still had it.

The stars were out when I stepped onto the courtyard
balcony. The air was crisp. I lowered my right knee and

extended my left leg in front of my right, up on my left foot, *hop!*, down, up, *hop!*—dancing toward the kitchen. The dancing was sure to be my favorite part.

Aljohar was bustling about the kitchen by candlelight. She set me to work peeling the eggs—seventy-three of them!—that had spent the night simmering in a cauldron of water with red onion skins and vinegar, the fire kept alive by Fatima, who had finally been allowed to go to sleep. Aljohar and I had cracked the shells in the evening, after they'd first been hard-boiled. Now as I worked, I admired the patterns of lines that had been created: ivory where the shell had remained, violet where the cracks had been. Yawning, Vellida came in and stood next to me at the worktable, transferring dried mackerel to a platter.

The party would be in the street outside our house, and most of the aljama would come. While everyone was singing, dancing, and eating, servants, hired for the occasion, would prepare more food to bring out later. The day would close with a meal after the ceremony.

I smiled at Vellida. "You're next."

"God willing. And then you."

"First Samuel."

"I meant girls."

God willing.

When I finished placing the 292 egg quarters on platters, Aljohar had me begin to bring them out to the street, where Dueyna, beautiful in a blue woolen cloak embroidered with silver artichokes, stood with her family.

She ran to me, saying, "How pretty you look . . ."

I realized she didn't remember my name. "Paloma—Loma."

"Loma, I'm happy to have a sister at last." Her voice was so breathy it seemed to have bubbles in it. "The first question I asked Papá was, 'Does he have sisters?'"

I smiled though I didn't believe her—it wasn't what I would want to know.

Her papá called her. She went to him, and I returned to the kitchen, where Aljohar told me Belo wanted me in his study.

When I got there, he was wearing his finery, a green silk overgown that was pleated down the front, but he was where he usually was: at his table, writing. He looked up. "Ah, Loma. Do you approve of this poem for the occasion of the engagement of my least-worthy grandchild?"

Because of the gambling, or did he know more?

He read the poem from a book at his elbow. This was the last stanza:

> *The gate is shut! Arise, oh, please,*
> *and open it! Oh, send to me*
> *the gazelle that ran away! Godspeed*

her to my side. Ah! Ah! You're here!
Your scent and honeyed voice hold me
and will forever please me.

I said, honestly, that it sounded beautiful. I didn't add that I'd break out in giggles if anyone ever recited it to me.

"Then I'll read it when the time comes."

Because of my opinion? If Bela could be here, she'd be smiling.

I hoped he'd say I looked pretty, but he returned to writing. I opened the door to leave.

"Where are you going?"

"To the party?"

"Stay for a little while. A party is noisy. I prefer studying and talking with you."

I closed the door.

"I'm considering how God chooses the children for each family. Why give Joseph to Jacob? Why you to us? Why Yuda? Why the others?"

Why did He give us to Mamá out of all the other mothers?

Belo was waiting, as if I could tell him.

"Samuel, Ledicia, and Vellida are good children." That didn't feel like enough. "Dutiful. Kind. We're nice to each other."

"But why did the Almighty, out of His goodness, give *you* to us? Sit." He pointed at my cushion.

I sat.

Voices drifted in through the windows. People were arriving. Someone began tuning a lute. I wanted to hear what Belo would say next, and I wanted to be outside. I wondered if the littles had come. It was their first party, and I wanted to help them enjoy it. And if Dueyna really hoped for a sister, she'd be missing me.

"The Almighty, when Bela died, made me notice you and realize that you may help me while I help the Jews." He said that before there were juderías, Jews and Christians and Muslims could live wherever they liked. "They'd celebrate together, grieve together, even write poems together. I and a few others keep that tradition of friendship. It's one way of helping."

Outside, the lute was joined by drums and tambourines, and the music began in earnest. I bounced my knees. In a little while, Yuda, with three other unmarried young men, would ride down the street on mules fitted with bells and would stop when he reached Dueyna, which seemed the height of romance, a moment—when it happened to me—that I would treasure.

My heart-hatred side wanted to see it, too, because Yuda would look ridiculous—an ugly camel head on a jingling mule.

But I also wanted Belo to keep talking about Spain and my part in helping him. If I stopped him and joined the party, he might never return to the subject.

I stayed. Soon, hooves clattered and bells chimed. I missed Yuda's arrival, but Belo started to talk about his childhood and his parents, who had died long before I was born. His papá spoke even more languages than Belo did, including Russian, and his mamá played the lute.

"Angels danced above her head when she played."

I knew he didn't mean real angels, but I wished I could have heard her. I wished she was playing for Yuda now, and we were both out there.

My brothers and sisters probably hadn't heard these stories. Would they be angry if they found out?

Another worry to keep me awake at night.

Belo talked until Papá rapped on the door and came in. "Oh, there you are, Loma."

I jumped up from the cushion, feeling guilty, though I wasn't sure why.

Papá turned to Belo. "It's time."

He rose smoothly. "We're needed, Loma."

In the street, my niece, Beatriz, ran to me. "Where were you?"

The dancing and singing were over. It was time for the ceremony.

"With your *bisabuelo*." Your great-grandfather. "Let's

watch together." I took her hand, and we went to where our family stood, in the middle of the cobblestones. Yuda had positioned himself on the edge of the group of us. Next to him was the new servant, Hamdun, who held an embroidered pillow. Atop the pillow were gifts for Dueyna: four gold rings and a silver pendant set with pale blue stones on a pearl necklace.

If they had been dressed alike, I would have guessed wrong about which man was servant and which bridegroom. Yuda stared off above the head of his wife-to-be and looked bored. Hamdun, by contrast, smiled a smile that almost embraced her, a few yards away, sitting on a bench beside her parents, with her five brothers standing behind her.

Belo took the space between the families and recited the poem he'd read to me. Dueyna's smile became fixed. At least she didn't giggle. The guests applauded.

Then the *hazan* took Belo's place. (The hazan sang for synagogue services and proclaimed at weddings and engagements.) Our hazan was a barrel of a man with a booming voice. "On this day, Guedaliah has engaged his daughter Dueyna to marry apprentice goldsmith Yuda." Guedaliah was Dueyna's papá. "They will appear for the wedding as arranged. If one or the other does not appear, their oaths to each other will not bind them; gifts will be returned; and a fine of one thousand *maravedis* will be paid to the aljama. They are now engaged."

I was disappointed. Nothing had been said about their lives together or their children.

Yuda took the pillow from Hamdun and brought it to Dueyna. He smiled down at her, and she smiled up at him, her eyes glassy with tears. The hazan began to sing, "'Blessed art Thou, O Lord our God, King of the universe . . .'"

Beatriz and I swayed with the lilting tune.

"'. . . Who hath created joy and gladness, bridegroom and bride, mirth and exultation . . .'"

When he finished, Beatriz and I and everyone else went to the tables and began to eat. I wished again that Belo hadn't made me miss the dancing.

8

The year changed to Christian year 1484. Everyone was healthy, which didn't stop me from worrying about a return of the plague.

In February, Vellida turned twelve and became a woman according to our law. Papá began negotiating for a husband for her, and she started to fluff out her pretty hair—at five-minute intervals. Alas, her hair was her only beauty. Ugly Camel Head's name for her was Nut-Cheeked Squirrel.

But her puffy cheeks and small eyes didn't stop Papá from finding an excellent match: Jacob, son of the lawyer Don Brahem, who argued in the courts for Jews, Christians, and Muslims. They were to be married the following April, more than a year away. However, the engagement party was to be in two weeks. I looked forward to it even more than I had to Yuda's, since Vellida was my beloved sister, as Ledicia was, too. I wanted to watch the face of her husband-to-be, to satisfy myself that he wasn't bored at the prospect of marrying her.

And this time, Beatriz and I would dance.

She danced, but I didn't. Belo delayed joining the party again and instead began to teach me how to play backgammon. I had longed to learn, and he had promised to teach me. Though he meant to please me, he had chosen the wrong moment. I forgave him. I loved him. By then, I loved him more than anyone else in the family, but he wasn't like Bela. He didn't understand children.

On a Tuesday morning in March, Belo's dear friend Solomon Bohor visited us. Don Solomon, like Belo, was a financier and courtier and another great protector of the Jews. Samuel, Vellida, and I met him at dinner.

Don Solomon could have been Belo's papá, he was that old, a slight man with a skinny beard and a round belly. His face was bright with good humor.

Actually, most of him was bright. His silk robe, which came down only to his mid calves, glowed yellow green, embroidered with gold thread in circles and squiggles. Below the robe, his red hose was embroidered with silver thread. Looking at him caused discord in my eyes. Belo and Papá dressed in fine fabrics, too, but their hues were more sober.

Samuel and I sat on either side of Señor Osua, Samuel's teacher. Vellida sat directly across from us. Belo gave Don Solomon his own armchair at the head of the table and asked him to say the prayers, which he did in a surprisingly deep voice for such a small, old man.

After prayers, Belo introduced us, starting with Vellida and mentioning her betrothal.

She blushed.

Belo went on. "This is Samuel. Señor Osua, he does well, doesn't he?"

Señor Osua nodded. "He finds the heart in the words."

"A future rabbi," Papá said.

I felt Samuel's pleasure.

Mamá passed the tureen to Don Solomon. "Lamb and fennel. We're good cooks in this family."

I wondered if Don Solomon heard the challenge in her voice. No one had better disagree.

Don Solomon ladled a generous serving into the bowl he was sharing with Belo. His eyes on me, he said, "Did you help your sister?"

I nodded. I had shelled the chickpeas.

Belo said, "Loma is my favorite grandchild."

Papá coughed. Mamá's eyes flicked to me and away. I sat frozen. Would Samuel and Vellida hate me? I was lucky

Yuda was with his master goldsmith.

"She's quick. If she were a boy, she could do anything. She's the comfort of my old age."

This was like the engagement parties—good and bad at the same time. I didn't dare look at my brother or sister.

Don Solomon just said, "From my many years, your age isn't old." He smiled around the table. "Joseph, Asher has been granted an audience with the monarchs when they're in Tarazona."

Asher was Papá. Belo had already had audiences with the king and queen, but Papá never had.

Papá put down his spoon. "I had barely dared to hope. Thank you!"

"Tarazona?" Mamá cried. "So far? With brigands behind every tree?" She was at her worst when Papá traveled.

"The guards will protect us, Violanta." Papá laughed. "If I don't come back, you can marry someone who never travels."

Mamá's face reddened, but she didn't speak.

Journeys *were* dangerous. Before Papá left home, he always gave Mamá a just-in-case writ of divorce, a legal document, called a conditional *get*. Belo used to give Bela a conditional get, too, when he traveled. They weren't divorced unless he didn't come back—that was the conditional part. But if he didn't, Mamá could marry someone else. Another worry.

Belo and Papá hired Jewish guards to protect them, and they were friends with the nobles whose land they traveled through. Neither of them had ever been attacked.

Belo said, "Asher, we'll take Loma with us."

I stopped eating with my spoon in the air. Traveling with Papá and Belo, the two I loved most; being away from Mamá and Yuda; seeing the world beyond the judería—could I go?

"If she dies," Mamá said, "remember I said she shouldn't go."

But she hadn't said I couldn't, just shouldn't. Could I?

Was that what my chart meant, that I'd die before I had children?

Papá pulled his beard. "She should be home, learning to cook and sew."

My face heated up. I was the cause of discord.

"The queen will meet her," Belo said.

Really? And the king?

He went on. "Queen Isabella will see a girl where girls usually are not. She may remember herself when she was a princess. Loma will raise us in her regard." He put his right hand on the table, palm up. "Loma will be good for the Jews." His voice dropped. "And she's a comfort to me. Son"—he turned to Papá—"you know how much I miss Esther."

That settled it, as Belo must have known it would. I was going!

Don Solomon smiled at all of us. "What a wonderful family you are, benignly ruled by Don Joseph." He turned to me. "Loma, your belo and I are respected because our friendships with Christians protect the Jews, but he's honored for being a thinker and philosopher, a writer of books."

I'd never seen Belo blush before.

That night, I forced myself to stay awake until Vellida came in, and then I asked her if she was angry at me.

When her gown dropped to the floor, she said, "Before, I would have wanted to be the one to go with Papá and Belo, but now I'm getting married." She blew out our candle and slipped into bed.

"I didn't mean to be Belo's favorite."

In the dark, I could hear the smile in her voice. "That's an honor I never would have wanted."

"Why not?"

She rolled onto her side. "Belo giveth; Belo taketh away. It isn't bad to lose what you never had." In a minute or two, her breath became regular.

I lay awake. Vellida was right. Now that I knew I was his favorite, I would be miserable if Belo chose someone else. If I had to miss every engagement party in the judería to keep my place, it would be worth it.

The next evening, when we were studying together,

Samuel said he wasn't angry at me, either. He blushed. "I think I'm the rabbi's favorite, outside of his children." He added, "When Yuda figures it out, he'll be angry, or he'll find a way to use your specialness to help him. Be careful."

As if he needed to tell me.

Don Solomon stayed with us for three days. At Belo's prompting, he told us stories at dinner about the monarchs.

From one I learned that King Ferdinand's great-grandmother was Jewish—and that she and I shared the same name! Hers—Palom*ba*—wasn't spelled exactly like mine, but still!

The Jews were happy he was on the throne and not any of Queen Isabella's other suitors.

Don Solomon said he'd had a hand in the royal marriage, which made his presence in our dining room seem miraculous. "Before they were married, King Ferdinand was poor, even though he was the prince of Aragon. I gave him trinkets and money so he wouldn't go to her empty-handed." He told Mamá, "He was handsome, and the princess was comely."

Mamá didn't smile.

Undeterred, Don Solomon added, "Love is rare between a king and a queen."

I relished the romance. They first met in the middle of the night, when he came to her boldly and she received him—boldly, too, because King Enrique, her brother, who had died when I was a baby, hadn't approved the match. They married without his permission, which hardly seemed possible.

They were exotic creatures. If Don Solomon had said they had peacock feathers growing out of their ears, I would have believed him.

Papá's audience with the monarchs was to take place a week after Don Solomon left us. The night after he left, Belo gave me back Bela's amulet, which both pleased and frightened me. Did we need its protection on the trip?

Our family—including Ledicia, her husband, Beatriz, Todros, Yuda, and Dueyna—saw us off the next morning, standing in a knot outside our door, where six guards, mounted on mules, waited. Beatriz wailed and hugged my waist. She and Todros were my only regrets about leaving.

I stroked her hair and felt like I was playacting Bela. "When I come back, I'll tell you stories."

A yard away, Todros bounced on the balls of his feet. I crouched and hugged him.

"Tía Loma will return soon." Ledicia backed her children away from me.

Papá and Belo mounted their horses, Belo as nimbly as his son.

Hamdun helped me up in front of Papá. "Comfortable?"

I nodded, and he smiled as if I'd given him a gift. Then

he climbed on a mule and took the ropes to lead the two donkeys, which carried supplies for the journey. They'd be happy, because animals loved Hamdun.

Along with a crowd on their way to the market, we passed through the judería gate. I touched Bela's pendant and hoped it would keep Señor Mateo and Señora María indoors or at least away from us.

The narrow street opened onto a plaza. We clattered past the church, where I might have been baptized. A white stork flew overhead. Bela would have called it an omen, but of what?

9

We left the city, *clip-clopping* on a road paved with broad, flat stones. As the luckiest girl in all the aljamas, I swore to remember everything.

The road was bordered by pastures, where the green seemed improbably bright. Absently, I started counting the grazing sheep and goats. The morning was pleasant, sunny, cool, with a light breeze.

Entwined with my joy were strings of worry. Would brigands attack? Would the monarchs be angry when I appeared before their persons?

Belo kept the horses to a walk. Papá prayed softly or sang softly, just as he did at home. I felt as if I were nothing but my eyes, my ears, and the part of me that always counted things. Three, seven, eleven riders pounded by, galloping toward our city. A single beggar stood in front of the horse Papá shared with me, forcing him to rein it in. The man, in a threadbare linen cloak, held out a dirty hand for alms. Papá opened his purse and gave him a reale.

The beggar stepped aside, and we set off again.

"Papá," I said, "I didn't see him until he was right there!"

"People often don't see the poor."

Maybe because no one was afraid of them.

Two oxen drawing a cart clattered toward us. The sky seemed bigger here. Our guards talked among themselves. The road followed our Henares river, which chattered to itself in a language of gurgles and whooshes. The paving stones ended, and the roadway became dusty dirt. No brigands.

As the sun was setting, we arrived in Medinaceli, where we spent the night in the house of the rabbi, and our guards stayed in other Jewish homes. I slept in a bed with the rabbi's two daughters. In the dark, I pretended they were Vellida and Rica and that Bela had just kissed me and left.

After prayers the next morning, we set out again, in a rainstorm. We put the hoods up on our cloaks, and I was grateful for the warmth of Papá behind me.

Beyond the town, Belo said, "Loma, you'll meet the

Duke of Medinaceli in Tarazona."

A king, a queen, and now a duke. "Will they mind that I'm with you?"

"His Grace has children and grandchildren of his own," Papá said. "He is a friend to the Jews."

Belo added, "He likes people who make money for him."

Feeling bold, I said, "Belo, would you please snap your fingers?"

Papa said, "Why do you want him to?"

I swallowed, nervous now. "Er . . . Because Mamá says Belo makes golden ducats that way, and he makes them for the duke." I wanted to see him do it.

Belo and Papá laughed. I felt foolish. Mamá had set this trap for me to fall into.

Papá said, "Loma, we do what the Christians let us do—lend money, collect taxes, run enterprises, like their silver mines, for them."

"Better than they do, and everyone gets rich," Belo said. "The Christians can be corrupt, but everybody watches the Jews. We have to be honest."

How kind Belo and Papá were, to explain everything to me. I felt lucky twice over.

The rain lightened to a drizzle.

"We'd be honest anyway." Papá kissed the back of my head. "Jews used to be allowed to do more than they can today. We have the best physicians, but they're kept from treating Christians. The doctors make less, and Christians die. The Almighty shakes His head."

"In some towns"—Belo pushed back his hood—"Jews can sell hardly anything to Christians. The Jews there are so poor that kind Christians give them charity."

Papá said, "Some Jews become Christian just so they can earn a living."

We stopped for the night in the village of Gómara and stayed in the house of one of the five Jewish families, where pallets were set out for us in the living room. After the family retired to bed, Belo pulled his foot salve out of his saddlebag and asked me to rub it in. He took off his shoes and hose.

Papá said, "Loma is tired."

"She'll be rested in the morning and my feet will still hurt. She doesn't mind, do you, Loma?"

I shook my head, though I didn't want to do it. I knelt as Fatima did. The salve smelled of peppermint, and Belo's feet smelled of feet.

They were cold!

"Rub harder. Dig between the bones."

I tried. The tips of my fingers whitened. "Did Bela do this?"

"She refused."

Could I refuse? No.

"Thank you for coming," Papá said, "or I'd be kneeling where you are."

A wave of homesickness engulfed me. What were the littles doing? Did they miss me? I wished I could hug them and breathe them in rather than feet!

Later, on my pallet, my first worry was that plague had entered Ledicia's house.

The next day dawned warm and sunny. No bandits accosted us. Time passed peacefully. At dusk, we reached Tarazona and went straight to the house of the rabbi and his wife, where I shared a bed with their five-year-old daughter.

Worries marched into my mind like soldiers. Would the king and queen be angry that I was there? What if they disliked children? Would I disgrace Belo and Papá? Would priests come and baptize us?

My imaginings grew wilder. Did the monarchs look like ordinary people, or were they bigger? Did they speak or just roar?

The rabbi's daughter rolled over and pressed against my side with her nose pushed under my shoulder. Comforted, I finally slept.

My worries woke up with me.

Belo and Papá left me in the morning, first to pray at the synagogue and then to spend time with the rabbi. I helped the rabbi's wife prepare dinner and made a game with her daughter of mashing garlic and spices together.

But when Belo and Papá returned with the rabbi, they said that we had been invited to take our dinner with the Duke of Medinaceli.

With a Christian? I wondered what we'd be able to eat.

We followed narrow, winding streets out of the judería into other narrow, winding streets. Some of the streets were stone stairs going upward. Once, we had to flatten ourselves against a shoemaker's shop to make room for a rider on horseback.

Papá said, "The duke is our host for dinner at the Singing Chicken."

Chickens could sing?

"It's an inn," Papá added. "A good place for conversation."

When we got there, Belo stopped Papá's hand on the door latch. "Do what we do, Loma, and call the duke 'Your Grace.'"

We entered a small vestibule: stairs facing us, closed door to the right, open door to the left. We crossed the threshold on the left into an empty room—empty of people, filled with a table that ran the length of the chamber and was covered by a stained white tablecloth. A pillow-covered bench flanked the table. An armchair stood at the end farthest from the vestibule door. A window, shutters open, let in light and cool air. Nailed to the wall above the fireplace was a wooden crucifix. I knew what it was, but I'd never seen one before. I touched the little bulge in my bodice where Bela's pendant was hidden.

A door on the wall to our right, which would lead to the back of the inn, squeaked open. A very short man entered, a servant, I supposed. He bore a tray that held a small bowl of almonds and one of dried apricots, three pewter mugs, a large ewer, and a small ewer. "Wine for the dons and small beer for the señorita. The duke sends his apologies. He'll come as soon as he can." The man left.

Papá poured wine from the big ewer for Belo and himself and beer from the small one for me. He said the prayer and added, "Loma, a grandee makes people wait."

Belo sat on the bench with his back to the table. Papá sat, too, leaving room for me between them. I sipped my small beer, which tasted like small beer at home, not seeming to be particularly Christian beer. My stomach rumbled. At home, we would have eaten by now. Ledicia might have brought the littles. I'd have encouraged picky Beatriz to eat.

Christ looked so skinny! I counted five ribs sticking

out on each side of him. Perhaps he'd been waiting for his dinner, too. I stifled a giggle, put down my mug, and circled the table, counting the wide floorboards that ran the length of the room. Eighteen. I circled again and again. We could have covered four miles on our horses by now.

The door flew open. Belo and Papá jumped up, but I was standing already. I made fists of my trembling hands.

A tall man came in. Standing very erect, with his feet close together, he proclaimed in a voice that was too loud for the room, "Luis de la Cerda y de la Vega, the Duke of Medinaceli."

10

Two other tall men followed him in. Belo and Papá bowed. I curtsied, wondering if I was doing it right for Christians. With a rustle of cloaks, the men bowed back. The one who'd announced the duke hurried to the back door and passed through it.

"Apologies!" The tallest of the men turned out to be the duke. "I'm not the ruler of my time."

He looked younger than Belo but closer to his age than to Papá's. He had pale blue eyes and was clean-shaven with a squarish face and a cleft chin. Below the wide brim of his hat, strands of light brown and gray hair fell to his shoulders. His green cloak was embroidered so lavishly with gold thread that I saw more gold than green.

"Your Grace, we're glad to see you now," Belo said, "and whenever you like."

The duke sat in the armchair. "Please sit."

His companion sat on the bench near the vestibule door. Belo sat on the duke's right and patted the cushion on his right for me.

But the duke said, "No, my friend. She'll sit with me." To my astonishment, he lifted me onto his bony knees. He smelled of fried fish and mustard. "She's healthy!"

He meant stout. I was too old to sit on anyone's lap, and I didn't like it.

"Her mother's cooking, Your Grace," Papá said, looking a warning at me and sitting on Belo's right, where I wished I could be. He chuckled. "I'm healthy, too."

I didn't know what he was warning me against.

"Paloma is the favorite, Don Joseph?" the duke asked.

"She reminds me of my wife of blessed memory. Paloma—Loma—is clever."

"As all my children are," Papá hastened to say.

The duke shifted me on his legs. "Tell me, Paloma, do you like being clever?"

I touched Bela's amulet chain and nodded, afraid to speak.

"Is there anything you want more than cleverness?"

This was like asking me to choose between sleep and the moon. My voice came out tiny. "I want to be a good mamá someday, but—"

"I can't hear you." The duke tilted his head.

My heart hopped like a sparrow. I managed a little more volume. "I want most to be a good mamá someday. Being clever will make me good. Being clever helps me be good at"—I thought about it—"almost everything." There had to be exceptions, even if I couldn't think of them.

The duke pursed his lips. "A clever answer."

The door to the back whined open again. The duke's other companion returned with the small man who'd come in before and another not much larger man. The short men bore trays. The companion joined his fellow on the bench.

The muscles stood out in the forearms of the two servants as they lowered their trays.

A ladle protruded from a large covered bowl. Platters held fried chard and eggplant; black-eyed peas with mint; cod with cilantro and olives; glistening grilled sardines; smoked mackerel; white rolls; and a salad of watercress, lettuce, and pistachio.

The servants returned to the kitchen, and one came back with a tray of cutlery, three two-handled bowls, a stack of stale bread, and a pastry shaped like a fish, probably a fish pie. The man lifted the lid off the big bowl, revealing white bean soup.

My mouth watered.

"Lent," the duke said to Belo. "No meat."

Papá said, "We're happy to share a meal with you, Your Grace, no matter the menu."

The servant passed out the cutlery and the bowls: one for the duke, which I had to assume he'd share with me if he kept me on his lap; one between Papá and Belo; one for the duke's two companions; a bread slice in front of each of us—two slices before the duke. The man distributed spoons. We all had our own knives in our purses.

But oh no! The bowls had probably held both milk and meat, and the spoons had likely touched both. Had the duke invited us to share a meal we couldn't eat?

Papá had said he was happy to break bread with the duke.

Ah. This had to be a Jewish inn. The duke was a friend of the Jews, so he chose a Jewish inn.

Then why the crucifix?

The servant ladled soup into the bowls and began to place a portion of everything except the fish pie on each slice of bread. When he reached me, the duke held up a hand and asked me what I liked most and what I didn't like.

This was kind, but I had to speak again. I said I liked everything, especially the eggplant and the sardines. The servant gave me more of those, moved on to everyone else, and stood away from the table.

The duke crossed himself as did his companions and

the waiter. Belo and Papá lowered their heads, so I did, too.

The duke thanked Jesus Christ for our meal.

I went hot with embarrassment. Belo and Papá echoed the duke's *amen* at the end, and I did, too, though a moment late.

The duke lifted me off his lap and set me on the bench next to Belo, who said our prayer, thanking the Almighty for the food. The Christians echoed our *amen*.

Everyone began to eat. I did, too.

Between bites, the duke said, "What have you been writing about, Don Joseph?"

Belo put down his knife. "The Book of Samuel, monarchy, and law."

"Whose law?" the duke asked.

"Religious law or the law that assemblies have passed." Belo sounded happy, as if we were in his study at home. "Laws are to be followed."

Was I breaking *our* law by eating? Were Belo and Papá? To comfort myself, I counted the times the duke put food in his mouth. He was a quick eater.

Gradually, I calmed.

"Don Joseph . . ." The duke sounded happy, too. "I beg of you: a poem."

"Hmm . . ." I heard Belo's feet move on the floorboards. He was extending his legs, as he did when he felt especially at ease. "If I may, Your Grace, I'll put the words of the poem in your voice as our host—your voice, if you were a country bumpkin."

"I'm eager to hear myself that way."

"This poem was written more than two hundred years ago," Belo said, and then recited:

> *Hospitality tastes sweet, as milk wrung*
> *out of cattle-curds and as cake crumbs*
> *steeped and heaped, without number,*
> *plunged in cream. When guests come*
> *in the night, I cry to my sons*
> *to throw open the gates. I exult,*
> *as a wolf does, stalking a buck,*
> *like a plowman whose seeds flung*
> *in earth will yield barley for the hungry.*
> *To see guests makes me the wealthy one.*
> *You are here. You are welcome.*

Everyone was silent. I worried that the duke didn't like being compared to a wolf. Had Belo caused discord with this powerful Christian?

But after a moment, he clapped and laughed. Instantly, his companions and Papá joined in. I didn't find anything funny, but I clapped, too.

"Ah, Don Joseph," the duke said, "we're relics, you even more than I, of an earlier age. I do exult in your company."

I hadn't been sure if I liked the duke, but now I decided I did.

The servant cut the fish pie in six pieces, not as evenly as I would have.

I was full, but I ate and discovered that the pie had no fish. It was a fish-shaped apple pie with cinnamon and saffron, a surprise of a dessert. My appetite came back.

The duke pushed away what was left of his bread. "Your audience will take place on Monday. Her Majesty requested of me that I inform you. I suggest you arrive early."

"Thank you for telling us," Belo said.

The duke brushed a crumb off his doublet. "The monarchs' ambition for victory is my ambition, too. Alas, their poverty is my poverty as well, but they expect a gift or a loan from me, as well as my sword in battle."

I learned later that loans to the king and queen were rarely repaid.

"And," he went on, "I am planning my palace, which is a heavy expense. I must squeeze a little more from my suffering people."

"That is regrettable," Papá said.

The duke nodded. "They feel pinched already. I don't want riots." He turned to me. "Paloma, if you really are a clever little Jewess, what should I do?"

Papá coughed. "She's just a child."

"Yet you're introducing her to our sovereigns."

"Answer His Grace's question, Loma," Belo said.

How many ducats did the duke need? How poor could he be? He was a duke!

The silence stretched.

What if I were one of the duke's people? I thought of myself at home, and Yuda came to mind. An idea formed.

"Your Grace . . ." Speaking came easier now that I liked him. "When my brother Yuda is expected for dinner, I know I'll have to share." I blushed and realized where my thoughts would take me. "But when he surprises us, I'm angry that I have to share."

Papá made a strangled noise.

The duke waved a hand in the air. "No one is surprised to have to part with money. Not much of a pronouncement for a prodigy."

If people weren't surprised, I thought, why would they be angry?

"But," I said in a smaller voice, "your people don't know when. Yuda has surprised us in the past and probably will do it again, but I don't know when."

The duke bit down on his lower lip, which I hoped meant he was thinking.

My blush deepened. "If I know Aljohar cooked eggplant for dinner, I decide ahead of time how much I can have without"—I paused, then went ahead—"Mamá calling me a glutton. I look forward to that amount."

Belo helped me. "Suppose one of your farmers decides he can afford to buy another ram. Then—without
warning—he finds out there will be a new levy and he'll
have to sell a ram instead. You know he's angry, Your
Grace."

The duke nodded.

I spoke again. "But if he knows about the tax, he doesn't
picture a new ram."

Belo went further than I would have thought to go.
"This farmer is a good fellow. He wants, as we all do, victory in the kingdom's wars. He also wants you to have
your palace, which will reflect glory on you and all your
people, including him."

The duke stood and bowed to me—not deeply, an incli-
nation more than a bow. He tipped his head to one of his
companions. The man reached into a slit in his cloak and
produced a purse, which he presented to Belo.

"For the dowry of Paloma," the duke said. "Don Joseph,
until the next time we meet. May your audience go well."

My dowry!

The audience!

11

We sat on high-backed chairs in the courtyard of the Episcopal Palace. My fear had changed to boredom and hunger. Papá had said I mustn't walk around. To make sitting more active, I swung my legs, counting each swing, until, after just fifteen, Belo told me I was wasting my energy in foolishness.

I counted the potted plants that circled the fountain in the middle of the courtyard: 16. I counted the big ivory tiles that I could see: 57. And the small ivory tiles: 128—maybe. I kept losing my place, which was maddening.

Since our arrival just after dawn, we had been assured repeatedly by men in silk doublets and velvet capes that the monarchs would see us "very soon." Belo called these people *noble riffraff.* Papá said they were low-level lords who worked as secretaries to the monarchs, handling their appointments. I wondered how many appointments the monarchs had in a day.

I wore my best gown—mauve silk with flowery embroidery in green thread. Around my neck hung a necklace of glass beads and a gold pendant set with a yellow stone. Bela's pendant hid under my gown.

Papá whispered prayers. Belo stared straight ahead.

Finally, a young man rushed to us and bowed stiffly, as if his upper half were the lid of a box, folding down. "Their Majesties will receive you in the throne room."

My hunger vanished.

We followed the secretary to a stone staircase. I wondered why the staircase divided, even though both sides led to the same balcony. The secretary led us up the left side, perhaps the side reserved for Jews.

Was the queen always angry, like Mamá?

Beyond the balcony, the secretary turned smartly to the right. I watched the hem of his crimson cape, his legs in green and gold bicolor hose, and the backs of his shoes, which were tan with low heels.

Close behind him, we crossed a threshold flanked by open double doors. Seven steps in, the secretary halted abruptly. We stopped, too. My nose was an inch from his cloak, which smelled musty.

The secretary barked, his words as clipped as his

movements, "The Cantala family attends Your Majesties."

Belo took my right hand, and Papá took my left. Belo's grip was so tight it hurt. Papá's hand was slick and slippery. He was sweating! And my hands were freezing. We marched forward. I closed my eyes, relying on the hands to keep me from falling.

I managed to count, though I could hardly feel my feet. Twenty steps.

Belo hissed furiously, "Loma, open your eyes!"

I did, though I turned my head, afraid to look forward. The walls were made of carved wood. There were no windows on this side, but candles burned in candelabra atop posts that lined the wall. How many posts? How many candles?

"Don Joseph!" The voice, deep and velvety, came from a man.

Still holding my hands, Belo and Papá bowed deeply. I curtsied despite my weak knees. When I rose, I dared to look at the monarchs—

—who were smiling at us, showing ordinary teeth rather than fangs. They sat perhaps four feet above us on a wooden dais, on matching high-backed thrones covered with tapestry and topped by scalloped canopies.

Orange-red hair rippled to the queen's shoulders. Her gown was burgundy velvet studded along the neckline with pearls set in gold. The king was more soberly dressed in a brown cloak that fell open to reveal a black doublet and ivory hose. He wasn't stout, but his face was fleshy and his lips plump. Though he had no beard, his cheeks were stippled with black dots.

The monarchs' smiles seemed happy. They were either pretending or were truly glad to see three Jews standing before them.

"Who is this?" Queen Isabella cried.

This was me.

Belo said, "My granddaughter Paloma, the pride of my old age."

"Surely," the king said in his velvety voice, "all your children and grandchildren are your pride."

"Certainly, sire, and, most of all, Paloma."

"Come to me, Paloma." The queen's voice, now that she wasn't shouting, was soft and insistent.

Belo and Papá nudged me forward. I stumbled, caught myself, and climbed the dais.

Queen Isabella held out her hands. I went to her and clasped her hands despite my terror and, really, horror, as I catapulted back to the moment when Señor Mateo grabbed me.

"How old are you, child?"

I whispered, "Seven." Her hands were paler and pinker than mine, which were tan and yellowish.

"Three years older than my Juana and six years younger

than Isabella. If matters were otherwise, you could be lady-in-waiting to one of them. Would you like that?"

I nodded, afraid to say no.

"What kind of husband do you hope for someday, Paloma? Handsome? Kind? Rich?"

I nodded again and, since this was a topic I'd considered, I found the courage to add, "And wise."

"Not an impossible combination." The queen smiled at the king. "Such a man chose me."

King Ferdinand smiled, too. "You would marry a great lord. Your abuelo would become a lord or a bishop, and who knows how high your papá could rise?"

Belo a bishop? In a church? I realized he meant *if we became Christians*.

"My husband and I love your abuelo as if he were part of our family." Queen Isabella let my left hand go and covered my right in hers. "Are you good, Paloma?"

I whispered, "I don't know." I thought of my heart-hatred for Yuda.

"Do you want to be good?"

"Yes."

King Ferdinand chuckled. "It isn't easy."

"Sometimes," his wife said, "it's hard even to know what course is good, but Jesus and my confessor show me the way. Best of all, when I sin, my sins are forgiven."

Ice seemed to run through me. Were they going to force baptism on us?

"Look at me, Paloma," Queen Isabella said.

I did.

Her eyes were blue. "Tell me your latest good deed."

What good deed? I obeyed and respected my parents and Belo, but those weren't deeds. "Er . . ." I took three shallow breaths and remembered. "On the way here, I massaged my abuelo's feet."

After a moment of silence, a squeak escaped Queen Isabella. King Ferdinand cried, "Ho!"

I hoped I'd said something dreadful enough to make the queen stop wanting me for a Christian but not so awful that I'd be killed.

Then Papá laughed his boisterous laugh. An instant later, the king drowned him out with his own laughter, and Queen Isabella proved to have a gurgling laugh. She let go of my hand.

Belo didn't laugh. I turned to see his beard jutting. He was angry—probably at me.

The queen wiped her eyes. "More of our guests should bring progeny. Don Joseph, I see why you prize your granddaughter so. Paloma, you may go back to your grandfather and father."

I hurried to Papá, who put his arm around me and

spoke for the first time. "Majesty, she's a truthful child."

Belo said, "Paloma is an unusual girl, but, my queen"—
he swept a bow—"unusual females aren't unprecedented."

Queen Isabella nodded, and I decided that Belo had
brought me on this trip just so he could say that sentence.

"Spain's need is great." King Ferdinand leaned forward
and put his forearms on his knees. "It won't be satisfied by
a small sum."

"Not if we are to defeat the infidel," Queen Isabella said.

The infidel meant Muslims, who ruled in the south. The
Christians had been fighting them for hundreds of years.
Jews weren't the infidel; we were the heretics. Just as bad.

The queen stood. "Dine with us tomorrow."

The king stood, too. "Bring a proposal. Leave the child
behind."

12

At noon the next day, Belo and Papá dined privately with the monarchs, and Papá offered his proposal. Late in the afternoon, when they returned, the three of us sat on a stone bench in the courtyard that the rabbi shared with three other families.

On one side of me, Belo yawned. On the other side, Papá wriggled his shoulders. I sensed how relieved both of them felt.

Papá had suggested a new head tax, that is, a tax on every Christian who paid taxes (not nobles or church officials, who didn't). Jews already paid a head tax.

The Church would increase its tithes, too. Tithes were a religious kind of tax. Most of the money went to the Church, but the monarchs got a share, which few people knew.

The monarchs had appointed Papá chief tax farmer for the new tax. He'd first have to give the monarchs the tax out of his own money—and Belo's—and then farm (collect) it from their subjects. He'd be allowed to collect more than he had laid out and keep what was left over. But sometimes the tax farmer wouldn't be able to collect as much as he'd given the king and queen, and then he'd lose money. The monarchs always got the amount they expected. Tax farming was risky!

"It was a good day," Papá said.

I took advantage of how relaxed they were. "Why do any Jews become Christians when they aren't forced to? Do they believe in Jesus?"

Papá said, "Some may. The Christians say Judaism is the way of the past and theirs is the way of the future. Some believe that."

I wondered what conversion felt like: the baptismal water soaking my head, believing that God had a son, eating pork, marrying a Christian, having Christian children, not needing Bela's amulet, because no one kidnapped Christian children.

Might I like it?

When we returned home, my nephew Todros was shy with me for a week. I had a lump in my throat the whole time.

In June, Yuda and Dueyna were married. This time, I spoke to Papá before the wedding. Whatever he did I don't know, but Belo let me go to the celebration. I danced for hours, sometimes with my sisters, but mostly with Beatriz and Todros.

In August (a month after I turned eight), I went with both Belo and Papá to the city of Burgos, where Belo helped Papá be a tax farmer. Belo had me come along for another meal at an inn with a wealthy Old Christian and for a dinner at the home of a New Christian.

Before, I hadn't realized there were two kinds of Christians. Old Christians had believed in Christ for a century or more, while New Christians, also called *conversos*, had for less than that—if they really did believe. Many New Christians had converted to keep from being killed by mobs, but if they went back to being Jews, they'd be executed.

At the inn with the Old Christians, we were served a dish of chicken baked with cheese. Belo and Papá ate, so I did, too, even though we were breaking Jewish law.

Afterward, Belo said, "If we can't eat with the Christians, we can't do business with them. The rabbis say it's all right, if it's good for the Jews."

I didn't mention how delicious I thought the dish had been.

At the New Christians' house, however, dinner followed our law in every way, including prayers in Hebrew. The servants were Moors—Muslim, not Christian, as I could tell by the women's pants and the men's turbans—because the conversos were in constant danger of being discovered practicing Judaism, called "Judaizing." Moors would be less likely to report them to priests than Christians would. If the conversos were caught, the Holy Inquisition—the Christian religious court—could make them pay a fine or take their belongings or even have them killed.

Back home, Mamá and Ledicia were growing big bellies. Hooray! I was going to be an aunt and an older sister again. I hugged Mamá, who tolerated my arms and yelled at Fatima for not dusting carefully enough.

The next Friday, I cooked the Sabbath stew myself—soaked the white beans, simmered the lamb and onion, added the beans, mixed the spices, stirred and stirred.

When he tasted it, Papá said, "Aljohar should be jealous."

Aljohar smiled. "She's a credit to Doña Violanta and me."

Samuel said, "Your husband will be a lucky man."

Belo said, "Esther used to put in extra garlic for me, the way I like it."

Next time, I thought. I always wanted to please Belo.

But the next time, he said I'd made the stew too salty.

In November, Yuda was caught gambling again, this time with Zemah, the rabbi's son, who was only eleven.

I don't know what happened between Yuda and his wife and her family, but in our house, Mamá's shouts resounded.

She called Yuda a serpent from the moment he was born and blamed Papá for not supervising him more. "You can't take your eyes off a serpent."

Even though Papá had said he wouldn't be able to once Yuda was a man, he and Belo did protect my brother as much as they could. Money was given to the synagogue and the aljama council. A gift went to Don Ziza, the goldsmith, to stop him from dismissing Yuda. Belo sent a heavy purse to chief constable Don Rodrigo to forestall punishment from the Christians. And a donation was made to the aljama poor, because gambling wasn't a sin if the winnings went to the poor.

On the day following the discovery of the gambling, Samuel, Vellida, and I were included in a family meeting with Yuda in Belo's study.

Belo sat in his chair; Mamá and Papá shared a settle that had been carried in. Samuel, Vellida, and I sat on cushions. Yuda stood.

He resembled a camel's head less than he used to. He'd grown plumper than I was, and now had a roll of fat that suggested a chin buried somewhere.

He wore gold and silver rings on every finger. Around his neck hung an emerald pendant—goldsmiths wore their wares to show what they could do. He produced silk packets from his pocket, which he distributed to Belo, Papá, and Mamá.

"What's this?" Belo said.

"Rings I made for you. I was saving them for Hanuk-kah, but you've been so kind." He turned to Samuel and me. "I'm going to make rings for you, too."

Belo and Papá instantly gave them back without looking.

Mamá emptied her packet into her palm, revealing a pearl set in a silver ring, which she drew onto her index finger. "It's little enough for all I've done for you."

Belo's eyes went to his bookshelves. I knew he wanted to get back to his books and his writing. "Tell us what happened."

Yuda sat on a cushion. "Zemah begged me to teach him the rules of dicing"—he blushed—"which I barely remem-bered."

It was Zemah's fault?

He went on. "I just wanted him to enjoy himself, so we played for a few coins. It won't happen again."

"The sum doesn't matter," Papá said. "It was gambling. We've managed to keep you from being excommunicated."

Excommunication for even a day was terrible. The whole aljama would shun the person.

Belo said, "You won't be excommunicated, but you may be flogged."

Yuda's eyes filled. "I didn't harm Zemah. I didn't harm anyone."

"The rabbi and the council will decide," Papá said.

"The aljama is angry. They don't want a rich man's son to be able to do whatever he wants."

Samuel said, "Papá, why is gambling a sin, since God decides how the dice land?"

"There's more than one opinion, son," Papá began, "but—"

"Did Zemah expect to win from you, Yuda?" Belo said.

"I told him it could go either way, and he knew that anyway."

Yes. I was only eight, and I knew. But I was sure Yuda had enticed Zemah with the likelihood of winning.

"Gamblers don't expect to lose," Belo said. "The winner is a thief, who steals the loser's coin. Gambling is a sin because it's thievery." He could have stopped there, but he added, "Judaism is a light to the nations, but you, Yuda, are a darkness."

It sounded like a curse.

Papá said mildly, "Son, I only want to be proud of you."

His anger seemingly over, Belo said, "I want that, too. Nothing more."

Yuda stood and kissed Belo and Papá on the cheek. "I hope to surprise you."

That sounded ominous to me and to Samuel, too, from his glance at me, but both Belo and Papá took Yuda's hands and pressed them.

Didn't they see his malice?

13

A year earlier, in our courtyard, Yuda himself had described a flogging to Samuel and me, which he'd witnessed the day before in front of the synagogue.

"First Don Israel examined Señor Ezmel."

Don Israel was a physician, and Señor Ezmel was a locksmith.

"What did Señor Ezmel do?" I said, sitting on a bench.

"Cheated customers. Don Israel said he was healthy, so he had to bend over and raise his shirt."

Yuda told us the whip was a leather strap folded in half with a handle in the middle, so that both ends struck Señor Ezmel's back.

Grinning, Yuda raised his arm and slashed down. "There was blood right away. Señor Ezmel yelled that he was sorry and he'd never do it again, so they stopped. I pity him."

That night, during my worry time in bed, I tried not to picture the whip lashing Yuda's pudgy back. Though I hated him, I didn't want him to be flogged.

And he wasn't. The next day, we learned that the aljama council, awash in gifts from Papá and Belo, decided that Yuda's offense hadn't been serious enough.

In February 1485, Mamá and Ledicia had their babies. Ledicia had a daughter, named Jamila, and Mamá had a son, named Jento.

Thanks to the Almighty, all lived and were healthy. I spent as much time as I could going back and forth between houses, hovering over one crib and then the other.

In March, Samuel turned eleven, and in April, Vellida married her Jacob.

I discovered, while dancing, that Beatriz, at age four, had begun to worry. She stumbled once, pulled her hand out of mine, and left the circle.

I followed her. "What's wrong?"

"I don't like to dance."

She loved to dance! After coaxing, she told me she didn't like to stumble when she danced. "I did it wrong, Tía Loma."

"We don't have to dance."

"Good."

But I wanted to, and I wanted to with her. I had an idea. "Watch."

"Stay with me!"

But I joined the circle again, clasped hands with two women, and stumbled on purpose. The hands held me up. I kicked when you weren't supposed to and failed to kick when you were. I added a jump that didn't belong at all—

—and a laughing Beatriz broke into the circle. We danced together until the music finally stopped.

At the end of May, when the whole family went to the synagogue to celebrate Shavuot, a priest and a Christian scribe in a voluminous white robe leaned against the north wall. The congregation waited for the usual diatribe, but neither of them spoke, so the hazan began the service.

I missed the haranguing! At least that was routine— death, hellfire, demons—I hated it, but I was used to it. This was alarming because it was unusual. I put my arms around Beatriz and Todros. If they became frightened, I was ready to comfort them.

After the service came announcements by the head of the aljama council—of weddings, engagements, births. Flies buzzed. My scalp itched.

When the last announcement was made, the rabbi mounted to the tevah.

"I am told to say this: All the Jews of Spain are instructed by the grand inquisitor, Tomás de Torquemada, to report any Christians that you know of who are Judaizing. For instance, they may ask you how to observe the Sabbath, or when one of our holidays is. Anyone who doesn't tell the priests"—his chest rose in a deep breath—"will be excommunicated. If you know such conversos, I urge you not to protect them. But any who accuse falsely will be punished by the Inquisition." He left the tevah.

Belo and Papá knew Christians—New Christians— who Judaized, who were really secret Jews, as much as they could be. *I* knew them. Was I supposed to go to the Tribunal?

We weren't the only ones who did business with conversos. Shopkeepers had New Christian customers. Artisans did, too. Yuda's master, Don Ziza, did. The converso customers of Señor Lauda, the butcher, came to him for kosher meat. Every single one would be a Judaizer! Did he have to inform on them?

The priest ascended the tevah. "Do not add to your own heresy the sin of destroying Christian souls." He began the usual speech but stopped after only a few demons had tormented us. His voice softened. "I've warned you many times, week after week, but you don't believe in hellfire. You know excommunication, though, and the life of an outcast. I beg you, don't bring that down on yourselves."

He left with the scribe.

If Belo, Papá, and I became outcasts, could we be outcasts together?

When we got home, Fatima was standing in the vestibule. She told us that a priest was waiting in Belo's study. "He asked for Loma, too."

Ai!

Papá kissed my forehead. "Don't speak unless you must."

Mamá said, "This is what comes of taking a child everywhere."

Belo said, "'I don't know' is an excellent answer, Loma."

In the study, the priest had taken Belo's chair. On Belo's desk rested a plate of dates, figs, and almonds, which a servant must have brought.

Servants had also carried in a settle. Belo and Papá bowed, and I curtsied. They didn't sit, so I didn't, either.

"Welcome to my house," Belo said, which I knew he meant to be funny, because the priest was acting as if it were *his* house. "Please eat. The figs are especially good."

The priest took a single date and a single almond.

"We're honored by your visit," Papá said.

"I'm visiting no one else."

Did he mean we should feel honored or frightened?

Belo sat on the settle, and Papá and I did, too.

"Don Joseph, you serve the Church."

Belo collected tithes for a cardinal, and he gave gifts to bishops and cardinals.

"And the monarchs." Belo took two figs and passed the plate to Papá.

A breeze wafted in. Outside, hooves *clip-clopped*. Papá handed the plate to me, and I rested it in my lap, because I didn't know what else to do with it. If I tried to swallow, I'd choke.

The priest waved away a fly. "You eat in the homes of New Christians. If they're practicing Jewish rites, you would see." He turned to me. "Child, you've been there. Have you seen it?"

Ai! I couldn't ignore a question. And I had seen it.

"Child—"

"Her name is Paloma," Belo said.

"Paloma, nothing will happen to you if you tell me."

What would happen to Belo and Papá? "I d-don't know."

"Did they eat cheese and meat together?"

"I d-don't know."

"Did they serve bloody meat?" (Kosher meat was never bloody.)

I repeated that I didn't know.

"What is the weather today?"

"I don't— It's hot and sunny."

"Did they talk with your abuelo and Papá about the law?"

"I don't know."

"Don Joseph, I'm aware how dear this child is to you. Soon you may have to bring her to the baptismal font as the only way to save her. You can go, child."

I looked at Belo. He nodded, and I fled.

The Holy Inquisition joined my list of nightly worries.

The priest didn't return to our house, and I wasn't called to the Holy Tribunal, but Señor Lauda, the butcher, denounced three converso housewives for buying kosher meat. One lost half her property and had to spend six months in prison; another had to wear the *sanbenito*, a yellow tunic, and a tall conical cap, for a week; the third was found innocent. For informing falsely, Señor Lauda was sentenced to death by stoning and was killed.

I heard about it when Mamá told Aljohar in the kitchen, where I was stirring bread into the stew to thicken it. The spoon slipped out of my hand.

Aljohar, who bought the family's meat, cried, "Woe!" After her lamentations, she added, "Such a kind man. And honest."

No one else from the aljama came forward to the

Inquisition, but Old Christians informed on New. People were tried for what seemed to be minor failings. A man lost all his property for washing his hands before praying—a Christian prayer!

In April 1486, when I was nine and three-quarters, the town council of Valmaseda, far in the north, expelled its Jews, despite the queen's order that they *not* be expelled. Belo went to persuade the council to change its mind and took me, Hamdun, and six guards with him.

I half didn't want to go. Vellida was pregnant with her first, and the baby could come any day. Of course I did go. No one asked my opinion anyway.

On the ride there, Belo was jubilant. "Loma . . ."

"Yes, Belo?" I rode next to him, because I was old enough to be on my own mount, a mule for this trip since the terrain was mountainous.

"Now we use our wealth." The gold ducats in his saddlebag clinked softly. "We'll spend whatever we need to to return the Jews to their synagogue before the gentiles can make it into a church." Holding the reins loosely, he turned his hands palm up in his lap, as he did when he was about to bargain with someone. "Everyone will be delighted. Did I ever ask you this riddle?"

"Which one?" We both loved riddles.

"The wise men of Athens tested a rabbi by ordering

him to show them the center of the world, so the rabbi pointed at the ground at his feet. 'Down there.' The wise men were amazed and made the rabbi say how he knew. How did he know, Loma?"

That was the riddle? I laughed and admitted I had no idea.

"Ah. The rabbi said to the wise men, 'Prove me wrong.'" Belo started laughing, too. "They couldn't!"

That was the answer: they couldn't. Clever rabbi! It became my favorite riddle.

No other Jewish girl had my adventures. An hour later, I experienced snow up close. Snow! As in my plague delirium. Not coming down, but on the ground near the road. I dismounted and touched it, the coldest thing I'd ever felt.

The next morning, the town councilors of Valmaseda met with Belo, and I was there. They didn't want a new door for their church or a monument in their square, and they wouldn't take money outright. They just wanted to be rid of their Jews.

When we left them and crossed the town's ancient bridge, Belo said, more to himself than to me, "How are people staying warm?"

The breeze was chilly. I was snug in my heavy cloak, my hat, and my plumpness.

The expelled Jews were camped in shabby tents in a

green valley watered by the Cadagua River. A flock of thirty-five sheep grazed nearby.

I counted fifteen tents and fifteen wavering fires. In sight were twenty people, tending the fires or gathering brush from the bushes along the river, but more people were probably in the tents, out of the wind.

A straggle of seven Jews, four men and three women, ran toward us, led by a youngish man in a gray cloak and a knotted wool hat, who introduced himself as Rabbi Huda. Belo said who he was and who I was.

The rabbi bowed and turned to his companions. "Don Joseph! God heard us! Do you come from the king and queen?"

"Don Solomon Bohor is hurrying to them." Belo dismounted from his mule.

I dismounted, too. Don Solomon was Belo's friend who'd visited us.

Belo added, "Show us how you're faring."

"Your granddaughter, too?"

"Yes. She wants to come."

I did want to.

The guards and Hamdun stayed behind. I noticed Hamdun's sad face.

As we walked to the tents, the rabbi said, "We have fish from the river, but not enough. We don't dare slaughter any of the farmer's sheep, even though we'd pay him back." He pointed at a farmhouse perched on the hill above us. "Señor Diego hates Jews."

We stooped to enter the tent the rabbi led us to. I heard mewling and was transported into the past. A sick kitten!

But the whimper turned out to come from a baby. In the back of the tent, a woman sat on a carpet with a blanket around her shoulders and a baby in her lap.

The rabbi said, "Our son won't nurse. We have no medicine, no physician."

I crouched by the mamá. How thin the baby's arms were! And how big his eyes. Beautiful! "Can I hold him?"

The woman shook her head. "I have him."

The rabbi led us to other tents. We saw a woman with a swollen leg, a man who hadn't stopped weeping for two days, and a woman who was guarded by her husband because she kept trying to return on foot to Valmaseda, where her married daughter lived as a Christian.

I could think only of the sick baby.

Belo gave half our ducats to Rabbi Huda and told him to use the money to buy food and whatever the aljama needed to better their situation.

The rabbi thanked him. "This will help us find new homes."

We left the camp to return to the city of Vitoria, which we had passed through on our way here. Belo prayed for half an hour. I felt comforted until he began to talk.

"As soon as I saw those councilors, I knew we'd fail."

We? Had I failed?

"But there must have been something we could have said—how much money we had. They probably didn't think we had so much. Should we go back? I've already given the rabbi half, so we no longer have it. We shouldn't go back."

"Why did you give the rabbi only half, Belo?"

"Half was more than enough! Who knows what else our purse will be needed for tomorrow or next week?"

"Oh." I asked my most important question: "Belo? Is there a physician in Vitoria?"

"Yes. Why?"

"Can we send him to the rabbi's baby?"

"That baby is past saving."

He would die? I wept until I had no more tears.

14

As we rode, Belo continued going over what had happened. I'd never seen him so agitated. Finally, he said, "You're quiet, Loma."

"What was wrong with the baby?"

"Even a physician might not know. Babies aren't hardy. Sometimes they die."

As my baby sister, Soli, and my brother Haim had during the plague. I wished Papá or one of my sisters or Samuel was here.

Were baby Jento and Jamila all right? Had Vellida given birth to a healthy baby? Were all of them well? A noisy sob escaped.

"Loma . . . your bela was always the one to comfort the children."

Meaning he didn't know how.

Hamdun maneuvered his mule close to mine. "Mistress, it's very sad. Babies should live to grow up."

I nodded at him and felt a little comforted.

It was dark when we reached the rabbi's house in Vitoria. The guards and Hamdun stayed in the house next door. I slept in a bed with the rabbi's twin daughters, who were three years old. When I woke once in the middle of the night, their easy breathing sent me back to sleep.

Belo always wanted an early start, so I wasn't surprised when the rabbi's wife woke me at dawn. But he wasn't in the dining room, and the rabbi's wife said he wasn't feeling well.

"What's wrong with him?" He was fine yesterday!

"Don Shemaya is looking at him."

I understood that was the physician.

"Have some food." She cut me a slice of bread and a wedge of cheese from a tray on the table and put them aside for me on the tablecloth.

My stomach insisted I eat. I swallowed a bite of cheese. "Is he very sick?"

"The doctor will tell us."

One of the twins wailed, and the rabbi's wife ran to their bedroom. Alone in the dining room, I made myself concentrate: three open cupboards for platters and bowls: one for meat, one for dairy, and one for Passover. A silver menorah stood atop one of the shorter cabinets.

Was Belo in pain?

To quiet my fear, I counted the wooden floor planks, walking around the room so I wouldn't miss any.

"Paloma . . ."

I turned. The rabbi and an old man stood under the archway to the room.

The old man, Don Shemaya, said that Belo was resting. "I bled him and cupped him. He's tired, but he asked for you."

I entered the bedroom, where Belo had spent the night. He was sitting, propped up by five pillows.

He smiled at me—or meant to. His mouth went up only on the left side. His right eye seemed droopy but his left eye was as ever.

"Lo . . . ma. Hard . . . to . . ." His mouth worked, but more words didn't come.

"A paroxysm," Don Shemaya said. "I suspect he's had them before. We have to see how he takes the treatment."

Belo's good eye went from my face to his right. Did that mean anything? He did it again. And again. And tilted his head to the right, too.

"Is he trying to say something?" I asked.

Don Shemaya said, "I don't know."

I walked to the side of the bed he'd tilted his head at and saw the saddlebag with the ducats on the floor. Did he want it? Did he want me to take it? The rabbi would never steal from him! Did he mean the saddlebag at all?

Don Shemaya said, "I'll stop by this afternoon to see how he's doing."

Belo's head became almost violent. "Lo . . . Lo . . ."

The physician left.

Belo squealed, "Lo!"

I realized. "Wait!" I cried.

Don Shemaya returned.

How many ducats? Belo wouldn't want me to give too many or too few. I took out five ducats, which jingled in my hand. Belo's eye bulged.

Too many. I dropped three back in. "Don Shemaya, thank you." I held out my hand.

He took one ducat. "Thank you. I'll be back."

The rabbi left to go to the synagogue. The rabbi's wife said she'd bring a tray of food for Belo, and she left, too.

When we were alone, Belo started the morning prayers. I couldn't understand him, but I recognized the cadence. I said the actual words along with him, enunciating each one especially clearly.

The rabbi's wife bustled back in, set a tray of bread, cheese, and dried figs on the bed, and slipped out.

When Belo finished praying, he tried to pick up the wedge of cheese with his right hand, but it slid across the tray and knocked the food onto the blanket. I put everything back on the tray. He patted the bed next to him. I sat and watched anxiously, but he ate without difficulty, using his left hand.

He chewed on that side for a few minutes but then began to chew on both sides. After he finished, he said, clearly, "I was hungry. Look!" He made a fist with his right hand, opened it, closed it. "It was just a spasm, Loma, an attack. This isn't the first one. Leave me so I can dress."

Relieved and happy, I found my cloak in the living room and discovered the rabbi's wife in the kitchen. "Belo is well again. Thank you for your hospitality. We're leaving."

"No!" She ran out, calling over her shoulder, "I'll get Don Shemaya. Don't go until he comes."

I knew I couldn't stop Belo, but dressing took him longer than usual. By the time he emerged from the bedroom, both Don Shemaya and the rabbi had come.

Belo ignored the physician's warnings that he should rest. After thanking him for the cure, he took my arm and led me outside. I doubt anyone could have seen that he was leaning heavily on me.

He was frightening me, but I knocked on the neighbor's door. Soon enough, the guards and Hamdun went for their mules and ours, and we were off.

As we cantered out of the city, my hands squeezed the reins. I wondered if Belo had been close to death during the night, if he would have died without Don Shemaya's treatment, if he might get sick again while we were traveling, miles from a house, miles from a doctor, where I wouldn't know what to do.

We arrived home safely, with Belo in seeming good health, and discovered that Vellida had given birth to a baby girl, named Clara.

Blessed are You, Eternal One, Who brings us to this moment for blessing.

I visited Vellida and the baby as soon as I could—half an hour after we got home. My sister looked radiant in her and Jacob's big bed, propped up by a bolster, the baby against her stomach.

Clara was beautiful, with gray eyes and a fuzz of brown hair. I put my finger to her tiny hand, and she held it. My heart beat wildly. Let her stay healthy! Let the Christians not harm her!

"Isn't she sweet?" Vellida said. "Her favorite thing to do is stare."

Clara's eyes closed.

"Next favorite is sleep."

At home, Jento had taught himself to walk a few steps. When he saw me, he trundled toward me, toppled, looked astonished, and then laughed. I threw myself on the floor with him and kissed his forehead and his lovely ears. His favorite activity, as I discovered when I returned to the rhythm of home, was to take stale bread cubes carefully out of a bowl onto a platter and then put them back in the bowl, eating as he went. I watched him while I worked in the kitchen. My eyes couldn't get enough.

I hated having the secret of Belo's illness. What if he still needed to rest? What if he didn't rest and he died?

He had made me promise not to tell Papá that he'd been sick, but he didn't say anything about Samuel, so I mastered my dislike of discord and told him. As I hoped, he reported the news to Papá, who went straight to Belo.

Samuel and I heard the argument from the courtyard balcony, where he had been explaining his latest lesson to me, this one in Latin, the language of Christian prayers.

From Belo's study, Papá yelled the question I'd wondered about. "What would have happened to Loma if you'd died?"

Samuel looked up from his book. I hunched my shoulders and stared down at it. Ledicia, who had come for the day, entered the balcony and joined us on our bench, sitting so that I was between her and Samuel.

"Thank you for your concern for *me*." Belo sounded sarcastic, as if Papá didn't care about him. "Someone would have brought her home."

"Who? Nobody loves her as we do."

Ledicia put her hand on the back of my neck.

"Where are the children?" I whispered.

Ledicia tilted her head.

Mamá cried from the living room, "Todros!"

Belo yelled, "I care about her welfare more than anyone. I love her more than anyone."

"You can't take her with you anymore unless I'm there, too."

I didn't want to be left behind!

"I can and I will. She's a comfort to me."

"Loma . . . ," Ledicia whispered in the silence that followed Belo's declaration. "We all love Belo."

I knew that.

Samuel put his book on the bench. "I'm hungry." He left us.

"Belo is good for our family," Ledicia went on.

"And for all the Jews."

"Yes, but . . ." She trailed off.

From his study, Belo added, "Think before you cross me, Asher."

Papá's voice rose in pitch. "Are you threatening me?"

I started to cry. Did Papá and Belo hate each other now? Because of me?

15

Ledicia put her arm around my shoulder and held me while I sobbed. She said into my hair, "Belo can be a little selfish. Keeping you safe should be the most important thing."

I just didn't want him to be sick when we were away from home, with me not knowing what to do. When I finally finished weeping, I looked down at the wooden balcony floor and told Ledicia about the sick baby and everything I'd seen in the tents.

"Belo said the baby would die. He said babies aren't hardy, and I remembered Haim and Soli. I couldn't stop worrying about Todros and Beatriz and Jento and Jamila."

Ledicia stroked my forehead. "Belo forgets how young you are, because you're so clever."

From now on, I'd have to be clever enough not to be my age.

That night in his study, while Fatima massaged his feet, Belo said, "You betrayed me, Loma."

I said, "I want to keep traveling with you."

"Then keep my secrets."

I promised I would, but he was cold to me for two whole days. I could hardly bear it.

Belo and Papá didn't speak to each other for a week. Then everything seemed to return to normal.

Belo had his way. In January 1487, I traveled alone with him to Sigüenza, where he tax-farmed for Cardinal de Mendoza, his great patron after the monarchs.

Papá told me what to do if Belo got sick again. If we were in the countryside, I was to leave him with one of the guards and ride with Hamdun and the other guards to the nearest town where Jews lived. If we were already in a ju-dería, I was to stay there until someone in the family came for me or for both of us. I was not to travel with Belo after he'd been ill, no matter what he said.

I said I would, but Papá shouldn't have believed me. He should have known I'd never leave Belo when he was sick.

Never mind. He stayed healthy, perhaps because he'd received word that the monarchs were making the town of

Valmaseda take back its Jews.

"Loma, I did good by going there. My presence must have mattered to the king and queen."

He didn't mention the baby, and I guessed he'd forgotten.

In February, we visited Calahorra and Toledo. While we were away, both my brother Jento and my niece Jamila mastered the art of climbing stairs unaided. Baby Clara wailed whenever I approached.

Ledicia promised that her fear would pass. She laughed. "When they're old enough, they'll want you to leave so you can bring back presents."

She saw my face.

"They love you! You're Bela to them, even though you're Tía Loma." She sobered. "And you're young, and you survived the plague, so they'll have you for a lot longer."

We all still missed Bela.

She added, "Beatriz wants to sleep in the snood you brought her."

I smiled. It *was* pretty, a silver net sprinkled with tiny pearls.

Samuel turned thirteen. The entire family, including Yuda and Dueyna and my married sisters and their families, came for dinner.

How deep Samuel's voice sounded when he thanked his

well-wishers. As little as a week ago, it was still cracking sometimes. Perhaps God had waited for this day to entirely give him a man's voice, a rabbi's voice. Anyone would be rapt, hearing teachings delivered in such a voice.

Mamá, Ledicia, and Vellida balanced their babies on their laps. My lap felt empty, but my niece and nephew had clamored to sit next to me, six-year-old Beatriz on my left, and four-year-old Todros on my right.

Beatriz slipped her hand into mine and tilted up her chin. "Tía Loma, I—"

I whispered into her curls. "You don't like meat. I know."

She nodded solemnly. I glanced at Mamá, who was scolding Jento for wearing what she called an angry face. He began to wail. Papá took him, and he quieted.

Aljohar brought out the Sabbath stew, which I had pre-pared—Samuel's favorite. The recipe came from Mamá's mamá of blessed memory. I loved the spices—the saffron, pepper, ginger, and cinnamon—which made the lamb taste, to my mind, like gold, if gold were edible.

I'd prepared extra against gluttonous Yuda, so there would be enough for a big helping for Samuel. The bowl went around the table. When it reached me, I took enough for me and Beatriz and pushed the meat to the side.

Everyone but Belo gave the traditional compliments on my cooking: the flavors were perfect; nothing over- or undercooked; my husband would be lucky to get me; my children would thrive on such meals—though in Yuda's mouth the words seemed to mock. Belo never praised my cooking, though he often praised Aljohar's.

Papá announced that he had hired a scholar from Ocaña to teach Samuel.

Belo said, "I'd like your opinion of my essay on history, Samuel. I should hear what the future rabbi thinks."

Samuel blushed and said he looked forward to it.

Belo added, "Come to my study after dinner." He didn't include me, which was right. This was Samuel's day. Still, I felt left out.

After dinner, I descended to the courtyard and sat on a bench. The March sun was sweet, and the myrtle had buds. Samuel's bar mitzvah had me thinking of my future. I was eleven. In as little as three years I might have my own baby.

I barely heard the footsteps. Yuda.

He sat next to me. "Dueyna is too timid with her spices, but I pay her the same compliments everyone paid you."

That was disloyal to his wife, and he meant that some of my compliments hadn't been sincere. He could stir up two kinds of discord in a single sentence.

"She may be barren. Mamá keeps asking about grandchildren. She doesn't know the pain she causes."

"I'm sorry," I said.

"Not painful to me. To Dueyna, who is a dutiful wife."

What else would she be? Didn't he want children?

"What does my clever sister think of Jesus?"

I frowned. "Me? I don't think of Jesus."

"Do you think God could have a Son?"

I shrugged.

He waited.

"God can do anything." I shifted on the bench. "He could have a daughter." The idea surprised me.

"He wouldn't. Suppose He did have a Son, His Son would be a gift, like the Sabbath is. People who believed in His Son would be His people, don't you think? God would be angry at anyone who didn't believe. He takes better care of Christians than He does of us. We may be feeling His wrath."

Why was he telling me this? "Do you believe in Jesus?"

"I don't know. I asked you for wisdom."

He didn't mean that, but I tried to think of a wise answer. "God gave us His law."

"And gave the Christians His Son."

I could hardly bring out the words. "Are you going to convert?" Belo might have an attack again. Papá would be beyond grief.

"Maybe." He stood and left.

A hoopoe pecked at a stripe of earth between two tiles. God made the hoopoe.

"Do you believe in Jesus?" I asked it.

It flew away.

Yuda would have relished knowing that his words poisoned my thoughts for a long while after we spoke. Were Jews wrong about everything? Would we all go to the hell the priests shrieked about?

16

The Christians' war to win all of Spain from the Muslims continued. Belo and Papá wanted the monarchs to win. Papá said that the Jews would pay lower taxes if there were peace. Belo said there would be new wars but that God had given us these rulers, so we should be on their side.

I wanted the Christians to lose, as a sign that God wasn't on their side.

In mid-August, Belo was summoned to the city of Málaga, which the monarchs had captured from the Moors. Papá argued against my going with Belo: the fighting was barely over; the soldiers would still be armed; I was too young.

Mamá alarmed me by wondering who would marry a girl as worldly as I would become, indeed already was.

Jento cried when I mounted my horse.

We traveled through the province of Andalusia, where no Jews had been allowed to live for four years. I looked for signs of God's favor on this Christians-only land, but the olive trees and the grape vines, laden with fruit, were no heavier here. The sky was the same relentless blue, and the heat grew more oppressive as we rode south.

I begged for a sign. Show me, God, I thought. If Jesus is Your Son, show me, and I'll convince Belo, and he'll convince the whole family. We'll be perfect Christians. The Inquisition will have no cause to accuse us.

We slept in tents in fields, since there were no juderías, but our tent was beautiful: on the outside, tan canvas; on the inside, brocade in green, coral, and ivory thread. Hamdun spread carpeting and smoothed out the bumps.

One night, I massaged Belo's feet while he used his knife to repair his pen.

"Belo? Why do the Christians care if Muslims and Jews convert?" I worked in the clove oil Fatima had given me. The tent filled with the bracing scent.

"Christians push us to convert because they're acting out God's will. The Almighty sends tribulations to test us."

I stopped kneading in surprise. "God makes them want us to convert?"

"Didn't He harden Pharaoh's heart?"

Did God make Yuda tell me his ideas about Jesus and Christians to test me?

No. I wasn't that important.

"Please don't neglect my left foot, which has to walk, too. Loma, why do you think our converso friends wish they could be Jews again?"

I changed feet. "Because of the Inquisition?"

"Why else? What do the priests tell us in synagogue every week?"

"That we'll burn in hell."

"Do we think *they'll* burn in hell?"

"I don't know." Samuel's books, which I'd read, were mostly about how to worship and what to do every day, like massaging Belo's feet—not that his feet were in the Bible, but honoring parents was. "I haven't read about hell in Torah."

"Exactly. Keep thinking."

"It's good to be Jewish because we don't believe in hell?"

Belo took another tack. "Do you like Sukkoth?"

I nodded. Everyone loved Sukkoth.

"Do you like the story of Esther? Do you like Purim?"

I nodded again and began to understand. "It's more"— Was this the right word?—"*enjoyable* to be Jewish?"

"Yes! The law isn't about staying out of hell. It's about the way we behave and feel before we die. That includes joy. We don't have to wait to be blissful until we're dead and have entered their heaven—after torment in their purgatory." He put his penknife away, reached for the folio on the carpet next to him, and began to write.

I hugged Belo's words when I went to bed. It made people happy to be Jewish.

But I sat up with a new thought: Yuda wasn't happy. The comfort melted away.

Early the next afternoon, we began to cross the hills that watched over Málaga, passing through forests of elm, juniper, and evergreen oak. Because the tide of people was against us, we proceeded in single file, a guard in the lead, then Belo, then me, then Hamdun, followed by the other guards.

Soldiers in loose groups trudged past us, this one with his arm in a sling, that one leaning on a crutch. I counted fifty-three soldiers and then lost track. Parties of nobles and their attendants trotted by on their destriers, the horses' gay trappings dulled by dust. A squire in a red-and-gold doublet, the colors of Castile, carried out a tired pantomime: drooped in his saddle, jerked awake, rode erect, drooped again.

Occasionally, snatches of song broke out among the

soldiers, but mostly they were a silent horde, grimly marching back to their interrupted lives. The loudest sounds were footfalls, hoofbeats, neighs.

I sensed our guards' Jew badges, the bright red meant to draw Christian eyes. (I knew by now that Belo and Papá paid a fee so our family didn't have to wear them.) Belo waved his hand in greeting at everyone. I kept swallowing my fear. The Christians stared but didn't accost us.

In late afternoon, a pair of oxen filled the road ahead of us, with more oxen behind them. We swerved onto the grassy margin. The first pair went by, linked to the next by iron chains. More oxen followed. I began to count. Drovers walked beside the beasts, keeping the chains from tangling. What were they pulling?

After thirty pairs, a wooden cart grumbled toward us. In the cart was an iron tube big enough for plump me to slide inside. Belo told me later that the tube was a lombard—a cannon.

Behind the cannon were more oxen, pulling, as we discovered, another lombard. And more oxen after that. No wonder the Moors of Málaga had been defeated.

Late in the afternoon, we crested the final hill. Belo reined in his horse and held up his hand for us all to stop.

Below us spread the conquerors. A forest must have been chopped down to make room for this billowing, pulsing sea of tents, interrupted by aisles crowded with horses, mules, donkeys, people.

Past the tents stood Málaga itself, guarded by the Alcazaba, the city's stone-and-mortar fortification, which glowed orange-pink in the sunset. It looked indestructible, with its high, sheer walls.

But, of course, it had been taken. Another sign of God's favor toward the Christians.

Beyond the city sparkled the innocent sea.

I lowered my eyes to the scene nearby. "Are those prisoners, Belo?" I pointed at three corrals to the right of the tents—one enormous, one big, and one small, each holding people crowded together, with soldiers patrolling around them. From here, I couldn't see the people clearly.

"Yes, Loma." He pointed from the largest to the smallest. "Muslims, then Jews, and then, I'm guessing, conversos who went back to being Jews because the Moors let them." He spurred his horse. I spurred mine; the guards and Hamdun followed. The stink of the camp engulfed us. My eyes stung.

Skirting the tents, we trotted to the corrals, low palisades of vertical sapling trunks. From one corral to the next, the prisoners looked the same. Most were women; all were skinny, with knobby arms and wrists, stick legs below their tattered robes, and cheekbones making holes in their faces.

I remembered what Ledicia had said. Papá wouldn't have let me see the captives. Now was when I needed to be older than my age.

Among the prisoners were children but no babies, which I would have noticed no matter how old I was.

Babies aren't hardy. Had they all died?

17

The Jews surged toward us, extending their bony hands.

Belo asked a prisoner closest to us something in Arabic, which these Jews spoke, and which I knew little of. The man answered. I caught the word for *bread*.

A different man said in Spanish, "First food in a week and not much before that." He smiled, revealing a gap next to his front teeth. "A tooth stayed in the bread. Thanks to the king and queen for their bounty. Will you speak with them?"

Belo nodded. "I will."

"Tell them we'll be good subjects, loyal. We'll work hard. They won't be sorry."

Belo promised. He turned his horse, and I followed

him, but I kept looking over my shoulder.

No matter how kind the monarchs had been with food, it was their war that had starved the prisoners.

Belo reined in his horse to ask a soldier where to find Don Solomon's tent.

"The Jew?"

Belo nodded, and the soldier told him the way.

As we went, Belo said, "The monarchs want money again, Loma."

Don Solomon's grand tent was an outpost on the edge of the tent city. As soon as we entered, my eyes went to a big man, large-featured, blond, ruddy-complexioned, about Papá's age, who sat on a cushion across a low table from Don Solomon.

Smiling, Don Solomon heaved himself out of his cushion. The man rose, too, in a lithe surge despite his size, and stood head and shoulders taller than his host.

Belo bowed, and I curtsied.

The man bowed, too, not as deeply as Belo had. Christian? He wore no badge, but neither did we. His green woolen doublet fell in sharp pleats from the neckline to the hem just above his knees. His only jewelry was three silver rings.

Holding out his hands, Don Solomon went to Belo. His robe today was violet silk, and his hose was a dusky red.

On his head was an orange turban stitched with silver.

Belo and he embraced.

When they pulled away, Don Solomon said, "Allow me to introduce Don Christopher Columbus, who also has been summoned here. You know his purpose."

I didn't know.

Belo kindly explained. "Don Christopher proposes to sail west to where he's sure the Indies will be, and return with treasure."

"Treasure for the kingdom and my financiers." Don Christopher sounded hoarse, as if he'd been shouting.

"He'll use Abraham Zacuto's tables for navigation." Don Solomon smiled. "I'm one of the financiers. Treasure is always nice, and I want Don Abraham to be renowned."

Don Christopher crouched in front of me. "Zacuto's *Perpetual Almanac* will bring us there and back, sweet child, and never let us go astray—if we can find the funds to sail at all." He touched Bela's amulet. "Give me this, and I'll return it tenfold. The chain will be gold, the jewel as big as your fist."

I drew back. He couldn't have it!

Belo put his arm around my shoulder. "You'll do better to apply to me, Don Christopher. The pendant was a gift to Loma—"

"Then I *do* apply to you." He towered over Belo, too.

"My contributors will be known as men who recognized greatness, and my wealth will restore the coffers of the Jews." He bowed again and left.

Don Solomon whispered, "He's a pauper now, but he'll be rich. Some men are magnets for fortune." He chuckled. "Their puffed chests pull everything toward them."

I looked around the tent, which was as big as our living room at home. Cushions were scattered across the rugs. I smelled rosemary. A burly manservant stood at another low table on which rested a platter of roasted eggs, a wheel of yellow cheese, a loaf of bread dotted with sesame seeds, and a bowl brimming with sugar cookies. I thought of the starving prisoners.

Don Solomon held out his arms to me. Surprised, I went into them.

Releasing me, he said, "You're a pretty girl. Still your abuelo's favorite?"

"She's my best girl and better than the boys, too."

I blushed and wished I was somewhere else.

Don Solomon helped himself to an egg. "The monarchs like her, too. Tomorrow morning she has an audience with the infanta."

"Oho!" Belo said.

The infanta was Princess Isabella, Queen Isabella's oldest daughter.

Why did she want to talk to me?

"It's a great mark of favor for you, Joseph," Don Solomon said.

Followed by *dis*favor if I did or said something wrong. My fingers felt icy.

"Loma will make a marvelous impression," Belo said.

How would I do that? If I didn't, how disappointed he'd be in me! What would I say to her? How would I produce words at all?

While I worried, Belo and Don Solomon talked about their journey here. I hardly listened until Don Solomon said my name.

"I have a great-grandson Loma's age, a thinker with a head for numbers." He filled a bowl and brought it to Belo. "We must talk."

Oh! Was this how it would happen—a conversation, and my future (if I survived the audience) happily secured, babies likely, despite my horoscope?

And me, still only eleven.

Was the great-grandson kind and gentle, as Bela had promised my husband would be?

Belo said, "She's too young. There's plenty of time to talk."

"Don't wait long. A dozen mamás have their eyes on my Nattan." He chuckled. "They squeeze his cheek, as if he were a young bull."

"I'll remember," Belo said.

I touched Bela's amulet. What if Belo forgot even though he said he wouldn't, and this boy would have been the perfect father for my children?

Soon after dawn, a secretary, fashionable in silk and fragrant with rose water, came to our tent to announce that the princess *yearned* (he stretched out the word) to entertain me in her tent in two hours.

I dressed in the best gown I had with me: pale blue with daffodils embroidered in gold thread. On my head went a tight-fitting hood bordered with lapis beads. Don Solomon loaned me a heavy gold chain with a ruby pendant from which dangled a pearl. I'd never worn anything that weighed so much. My neck ached.

I complained, but Belo said I'd better wear it. "The infanta will feel more at ease if you look like the people around her."

When the hour came, I followed the secretary up the mountain to the exalted tents of the monarchs and their coterie, close on the walls of a fortification, the Gibralfaro. As we climbed, the sounds of the camp diminished, and the air freshened.

This appointment began as a repeat of Tarazona, with waiting, this time in a tent that seemed to be the cooling-the-heels place for courtiers.

As I was about to enter, Belo's friend the Duke of Medinaceli came out. He recognized me and took my hands in his. "Paloma! I'm pleased to see you. Your advice was excellent the day we met! Now you're here to advise the monarchs, too?"

I knew he was joking. "Belo may be."

"You'll think of something to add to his wisdom." He bowed and strode away.

A dozen men sat on cushions, which lined the tent sides. I lowered myself onto a cushion as far from the men as possible. I was the only child, and, I was sure, the only Jew. A table held platters of fruit, flatbread, and dried sardines. The men ate and talked among themselves. I could always eat, so I did, and counted each time I chewed.

After two hours or more, a secretary came for me.

Princess Isabella's tent was a few yards uphill. The tent flaps had been pulled back to make a wide entrance. Inside, a bouquet of three young women smiled from a single large cushion. When I curtsied, they flowed to me and engulfed me, cooing.

"How sweet she is."

"What pretty hair." Someone touched my waves around my hood.

Their perfume dizzied me. Which was the princess?

Someone stroked my cheek. "Smooth as a grape. I could pet her all day."

Fortunately, they didn't. Two of the women left, looking over their shoulders at me and still smiling.

Princess Isabella took my hands in hers. Our rings clinked. "Thank you for visiting me, Paloma."

As if I could have said no.

"I'm lost in happiness to make your acquaintance."

My own sisters had never been lost in happiness to see me. I murmured that I was happy, too.

The infanta gestured, and a woman came in with a tray loaded with plums and placed it on a table at the back of the tent.

Princess Isabella resembled her mother: tall with auburn hair. She was even paler, so fair that a ribbon of blue vein, highlighted by dark powder, stood out on her forehead.

At last, she let my hands go. "We must see you often. You are too sweet not to be close by. I think you'd like the court. My friends would pamper you. Mother would mother you."

This was familiar. The princess was talking about me converting. Her friends' embraces had been about conversion, too.

She went on. "My parents love your grandfather. They *love* him."

I called up an adult response. "He's honored to have their affection." There.

She echoed my syllables and inflection without the words. "Blah blah blah . . . You answer like an ambassador and not a darling girl."

Was this a terrible blunder? I apologized. "Belo is always glad when the king and queen want to see him, so *he* can see them."

"Come!" She led me to the big cushion and waited for me to sit. Then she filled a bowl with fruit for both of us and shared the cushion with me. I wished she weren't so close.

"Dear, if you recognize Christ, I'll see to it that Mamá gives you a few of the Málaga Moors."

For a moment, I didn't understand. Then it broke on me: Ai! The skinny Muslim captives were going to be slaves.

The infanta waited for me to say something.

I wished people would stop cajoling or arguing or trying to force me to be baptized. I took a baby's way out. "Belo won't let me convert." Meaning: Persuade him, not me. Don't make me decide.

Princess Isabella beamed at me. "Blessed child! This is marvelous! A miracle. Your words will make Mamá very happy." She clapped her hands, and the secretary who had brought me appeared.

He gestured for me to follow him. The audience was over.

I was puzzled. What had I said to please her so much?

We'd gone only a few steps before I realized. I whirled. "That's not what I meant! Your Majesty!" I didn't mean I wanted to convert and Belo was stopping me. He'd be furious with me for suggesting that.

But her tent was empty.

18

Belo would find out what I said during our audience with the monarchs in the afternoon. I had to tell him first, but when I got back to our tent, Hamdun said he was with Don Solomon. I ate a few almonds, which dropped like stones in my stomach, and read from a book of poems. These lines seemed to grow on the page:

> *Silence, fool! Take care not to anger a sage*
> *who will shake you like a puppy, whose name*
> *is Wisdom, whose thought encompasses the sky.*
> *To dolts and silly women, his scorn is a knife!*

Maybe I shouldn't tell Belo and hope the queen would understand what I'd really meant. I counted the roses in the carpet. Belo and my family aside, might I convert? If I converted, God's plan would include my baptism, since nothing happened without His arranging.

When Belo came in, he took his mirror and scissors out of one of the saddlebags. "I must be just so for the monarchs. Will you trim my beard, Loma?"

Fatima did this at home, and when we traveled, he trimmed it himself. If he wanted it to be perfect, why choose me, who'd never trimmed anyone's beard before?

"Your bela was an artist of the beard. She kept me from resembling a billy goat."

I did my best. This would have been the time to tell him what I'd said, but I couldn't find the courage.

When I finished, he said I had the makings of an artist, too. He patted my cheek. "Don't claim to the monarchs that you're virtuous because you cut my beard."

I smiled weakly.

The sun was low in the sky when Don Solomon, Belo, and I followed a secretary into the cooling-the-heels tent, which was deserted this time.

My hands were cold; my face was hot. I remembered what Vellida had said: *Belo giveth; Belo taketh away.* If Queen Isabella revealed my foolish words, would I no longer be his favorite? Would he hate me?

We waited long enough for me to hope that the audience had been canceled, but finally the secretary returned and led us to an enormous tent. The monarchs had brought their thrones with them or ones just like them. The infanta sat on a cushion at her mother's feet. Both she and the queen smiled warmly at me.

The king's expression was merely cordial. After Don Solomon and Belo bowed, and I curtsied, King Ferdinand said, "Dear friends, I'm sure you've guessed why we called you to Málaga."

Don Solomon protested that he and Belo had no idea.

Belo said how happy he always was in their presence.

I wished I could be anywhere else.

"We won't sell the Málaga Jews into slavery." Queen Isabella reached down to smooth her daughter's hair.

They could sell Jews? Certainly. They could do anything.

Belo's inhale was so loud, I heard it. "Yesterday, Paloma and I met one of the captives, who asked me to thank you for your generosity with bread. He said to tell you they'll be loyal subjects." He paused. "As your Jews have always been."

King Ferdinand said, "Food and drink for so many are no small matter."

Don Solomon put a hand on my shoulder and pressed down. "Majesty, you honored me by calling me an old friend. I'm also just purely old."

He'd seemed spry enough when we walked here.

Queen Isabella clapped her hands, and slaves brought cushions for each of us. When we were seated, it seemed that something had changed. The king and queen sat less stiffly. Princess Isabella stretched her legs in front of her. We had become guests rather than people keeping an appointment. That was why clever Don Solomon had mentioned his age!

"They'll pay taxes as soon as they're settled," Don Solomon said. "May they return to their homes?"

King Ferdinand's voice hardened from velvet to steel. "Our soldiers died for their homes!"

"The Jews weren't fighters." Belo put his hands on his knees, palms up. "In my great-grandfather's time, we were wanted in Spain for what we're still eager to do—create wealth for the kingdom. Spanish royalty is a flower—our bluebell, which grows nowhere else."

Queen Isabella nodded. Her husband's mouth relaxed. They exchanged glances.

Belo leaned toward them. "The beautiful bluebell assures us all is well and eases our heart. But the flower needs good soil. Your Jews are the good soil."

I felt proud of Belo for speaking so well.

Don Solomon broke in. "I'm not the orator my friend is, who speaks in poetry, but may I remind Your Majesties that Jews, unlike Christians, are able to travel everywhere, even to places ruled by the Muslims. So long as there is another Jew, we have a bed, and, no matter the local language, we can speak Hebrew to do royal business: arrange trade, propose treaties, whatever you wish."

Belo took over. "If we were coins, we would be in your purse, only in your purse. We are your golden ducats."

Don Solomon's turn again. I wondered if they had planned this out. "Your other subjects belong first to a noble or a town. Jews are entirely yours—"

"—and we bestow everything upon you," Belo said, finishing.

Princess Isabella clapped her hands. "That *was* poetry!" She smiled brilliantly at me. "Paloma, your abuelo's poetry is one reason we want your family to be entirely with us."

I could barely breathe.

The queen took over, as if they, too, had collaborated in advance. "And your family, too, Don Solomon, for practical wisdom if not poetry."

"Many from your great-grandfather's time," King Ferdinand said, "are Christians now."

"The Jewish captives will be taken to Carmona," the queen said. "They'll work, but their upkeep will have to be paid for. So many Jews are a burden on our purse."

Four hundred and fifty, Belo had told me.

Both Don Solomon and Belo said that they would pay for the captives' food and care until they could raise funds from the aljamas.

"I will, too," I said. Belo had told me money had been put aside for all his grandchildren. I hoped this would show the queen I wanted to stay a Jew.

Belo put his hand on my head. "She's an example to us."

Don Solomon said, "Where will they live?"

"In the castle in Carmona," Queen Isabella said, "until the ransom is raised."

Carmona was in Andalusia and had no Jews.

A ransom. Not sold into slavery, but sold to us, their fellow Jews.

Selling them at all was cruel and evil. Buying them was good and kind. My heart decided: God, You may favor the Christians, but I won't become one if I can help it.

I heard Belo swallow. "How much ransom?"

Sums flew back and forth. The monarchs demanded. Belo and Don Solomon said that this amount and even that lower amount were too much. I realized that the four of them were enjoying themselves. Princess Isabella winked at me. I smiled back.

Finally, they arrived at the ransom: twenty thousand ducats. I divided: 44.44 ducats for each Jew.

Belo asked that several captives be freed to travel across Spain, to appeal to the aljamas for the ransom money. Permission was granted.

Don Solomon and Belo stood. I jumped up, too, praying to God to let me escape without a reckoning.

He didn't let me.

Queen Isabella held up a hand. "Don Joseph, your granddaughter wants to ask your permission for something."

Words didn't come. Tears rolled down my cheeks. I should have told Belo, so he could get me out of this. I should have prepared him.

The infanta rustled to me, put her arm around my shoulder, and hugged me. "Brave girl, God will reward you."

Queen Isabella said, "Christians have courage, child. Jews are cowardly."

No words.

"I'll speak for you, dearest." Princess Isabella squeezed my shoulder even tighter. "Paloma told me this afternoon that she would like to convert if she had your permission."

That wasn't what I'd said.

But it was close.

She added, "Christ did good work with this one."

Belo stumbled back a step. "She'll never have my permission." He huffed as if he could hardly get air. "Thank you for your interest in her."

The infanta gave my shoulder a final squeeze and whispered, "We won't abandon you."

Queen Isabella said, "My friend, your granddaughter

is wiser than you are. Come into the fold with your whole family. Don Solomon, Christ welcomes you and your family, too."

Don Solomon thanked her. King Ferdinand reminded us that the sooner the ransom was paid, the sooner the Málaga Jews would be free.

The interview was over. Now, I had to face Belo.

He was silent on the way back to our tents.

Don Solomon said, "Children have a knack for surprising us."

"She isn't a child!"

"I see," Don Solomon said.

I didn't. I wouldn't be a woman until I turned twelve.

We left Don Solomon outside our tent. Inside, Belo sat heavily on the cushion next to the low table that bore his writing. "Loma, Lo—"

"I just meant—"

He held up a hand. "It doesn't matter what you meant. You gave the Christians a weapon against me. Bela would be disappointed in you." He took off his shoes and hose and extended his feet. "At least you're good at this."

I cried while I rubbed the balm into his feet. He wrote in his folio and ignored me.

19

The next afternoon, Belo would have fallen off his horse if a guard hadn't been riding near him, where I'd have been if he hadn't waved me away.

Another spasm.

We stopped. I thought of brigands. Our guards wouldn't be enough against a large band. How to get him to safety? None of the villages on our way had Jews.

Belo sagged against the guard. His face drooped, but not as badly as the last time. And now the left side rather than the right looked slack.

Should we put him on the ground? Would he feel better if he could lie flat? Would food help?

He said, speaking clearly, "It's nothing, though the

horse has two heads." He looked at me. "I see two grand-daughters, both traitors. We should go." He tried to kick his horse, but managed only with his right foot. The beast shied sideways, and Belo almost toppled.

Hamdun lifted a protesting Belo gently off his horse and onto the sparse grass on the side of the road.

I dismounted and pulled my flask of watery wine out of the pouch tied to my saddle. Maybe a drink would make him feel better.

Or it might be the worst thing for him.

Belo wouldn't let me near him, but he rolled on his side and drank when Hamdun gave him the flask. "I'm much better now." He tried to stand, teetered, and collapsed back. "Give me a minute."

We had to give him half an hour while I wondered: if we should pitch our tents, where to pitch them, whether anywhere was safe. Then the spell seemed to pass, and he managed to mount his horse without help.

As we set out again, he said, "You did this to me, Loma."

I wondered if the guards and Hamdun pitied me or thought me a terrible girl. I considered galloping back to Málaga and telling the queen I was ready to convert. Then Belo would be sorry. Then he'd understand how much he'd hurt me, who had only made a mistake.

But the idea of being a Christian had become loathsome, even if Belo never thought well of me again.

In the tent that night, after we'd each bedded down a yard apart on the rug, he said, "I miss my Loma. Your bela has been angry at me all day. She tells me you *are* a child, and I should remember that. Come."

I snuggled under his arm, where he'd made a place for me. "I don't want to be a Christian, Belo. The princess didn't understand me."

"Ah. She heard what she wanted to hear."

Exactly.

As I drifted off to sleep, he added, "The Almighty thinks I can do more for the Jews, but I don't know what. When He punishes me by making me sick, I can't do anything."

At the judería in Guadalupe on our way home, Belo told the rabbi about the ransom and was greeted with dismay. The rabbi agreed the sum would have to be raised, but the aljama was poor. They wouldn't be able to give much.

Belo shook his head. I feared he'd get sick again, but he stayed healthy. At home, I told no one about his latest spasm.

With my twelfth birthday approaching, I treasured my rare opportunities to observe the aljama's older boys and the young men who hadn't yet been betrothed. My chances came on holidays when women and girls went to the synagogue with their families, and during celebrations, like engagement parties and weddings.

After services, for example, the congregation would linger in the street outside the synagogue. Grown-ups would chat. Small children would dash about, and boys and young men would play together. Girls had to stay with their parents, but no one could keep us from watching.

The comeliest boy was Benahe, whose entire face seemed to glow whenever he smiled. My eyes always looked for him first, and my breath always tightened when they found him. If a game of tag broke out, he was as graceful as a gazelle in the Bible.

Eventually, I'd drag my eyes to the others. Toui, who laughed often, seemed happiest. Saul, usually leaning toward the others, was the most intent. Esdras, the hazan's son, constantly tripped, as if his feet belonged to someone else. Papá would love to have a hazan for a son-in-law, and Belo might be pleased, too.

I wanted Belo to be pleased!

How could I tell which of them was clever, kind, generous, gentle?

And what about Don Solomon's great-grandson?

On one of these occasions, Yuda oozed next to me. "A sorry crop of swains, Lizard. I see you watching Benahe. Have you caught him at his hobby, picking his pretty nose?"

Go away, Ugly Camel Head!

"Saul, who seems so interested in everyone, comes close just to hear. You'll have a deaf husband if Papá gives you to him. Esdras will be on crutches in two years if he keeps his legs at all."

Yuda ran through them all. This one was a miser; this one couldn't say a truthful sentence; this one was so foolish he could barely speak sensibly. All the vices and weaknesses of humanity fell from my brother's tongue, as if the aljama were a modern Sodom and Gomorrah. "If I still gambled, I wouldn't wager on your happiness with any of them."

I thanked him for worrying about me. I'd developed a knack for sarcasm.

But he was better at it. "It's what brothers are for."

Samuel, the brother who truly wanted me to be happy, joined me next. "If I were Papá, I'd choose Yose Serrano for you."

"Yose?" Yuda had just told me how bland he was. "Why?"

"We're friends. He's thoughtful. Watch him with his brothers."

I did. He stood out because he was the tallest, and gangling, as if he hadn't yet gotten used to the length of his legs and arms. He wasn't as handsome as Benahe, but his face pleased me: long, narrow nose; thin lips, but a wide mouth; greenish-brown eyes.

Though Yose's long legs made him fast, he was often tagged because half his attention was always on his two younger brothers. If one stumbled, Yose caught him. If the brother managed to fall, Yose comforted him. Sometimes he played with a brother riding his shoulders.

A promising future papá. Nothing mattered more than that.

But I made other discoveries. When the boys chatted, he listened more often than he spoke, but when he did speak, the others paid attention. When someone made a joke, he had a habit of shaking his head while laughing. When he made a joke, he blushed.

His papá was the physician Don Israel, and his abuelo sat with Belo on the board that governed the aljama. No one could object to his family.

Then, two weeks before my birthday, he smiled at me. I looked around, sure the smile was for someone else, but no one was looking his way. The smile was for me.

I smiled back. His smile widened, almost cracking his face in half.

On July 7, 1488, a Monday, I turned twelve and became a woman. When I woke up, I stayed in bed, assessing myself.

I felt exactly as I had the day before! Had I really become a woman months or even a year ago and failed to notice? Or was I still a child, and would I have to masquerade as an adult until the change actually came, if it ever did?

If I had to pretend to be grown-up, I would. My husband and children would never know.

Husband! Today it would begin. I imagined Yose Serrano's smiling lips coming close, kissing me. His lips were soft!

My birthday was noticed.

At dinner, Papá beamed at me. "Another young woman in the family. It's an occasion."

The littles sat by me, as usual. The youngest—my nieces Clara and Jamila and my brother Jento—sat closest so I could help them with their food. Flanking them were my five-year-old nephew, Todros, and my seven-year-old niece, Beatriz.

Sunny Todros said, "I like Occasion. Where is it?"

"Ignoramus!" said Beatriz, trotting out her latest favorite word.

Papá said, holding up a platter, "A young man should be the beneficiary of these eggs, but I don't know who's worthy of them." He touched his forehead. "I'm thinking, Loma."

I blushed. I had made the eggs, which were baked with carrots.

Had Belo mentioned Don Solomon's great-grandson to Papá? Could I? I wished Belo would say something—wish me joy, acknowledge the day. He had said the blessing and nothing after that.

"She's a beauty," Ledicia said. "Look at those eyes and those thick eyelashes."

My kind sister. Yuda was at his own home or at Dueyna's parents', or he'd have found a way to remind me that I was an unblinking lizard.

I had reminded myself.

Samuel helped himself to more eggs. "Loma's outer beauty will draw in her betrothed, but her inner beauty will hold him."

Oh my.

Vellida laughed. "Don't make the poor boy always lose at backgammon. I let Jacob win most of the time."

Belo pushed back his chair at the head of the table. "The eggs are cooked to death, and Loma is too undercooked to be ready to marry anyone. I'm going to the synagogue." He left the table, and I heard him stump down the stairs.

Mamá put down her spoon. "I blame her horoscope."

20

I swallowed hard and refused to cry.

Papá stood. "I'll speak with your abuelo, Loma. Don't worry." He left but didn't go downstairs. He liked discord no more than I did.

But he kept his promises. He'd talk to Belo.

In the silence, Todros said, "Tía Loma, if you get married and have your own babies, you won't have time to play with us."

I kissed the top of his head. "If I had a hundred babies, I'd find the time."

Belo wanted me to have children and be happy, I was sure of it. He loved me.

But he must have insisted I wasn't ready when Papá spoke to him, because days and weeks passed with no more mention of suitors. In August, Yuda completed his apprenticeship and set up his own shop four streets from our house, and he and Dueyna moved there from their first home.

We all went to see it. The shop filled half the first floor of the house. The upper window shutter, pulled out and supported by poles, created an awning; and the lower shutter, pulled out and held up by four legs, created a counter. There, on a length of velvet, Yuda had spread an assortment of his handiwork: buckles, rings, necklaces, clasps, and brooches. I picked up a pendant—a circle set with five emeralds.

"It's marvelous," I told him, meaning it.

But I didn't return. I doubt that Belo, Mamá, my sisters, or Samuel did, either. Papá may have.

In September, Yose was betrothed to Gracia, the daughter of another wealthy family. Had he smiled at her, too, or had I been his real choice?

I wondered if Don Solomon's great-grandson had also been betrothed by now.

Desperate to win Belo's approval, which, a year earlier, had seemed my birthright, I worked on my cooking, my sewing, and my foot massaging. In his presence, I hardly spoke, because I feared I'd say something undercooked. Whenever he tasted a dish I'd prepared, the breath flew out of me, and I waited, empty, for his judgment—

—which didn't come. He ate without commenting.

My appetite dwindled. I became less plump—a little less plump, because Aljohar noticed and plied me with treats.

Though my sisters had been betrothed quickly after their twelfth birthday, not all young women were, and families often waited a few years to make a match for their sons. A wife hadn't been chosen for Samuel yet. I had a while before my single state would be gossiped about.

Finally, one evening in October, Belo remarked on my silence. "Loma, you're like a deer lately, all eyes and no words. Have you stopped talking to your abuelo?"

We were playing backgammon in his study. Disconcerted by the question, I failed to send one of his counters to the penalty bar, and I suspected he'd brought up my silence only to gain an advantage in the game.

I shook my head and then remembered to speak. "I haven't stopped."

He moved two counters onto his home board.

"Belo? Did you like my honey fritters?" They'd been one of the desserts at dinner. Papá had called them balls of sweet gold.

While I waited, I took my turn throwing the dice and moving my counters.

"Loma, your cooking is fine. Excellent." He smiled into

my eyes. "You are my perfect granddaughter, and you have plenty of time to get married."

How did he know that was what I meant?

He went on. "God willing, I'll dandle your babies on my knees."

He never dandled the current crop of babies. But maybe for the children of his favorite, he would. I smiled back at him, relieved.

"You are in early youth, but only the Almighty knows how many vigorous years I have left, and I'd like to keep you with me while I still can travel."

Did he expect his spasms to get worse? I hoped he'd stay well!

But I wanted to get married. God, I thought, is that wrong?

In February 1489, Samuel was betrothed to the soft-spoken and sweet Josefina Bivach. I became the only adult child in the family not to be married or have a wedding planned. At dinner, I added my congratulations to everyone else's and shrunk my envy into a speck in the corner of my heart.

When the meal was over, I hastened to my bedroom and then to the courtyard, hoping Samuel would join me. We used to study together there, and only he and I would come out in winter.

He came. I kept my hands behind my back.

"You're happy for me, Loma?"

I nodded, smiling.

"What are you hiding?"

I brought out the prayer shawl I'd made for him for this occasion. I'd carded and woven the lamb's wool for the lower part of the shawl. The silk collar I'd bought, but I'd sewn it on myself. "Do you like it?"

He draped it over one arm and examined it. "I've never seen one so marvelous."

That couldn't be true, but I accepted the compliment. "None made with so much pleasure."

He took my hands. "God will make you as happy as I am, and your husband will be the luckiest man in Spain. Look what an angel you are to Belo, to this whole family."

"Belo is my benefactor!"

"He used to be, but you've changed places."

I didn't know if I liked this idea.

Samuel went on. "God sees your goodness. We'll both have happy lives."

This was the first time I was praised for traveling with Belo but not the last. It was never said in Belo's presence, but the same compliment came from Papá and Ledicia. Yuda, when he cornered me alone, called me Angelic Pitiable Lizard.

* * *

In March 1490, when I was nearing fourteen, our whole family drew pity. Yuda and his wife stealthily followed a priest after Sabbath services. I don't know exactly how it fell out, but I imagined the scene:

They slip through the judería gate.

Yuda coughs wetly. A cheep of fear escapes Dueyna.

The priest turns and smiles. This has happened before. "Yes?" He recognizes that Yuda is a prize. He bows. "Yes, Don Yuda?"

"Weekly we hear your words—"

"Christ's words."

"I can withstand anything, but I don't want eternal torment for my wife."

He might have put it some other odious way. We knew nothing until a priest visited the house and delivered the terrible news. The priest came during dinner, so all of us received the shock at once.

Mamá ran out of the dining room, shrieking, "He's always been a viper!"

Yuda was probably imagining this scene and grinning.

I hid it, but I wanted to do as Mamá did: scream, tear my hair, and spread blame. With a converso brother, who would marry me?

21

After Mamá left, the priest said that Yuda's and Dueyna's baptism would take place on Easter Sunday. "We're hoping that more Cantalas will follow them to the font." He bowed and departed.

Maybe this wouldn't have happened if I'd told someone when Yuda had suggested to me that God favored Christians.

Papá and Belo left for the cathedral to seek an audience with the bishop. Samuel hastened to the parents of his betrothed to make sure they still wanted him to join the family, which it turned out they did. Vellida and Ledicia remained at the table and spoke in whispers.

The littles came to me. Even Jento, Jamila, and Clara

were old enough to partially understand. I told them that Yuda was being silly and everything would be all right for us if not for him. "Want to play backgammon?"

They all nodded.

I took the bowl of almonds from the table and led them to my bedroom. They climbed on the bed, or I helped them up.

"Todros and Beatriz will play together as a pair against the rest of us," I announced. The rest of us were Clara, Jamila, and Jento. "No discord!"

I let Todros and Beatriz set up the counters while Jamila bounced on the bed and made their task more difficult.

"Winners get three almonds apiece," I said.

"What do the losers get?" Jamila asked.

"Tickled!"

Ledicia came in. "I'll take over. You're to go to the cathedral."

The breath caught in my throat. To see Yuda? Me, alone in the cathedral?

I left as Beatriz said, "Do you know how to play, Mamá?"

"Tía Loma isn't the only one who can play games."

Papá, Vellida, and Samuel were waiting in the vestibule when I came downstairs. I wouldn't have to be alone. I took my cloak off the peg by the door.

As we hurried toward the judería gate, Papá said, "The

bishop is letting us talk to Yuda. It's a great favor to Belo."

"Why are *we* coming?" Samuel asked.

"You may be able to talk more sense into him than we can."

We crossed the plaza in front of the cathedral. How much taller and grander it was than our synagogue. Belo stood under an orange tree about ten paces from the entrance. Next to him were a priest and a man I soon learned was the bishop, whose tunic was so elaborately embroidered that my eyes lingered on it rather than on his pale face and oddly pushed-out jaw.

The priest—young and thin as a tent pole—started for the side of the cathedral. "Come!"

Belo and the rest of us followed him toward a wall broken by an archway.

"It's the cloister," Belo said. "Not indoors."

We passed under the arch. Yuda and Dueyna sat on a bench under an olive tree. I couldn't bear to look at my brother, so I scanned the cloister, which was bigger but much like our courtyard at home.

"Son! Daughter!" Papá rushed to them.

Dueyna wore a gold cross half the size of my hand on a gold chain. She stood, and Papá kissed her forehead.

"We'll give you your privacy," the bishop said, backing through the archway. The priest followed.

Yuda stood. "Greetings, Belo, Papá . . ." He named us all.

Belo's voice was a groan. "Why are you doing this to me?"

Yuda rocked back and forth on his heels. "God is punishing the Jews. Christians are His chosen now, and I don't want Dueyna to be tormented in hell."

If this was the reason, why hadn't he converted when he first talked to me about it?

Papá stepped away. "Samuel, talk to him."

"I don't want to lose my brother." My sweet brother kissed my dreadful brother's cheek above his beard.

"I'm still your brother," Yuda said.

"I won't see much of you if you convert."

Quickly, as if the words had been waiting on his lips, Yuda said, "How often do you visit my shop now?"

Ah. That was one grievance, one reason for hurting us.

Samuel blushed. "I'll come more often."

Papá jumped on this. "We all will. The Christians won't love you as your family does. They'll use you."

Yuda added, "Now my shop won't have to be in the judería."

If a person didn't care about being Jewish, that was sensible.

Vellida said, "Dueyna, you've always been devout. Do you want to convert?"

She blinked her pretty eyes. "Yuda says the Christians have become God's chosen people. He says I don't have to cook pork." She shuddered. "I couldn't touch it!"

"Then you should fear the inquisitors, you fools," Belo said.

A suspicion landed on me. "Yuda, did you gamble again?"

Dueyna's head jerked toward him. "Did you?"

"No." He shrugged. "Yes, but I was going to convert anyway."

"Yuda!" Dueyna cried.

Belo smiled a tight smile at me. "Clever, Loma." The smile vanished. "How much is your debt?"

Yuda named a sum that widened my eyes. Samuel gasped.

"You're going to convert and leave it unpaid?" Papá said.

Yuda didn't answer. Of course he was. The aljama wouldn't be able to collect the money, because the priests would protect their new convert.

Belo stood. "We'll pay your debt whether you convert or not, but if you do, next time, you can face Christian justice, and you'll discover it's much harsher than ours." He started to leave. "And less just."

Yuda said, "Christ will save me."

Papá said, "Dueyna, if you like, we'll take you to your parents."

"I'm a dutiful wife. I'll convert with my husband."

At home, Belo retired to his study and didn't ask me to join him, so I went with the others to the living room, where we sat on cushions around the low table that always held bowls of nuts and dried fruit.

Vellida said, "Loma, young men will still want to attach themselves to our family."

I nodded, preferring not to argue.

Ledicia came in and said the littles were napping. When we told her what had happened she said, "At least, we won't have to see Yuda anymore."

"What will he call the bishop?" I said.

"Your Excellency Pale Lima Bean," Vellida said, laughing.

Papá's shout came from the direction of Belo's study.

A moment later, Fatima hurried in. "Loma, you're to go to your belo."

I ran, guessing what had happened. I heard my brother and sisters behind me.

We crowded into the study. Belo was on the floor with his shoulders propped up against the cushion I usually sat on.

He said, sounding like himself, "Go away, all of you except Loma." His face didn't droop on either side.

They left. I was sure Papá would send for the physician.

A man sang a Spanish song in the street.

"Can I help you into your chair?"

"I can get myself into my own chair!" He put his hands flat on the floor, pushed, his shoulders high and straining, and failed to rise. "You may assist me."

He was lighter than I expected. With one hand under an armpit and the other under an arm, I maneuvered him into his chair, where he fought to catch his breath.

When he could speak, he said, "There. I have my dignity back. Tell me, Loma: How did I get a granddaughter like you and a grandson like Yuda?"

I began to praise my sisters and Samuel, but he held up a hand to stop me. "They are as they should be, but you—"

The door opened. Papá came in with Don Israel, the aljama physician and the papá of Yose Serrano.

How soft Don Israel's voice was, how gentle his hands—lowering the skin under Belo's eyes and examining them, picking up his hand and taking his pulse. And how serene his face was as he ignored Belo's protests that he was well, that the good doctor had come for nothing, and how obliged he'd be if Don Israel would bestow his ministrations on those who needed them.

Don Israel's son would have been perfect for me, if he was like his papá.

The physician stood away from Belo. "I don't see much wrong that rest won't cure. A week in bed and a month of light activity. No travel. Then, Don Joseph, you can return to saving us Jews"—he bowed—"as we count on you to do."

Belo shook his head. "I'll be fine tomorrow."

Feeling like a traitor, I said, "You always get sick again."

Papá glanced sharply at me.

Belo said, "This is the lying viper I've nurtured."

Don Israel and Papá stood Belo up and supported him to his bedroom. I trailed them, carrying Belo's pen, ink, and folio, knowing he'd feel less helpless if he could write. That's the sort of viper I am, I thought.

That evening, I found Samuel sitting on a bench, studying on the courtyard balcony. I sat next to him, and he put his book aside. In a few sentences I told him what had gone before each of Belo's spells—though I could hardly get the words out to describe my foolishness with Princess Isabella.

Samuel laughed so hard tears ran down his cheeks. "I wish I could have been there," he said when he could speak again. "Those grandees after their great victory, waging a new war over a single Jew. A child!"

I couldn't see the scene as funny, but I felt better about it.

"Lions fighting for a speck of meat! Belo should have realized."

Don Solomon hadn't realized, either.

Samuel added, "We worry about you."

I stiffened. "Who?"

"Your sisters and I."

"That I won't get married and have children?"

"No. Not everyone marries and has children."

He thought I wouldn't!

"The little ones belong to you as much as they do to

their parents." He smiled. "My children will, too. With you, it's inevitable."

But they wouldn't be mine.

"Belo doesn't understand how tender you are. You take everything in, and he doesn't spare you."

"I don't want to be spared."

"We know. That's how good you are."

I didn't see it that way.

I could be tender and strong. If Belo needed me, I was happy to be there, until I had my own family.

Belo was better the next day and even better the day after that. Papá prevailed upon him to stay at home, rather than go to the synagogue for the Sabbath service. That night, he sat up in bed with a board on his lap, writing in his folio. A six-candle candelabrum at his side provided light.

I had a single candle next to my cushion, where I read—or pretended to read—one of Samuel's books of biblical commentary. Actually, I was gathering my courage.

Finally, I said, "Belo?"

He put his pen down. "Come, sit by me."

I climbed on the bed and sat cross-legged by his knees.

"What were you reading? Do you want to discuss it?"

I shook my head. "I couldn't concentrate. I kept thinking of Yuda."

Belo picked his pen up again. "The On-High was help-ing me *not* think of him. Read your book. *Read* it this time."

"Actually, I was thinking of the family more than of Yuda."

Belo answered me while writing. "We're healthy; I still have the ear of the monarchs." He looked up. "We can still aid the Jews; the Merciful One is still merciful. Your brother is unimportant by every measure."

Bracing myself for terrible discord, I said, "He'll keep us from marrying."

Belo settled himself back on his pillows. "For a few years. People will have forgotten by the time the little ones are ready to marry."

A few years would make me too old. "Belo, would you speak to a family on my behalf?" This usually fell to the papá, but Belo would be better for me.

He set his writing board entirely aside. "Loma, I've kept you near me for my comfort and my strength. You have more of your bela in you than any of my other chil-dren and grandchildren. They're good children, most of them, but diluted."

A lump rose in my throat, a complicated lump. I'd sort it out later.

"Jews in Spain have always needed men like me and Solomon. Too often the monarchs listen to our enemies.

Haven't you seen that?"

My stomach felt tight, waiting to hear what this meant for me.

"Suppose I live another twenty years. It could happen, God willing. Imagine I remain vigorous despite my spells, and we continue to travel together to aid the Jews."

In twenty years, I'd be almost thirty-four! No one would want to marry me.

"If you're with me, I'll live the twenty years. You're my talisman, my amulet, given to me by your bela. Your years with me will win you praise from the community."

Through a tight throat, I said, "Bela wanted me to marry. She told me." And hadn't he promised to bounce my babies on his knees?

He touched my chin. "She would agree with me. I know as well as if she were"—he waved his arm—"sitting on the other corner of the bed."

"You said you'd dandle my babies on your knee!"

"I thought I would dandle them. The prospect was more distant when I said it." He shrugged. "I may die tomorrow, and then you must marry. I don't believe Yuda will be an obstacle. What do you say, Loma?"

I didn't want him to die tomorrow, so I said that.

He didn't want for me what I wanted for myself. Was I wrong to want it?

22

That night in my room, I kicked the floor cushions, threw myself on my bed and pounded the mattress, pushed my face into my pillow, and muffled my wail. I pulled my hair, though, in truth, that was more to see how it felt. It hurt, so I pulled harder, liking the pain. My face was soaked.

For an hour, I counted by elevens and used numbers to wall off sadness and fury.

Then thoughts came.

Belo believed what he was doing to my future was right. Was it right?

Did he guess the pain I was in?

Probably not.

Was my pain wrong? Was I right or wrong to be angry? I sobbed.

Did I have to do what he wanted?

I wished I could talk to Bela. Should I speak to Papá—or to Samuel, the future rabbi?

No. Neither of them would be able to persuade Belo, and I didn't want to tear the family apart.

I had a choice, even though he hadn't offered me one. I could stop being the way he liked me to be. I could dig too hard when I massaged his feet. I could speak louder than he preferred. There were a dozen things. He'd be furious with me, which I didn't know if I could bear, but finally, he'd decide he could do better without me. I could marry as soon as the shame of Yuda wore off.

Belo might get ill again and stay ill.

God had His plan. Wouldn't Belo be more important in it than I was?

I walked round and round on the rugs, passing the bed, the low copper table, the two embroidered floor cushions, the door, the chest that held my gowns and my shifts.

Did the Jews really need me? Though that seemed a prideful idea, I breathed deeper.

Would Bela be proud of me?

Might I gain something in place of the loss of my own children, be a bigger Paloma than I'd ever hoped to be?

No, that was too grand.

But I might do more than my sisters and even Samuel could as a rabbi.

On the bed, exhausted, I lay back and was asleep.

But after a few hours, I awoke. Suppose the mob came to our door again, after Belo had died, because I had deserted him. Papá might not be able to send them away. The chief constable of the hermandad might not help us.

The friar and the mob would drag us to the cathedral to be baptized.

Or they'd set fire to the house.

Or take Jento and give him to Christians to raise as a Christian. If I had my own child by then, they'd take him or her, too.

I sobbed.

They'd continue to Ledicia's house and commit terrible acts there, too, and throughout the judería.

I couldn't catch my breath. If the mob let me live, I would have lost my littles.

Then I imagined mamás across Spain losing their children, too.

I writhed on the bed.

If I stopped traveling with Belo, I'd have no relief from fear that he'd die and I would be the cause and the cause of everything terrible that followed.

The answer—the only answer—was clear. I would continue at his side.

I slept again.

In the morning, I didn't return to my agony. The

decision was made. I would treasure my nieces and nephews and Jento. For the sake of our family's littles and all the Jewish littles of Spain, and because I loved him and was grateful to him, I'd be Belo's amulet. And I would try to count myself lucky.

Yuda and Dueyna were to be baptized on Easter Sunday and take the Christian names of Pero and Marina Díaz.

Belo was still in his bed. While he wrote in his folio, I sat on a floor cushion.

Had it happened yet?

Was the baptismal water cold or warm or scalding?

Did Pero feel God's wrath? Or His Son's love?

Was Marina suffering, as I would be?

The day passed.

Belo began traveling with me again, busier than ever, as the monarchs demanded more and more money to finance their war against the kingdom of Granada, the last Muslim foothold in Spain.

Papá traveled often, too, for the same purpose. He once said that his purse had a hole in it. Coins in, coins out, with the king's and queen's hands at the opening.

When Belo and I met with his friends over meals, someone usually asked if I was betrothed, and then, when

I might be. Belo always said I had plenty of time, and, for now, he needed me. The conversation would end with praise for my kindness in staying with an old man.

Every time, Belo looked as if he'd swallowed vinegar.

The praise sounded empty. I'd chosen my fate, or I was following the furrow God had plowed for me.

Vellida got pregnant again, and so did Ledicia, after five years. I prepared. Every time babies were expected, my heart built new rooms.

Late in May, Samuel and Josefina Bivach married. Everyone in the judería came, as well as Belo's and Papá's Christian business friends. Pero and Marina were there, too, because kind Samuel had invited them. I kept my distance.

Before the wedding, while Josefina took her bath, I danced happily in the street with Beatriz, Jamila, and Clara. I clasped the children's hands. The rhythm entered me, and I forgot myself in pleasure—

—and didn't expect my pain later during the wedding ceremony. Samuel and Josefina shared a tallit, a prayer shawl, and faced Belo, who recited the seven blessings. My brother looked purely happy: bright smile, wet eyes, a bloom in his tan cheeks.

Belo intoned, "Blessed are You, Eternal One, Who makes the bridegroom rejoice with the bride."

Shouts erupted. People rushed to congratulate the couple. I swallowed tears.

Nothing had changed, but I stood statue-still for several minutes before I could turn to the feast.

At least a hundred revelers stood, talked with mouths full of food, gestured, laughed. There, at the long table, seeming as if a sun shaft lit only them, were Yose and Gracia Serrano. Playfully, Yose was snapping grapes off their stem and lifting them, one by one, to his wife's smiling lips.

I had never seen him do anything that wasn't sweet. In a different world, I would have been his wife. The happiness they shared would have been mine.

"You would have been bored, Lizard. You would have tired of a diet of grapes."

I mustered words with grape sweetness. "Welcome, Yuda—I mean Pero. I'm glad to see you."

He looked as ever, smooth and oily, in a tan silk robe and, around his neck, a thick gold chain from which hung a ring of pearls circling a ruby. I inhaled the lavender perfume he still slathered himself with—but not pork. Not a hint. "How fares Marina?"

"Wishing for a child, but Christ hasn't graced us."

"Where are you living?"

"Near the market. It's smaller, but big enough. You should visit." He gave me directions.

As if I would!

"I've been looking for you. I have a message for Belo."
He began in his buttered voice, "If he doesn't stop spoiling
my business, I'll ruin his life and Papá's and yours."

I fought to stay calm. "What is Belo doing, and how
will you ruin us?"

"I could have sold this." He touched his necklace. "A
buyer was interested, until he wasn't. Few come to my
shop. I paid fifty reales to discover that Belo is telling his
friends not to buy my jewelry."

"He hasn't said anything to me. How will you ruin us?"

"I'll tell the inquisitors he leads his converso friends
in prayer in Hebrew. I'll say he reminds them how to be
Jews."

I could barely breathe. All the good deeds Belo per-
formed for the Jews of Spain would end.

"I don't want to do it." He removed the necklace. "Give
this to Belo. The workmanship is fine. Tell him to wear it
and say who made it. Tell him to say he's proud of me."

I nodded.

But Belo listened to no one. The Inquisition would kill
us.

23

In my bedroom after the wedding, I recited a prayer of forgiveness, acquitting anyone who'd sinned against me (Ugly Camel Head) and asking to be pardoned for my sins (my endless heart-hatred for him). Then I thanked God for the day—

—and began laughing.

Thank You, Eternal One, for sending my brother to frighten me out of my envy of the marriage of Yose and Gracia Serrano.

I slept for an hour and woke, gagging on horror. If Belo died during torture, his trial would continue anyway. When he was declared guilty, his corpse would be burned. That was what the Inquisition caused to happen. The priests themselves didn't burn anyone; they *relaxed* their victims into the custody of the constables, who carried out the murdering.

Bela, what can I do?

I buried my head under my pillow and heard her chuckle. "The pillow won't save you. Rest, little fritter. You need your strength."

Clutching her pendant, which I never took off, I fell back to sleep.

Birds woke me.

When did Pero plan to inform on us? He had to wait a few days at least to give Belo a chance to visit people, but he'd be impatient.

Belo wouldn't agree instantly. I needed time—a month?—to persuade him. Not that I'd ever persuaded him of anything.

Also, I wanted a month more of freedom, remembering to savor each moment. The Inquisition didn't sentence people right away, but it did imprison them.

My stomach was rumbling. Hunger was to be savored and so was eating. I said the morning prayer of thanksgiving, feeling it more than any time in the past.

In the kitchen, Jento sat on a high stool at the worktable, being plied with barley cakes by Aljohar. "Look!" He smiled.

He was missing a lower front tooth. Savor. "I don't see anything."

"My tooth fell out."

"Are you sure? I don't believe you. You're not old enough."

"Yes, I am! I'm a big boy."

"Open your mouth very wide."

He did, as wide as it could go.

I moved in close and smelled his sweet barley breath. "Ah. I see it now." I kissed his forehead.

"Big boys share." I picked up a barley cake from the platter and ate it in three bites.

He stuck a crumby tongue out at me.

In the dining room, I took a silver tray from one of the open cupboards. At the table, I placed four wedges of cheese and four slices of bread in a wide bowl.

Belo lay on his side in his bed, facing the door. When I came in, he opened one eye and recited the prayer thanking God for giving his soul back after sleep. I said it in my mind along with him, adding a special thanks for letting me sleep at all, considering.

I put the tray down next to him.

"What's this?"

"It's a pretty day. It should be celebrated."

He said the prayer thanking God for food from the earth and took a wedge of cheese.

"Belo, did you see Pero at the wedding?"

"My eyes had better people to fix on—Samuel and his beautiful bride." He smiled. "Loma, not many men live to have great-grandchildren." He sat up and stretched. "How old is Ledicia's Beatriz?"

"Nine," I said absently.

He got out of bed. His undershirt stopped just above his knobby knees. "I will not discuss your brother. His name has already marred the day."

"Belo . . ." I pulled Bela's pendant out from under the neckline of my gown. "Maybe it keeps away the evil eye— I'm not sure I still believe it does—but don't you want me to be a better talisman than a stone?"

"On the subject of your brother, I want you to *be* a stone."

There was little satisfaction in it, but I huffed myself out of the bedroom without another word.

I went to the courtyard, where I would no longer find Samuel studying. I counted the stone tiles, as I'd done many times before.

No one could know, but I had to talk to Pero.

I found Papá in his study and told him I was going to visit Ledicia. "I'll take Hamdun." I couldn't go unchaperoned.

Hamdun was weeding in our back garden. He left his task, and we set out. At the judería gate, he said, "Mistress?"

"It's all right," I lied. "Papá knows."

We skirted the market, where the few Jews sold wares along with the many Christians. Through the window of his shop, I saw Pero. Head bent over his workbench, he failed to see me, so I had a few moments to admire his beautiful handiwork on its bed of velvet. I leaned close to examine a gold pendant, diamond-shaped, on which were etched bells and roses entwined on a leafy stem in a space no bigger than a fingernail.

"Pero . . ."

He looked up. "I expected Papá." He came to the window.

"Everything is marvelous." I gestured at the display.

"What's your favorite?"

"That one." I pointed at the gold pendant.

"Look at this." He picked up a silver ring that had a square, protruding front, set with a ruby and an emerald. "Watch." He flicked a minuscule clasp, and the front opened to reveal a tiny space. "For a relic of a saint, or for poison."

He made such things? People bought them?

"I sold several before— You have a week to persuade Belo. I know you've come to ask for time." He smiled his toothy camel smile. "Marina will be delighted to see you." His display of jewelry rested on a tray hidden under the velvet. He carried everything inside, closed the shutters, disappeared from sight, then opened the door to the house.

I told Hamdun to wait and went in.

24

On the second floor, Pero led me through an arch into a living room, where a Moorish maidservant was polishing a silver floor vase. "Sit! Take your ease." He told the servant to fetch Marina. "Tell her Loma is here."

Next to the vase was a settle piled with cushions. I sat and looked around, taking a moment to gather my courage. Across from me, the room overlooked the courtyard. A painted wooden crucifix hung above the arch we'd entered through. The chamber's chief beauty was the ceiling, with its grid of beaded beams and the plaster between them painted a sea-foam green.

I took a deep breath. "I need more than a week."

"You can't have it."

"He won't come around in a week." If he ever would. "Please give me a month."

"A week."

"Bela would curse you."

"She would. I don't think even she could have saved me from gambling."

Marina bustled in. "Loma!" She took my hands in hers and shook them. "I'm so happy you've come! After Samuel's wedding, Pero said we might have a visitor, but I didn't suspect it would be you." Her eyes glistened.

"I'm glad to see you."

"And to see Pero, yes?" She finally dropped my hands.

"And his beautiful jewelry."

"Everything he does is a masterpiece. You must stay for dinner! I always make too much. We were about to sit down."

If Ledicia and her family didn't come to our house for dinner, as they often did, Papá would tell everyone I was with her. If she came, they would be frightened, but I doubted they'd look for me here.

If I stayed, maybe I could persuade Pero to give me more time. "If I can eat what you're serving, I'll be happy to stay."

"Let's see," Pero said. "What is it today?"

"Goose stew with cinnamon, as my mother makes it."

"Can someone bring Hamdun inside and give him a meal, too?"

"Yes!" Marina hurried out, calling behind her. "I'm so pleased you're here!"

When she was gone, I said, "Belo is angry. He'll come around, but by degrees. Not quickly."

"A week. Denouncing my own family will bring me Old Christian customers."

Marina came back, followed by two Muslim maids bearing trays. "Come."

We followed her through another arch into a pretty dining room, which also overlooked the courtyard. The maids set their trays down on the long table. One went to an open cabinet and lifted out a bowl. Between this cupboard and one just like it hung another crucifix—at least three feet long, big enough to show the whites of Jesus's eyes.

"Not that cupboard," Marina said. "The other one."

Pero looked sharply at her.

Blushing she added, "We should all eat from the same cupboard."

The maid went to the other cabinet and fetched a bowl that looked identical to the first. I understood. Considerately, Marina didn't want me to have to eat from a bowl that had held dairy.

Apparently, since she had two sets of dishes, Marina was still observing at least some Jewish laws about food.

"Ask Cook to make fritters for dessert," she told the maids.

Pero bent his head and began in a strong enough voice that the sound would follow the servants out, "Bless us, O Lord, and these, Thy gifts, which we are about to receive from Thy bounty through Christ, our Lord. Amen."

I murmured, and Marina echoed loudly, "Amen." She added, "There are more places to direct my prayers now: Christ, the Holy Mother, the Holy Ghost, God—although I don't know if He's the same God. And there are many saints." She giggled. "How can anything bad befall us?" Her expression changed. "Maybe one of them will send us a baby."

Poor Marina. We were both childless, and she had to endure Ugly Camel Head, too.

"Christ is a comfort," he said. "And church is a comfort, too, isn't it, Wife?"

She ladled stew into my bowl. "If I understood any of it. The singing is pretty, the incense smells nice, and they light as many candles as we—as the Jews—do."

The stew was delicious, moist, and with the flavors of home: cinnamon, ginger, pepper, garlic.

I'd never spent so much time with Marina. She was naturally chatty, or she was nervous.

"How do you pass your day?" I asked.

"Christian women go out more than Jewish ones do, so I go to the market myself every day, and I don't have to take anyone with me. Sometimes I sit in the plaza outside the cathedral and watch the pigeons. My family doesn't visit me, and my neighbors don't, either. I work in the kitchen a lot. I have to watch the servants—"

"Salad, Loma?" Pero passed me the plate.

Undeterred, she went on. "—or they do things wrong."

I didn't ask what things, because I guessed. If she weren't supervising, the servants might add milk to a stew or melt cheese into a sauce. Unless they were stupid, they would have seen enough to report her. Or perhaps they were so well paid they didn't care.

I could threaten to denounce her.

Would I do it to save Papá and Belo? I wasn't sure.

Would that save us? Probably not. The Inquisition would just pull all of us in.

The meal passed slowly. Pero took helping after helping. I told them about Samuel's new house. Marina asked questions, and the minutes ticked by.

Finally, Pero put down his knife. A maid came and piled the dishes on a tray.

"I'll see how the fritters are coming." Marina started to follow the maid out, then turned. "It's such a pleasure to have you here!"

When she was out of earshot, my heart began to pound. Could I threaten Pero?

"A week, Loma."

I swallowed acid. My breath came shallowly. I wet my lips.

Marina returned alone with a platter. "I didn't need help to carry just this."

I complimented the fritters, which I couldn't taste.

Pero spoke of the early summer we were having.

Marina smiled at us and burst out, "Loma, come often! I change the menu every day, and I never serve"—she mouthed the word without saying it—"*pork.*"

She had given me as many reasons to denounce her to the inquisitors for Judaizing as Pero had to denounce us for helping other New Christians do so.

When the fritters were gone, she offered me almonds or a tour of her kitchen, but I said I had to go home.

"First, Brother, would you show me more of your handiwork? Our sisters told me to see everything."

In his workshop, I said, "Pero . . ."

He shook his head. "You can't say anything that will change my mind."

"You don't know what I'm going to say."

He folded his arms. "What?"

"You gave me your hospitality."

"You're my sister."

"Then you still have family feeling for us. We're not so different." He and I were nothing alike! "We've both taken unusual paths. I'll probably never marry, and you converted." I was just talking to give myself time to think. Was there any way to lessen his malice? "Are Christians not supposed to be kind?"

"You have a week."

I shouldn't have come. "Then I'll fail. Goodbye, Brother." I collected Hamdun from the kitchen and started for the judería.

But halfway there, God or Bela sent me wisdom, and I told Hamdun we were going back. When we arrived, Pero was carrying his tray of jewelry to the window again.

He set it down. "A week."

"Belo is just angry. He loves his family, and you're still his grandson. Papá loves you. You may need their love someday, even as a Christian. If they're"—*dead*, but I couldn't say the word—"they won't be able to help you."

I meant, *You may need their money and influence.* Pero would gamble again, and eventually he'd lose again, or someone would denounce him for winning. Christian punishment was even harsher than Jewish. Belo and Papá had Christian friends.

"I won't be ruined now for future aid I may never need."

"Suppose I go to Papá? Belo is impossible to persuade to do anything, even to discard his worn-out shoes."

That won a smile. He decided. "Yes, go to Papá. It doesn't have to be Belo who speaks in my favor. A week, though."

I probably wouldn't need more than an hour for Papá.

The rest of my wisdom came purely from Bela. "Can't we continue to be brother and sister? I'll visit when I can. I want to see what you create next."

His face relaxed. "You'll be welcome when you come."

Another inspiration arrived from Bela. "Pero . . ." I touched Bela's amulet. "Would you make a dozen like it?" I could give one to each little and have a few left over for new babies, protecting them and appeasing Pero in one stroke. "Not exactly the same. Use your artistry, but don't make them so rich I can't pay for them by myself."

He smiled one of his rare, real smiles.

"Goodbye, Pero."

Hamdun, who'd been sitting cross-legged on the cobblestones, stood.

When we neared the judería gate, Hamdun said in his soft, musical voice, "Loma, there's a saying: The wise can herd lions." He smiled at me.

I wasn't sure what he meant, but it sounded well-meaning. "Thank you."

Luckily, Ledicia hadn't come to our house for dinner, so my lie wasn't discovered. I went to Papá in his study that night and brought the necklace Pero had given me.

Papá moved from his desk to a floor cushion and patted the one next to him. "What's this?"

I sat and told him what Pero had said at Samuel's wedding about Belo ruining his business. I didn't mention the threat, though I'd decided I would if I had to.

The necklace jingled in his hand. "Your abuelo is pitiless when he's angry. I'll wear the necklace, and I won't be shy about saying who made it. Belo doesn't have to know."

In two weeks, I picked up the amulets, each one made of quartz, not gems, in a different color, each incised, like mine, with the Hebrew letters for God, on thin silver chains—better than my velvet one. How pretty they were. I said so and got another real smile in return.

As a mark of favor because he was my brother, I let Jento pick his amulet before I distributed the others.

He closed his fist around the dark green pendant with flecks of red, a surprising choice because of its somberness. I remembered Belo telling me that Bela said I was a cabinet of hidden drawers. Seemingly, Jento was, too.

I lowered the chain around his neck. "Now nothing can harm you."

But my confidence in amulets was less than it had been.

I chose the other littles' pendants myself based on eye color, skin tone, and temperament. When each had one, I felt I had done what I could against the malevolent forces of the world.

At first, I visited Pero to keep him from being angry at us. But soon I went for his wife's company. We talked by the hour—about cooking, sewing, spinning, weaving. Then we began to play backgammon together.

Hers was a child's game, just a rush to the end, with no strategy to take advantage of the luck of the dice. I won almost every game, but she wasn't troubled. Her nature was happy, fortunate for someone married to my brother.

I'd never had a friend before, only sisters and Samuel, and we all knew everything about each other. With Marina, there was discovery, which I relished.

"We're going to Gerona," I announced a few days before we left.

"Exciting!"

It used to be. Now it was my life.

25

Alas, we didn't enter a paradise free of trouble from my troublesome brother.

Belo and I journeyed here and there for almost two months—away from the littles, who changed and grew without me. As we journeyed, I imagined their comings and goings and wished they could remain exactly the same when I was away—if the Almighty would accomplish that without harming them.

On July 29, 1490, we were back. Papá met us at the top of the stairs. Mamá was shouting from the living room about the misery of having a son like Pero.

In Belo's study, Papá told us. Marina had come to the house the week before. Three priests and two constables from the hermandad had taken Pero. When they left, she'd rushed to her parents and then to us.

Belo's face was untroubled. I saw he wouldn't have a spell again over Pero.

We all knew how the inquisitors proceeded. My brother would be imprisoned and tortured until he confessed to the sin he'd been accused of. He, who feared a mere flogging, would say whatever they wanted.

But he might manage to wait before confessing—to see if Belo would rescue him. If Belo didn't come—and quickly—he'd take revenge. He'd accuse us. The Inquisition would widen its net to draw us in.

Belo had to help him!

"Papá," Papá said to Belo, "we have to go."

"Where?" Belo sat at his desk. "This doesn't concern us. Loma, please have Aljohar make up a bowl of something for me. I'm hungry."

Swollen with heart-hatred for Pero as well as for Mamá, Belo, and even Papá, I went to the kitchen. Aljohar had a stew simmering over the fire. With trembling hands, I ladled a generous helping into a bowl, set the bowl on a tray, and added a slice of bread.

Bela, what would you do?

She wouldn't be furious with everyone.

But I was. What could I do?

On my way back upstairs, I heard Papá's low tones in the living room with Mamá.

In the study, Belo thanked me for the stew. "We've been gone so long, I forgot I wrote this. Let me read it to you: 'Eternity belongs to the Eternal One; all else—'"

"If you don't help Pero, I'll never come in here or travel with you again." My hand flew to my mouth. The words, which hadn't been on my tongue when I came in, wouldn't soften anyone's heart. "I'm sorry! I—" I stopped, unwilling to take them back.

"I won't help him. Go."

I left for my bedroom, where I threw myself on my bed and stared up at the wooden ceiling, my eyes dry. Pero would die, after turning the gaze of the inquisitors toward us. We'd all be killed, and I wouldn't be able to stop any of it.

Fatima's soft knock interrupted my circling thoughts. She said Belo wanted me in his study.

I went, resolved not to stay if he hadn't decided to help Pero.

He stood at his window, looking out over the street. From the doorway, I could see only the clay roof of the house across the street and a square of blue sky.

"Why do you believe I should attempt to save my worthless grandson?"

"Because Bela would want you to." Because otherwise he'll kill all of us. But I was afraid to say that for fear of bringing on a spell.

"How old were you when your bela died?"

"Seven."

He sat heavily in his chair. "She showed her soft side to children. She'd be as angry at Pero as I am."

That might be true, but I had an answer from watching Ledicia, my model of a good mother.

"Do you remember when Jamila's skirt caught flame in the kitchen?"

"I heard about it."

"Ledicia had told her a dozen times to stay away from the fireplace. When the fire was out and Ledicia saw she was fine, she yelled for half an hour." I smiled at the memory. *Do you think I speak just to hear noise come out of my mouth? Do you think I'm not worth listening to? Your mother is your mother, so you have someone to obey.* "Bela would have wanted you to save Pero so she could punish him afterward."

"You're right. Bela would have felt as you say. I'll do what I can to rescue him, but I'll leave the yelling and punishing to you and your papá, and if I fail—"

He saw my face.

"I'll do my best, but if my best fails, I won't suffer. He's a worm to me."

I wondered if I could ever become a worm to him.

Belo took Papá with him to the hermandad, and when they returned, it was with the news that the three of us were to travel to Segovia, where Don Solomon lived and where Pero had been taken. I'd been to Segovia twice before, but never to see inquisitors!

This time, I had to leave the littles, not to help all the Jews of Spain but to save one worthless brother.

Before we left home, I pulled Ledicia aside and asked her to find out if Marina was all right. "Nothing is her fault. Help her if you can."

Ledicia promised she would.

Mamá followed us down to the street and astonished me and probably everyone else by hugging me. "The Almighty sent you to comfort this family." She stroked my cheek before she stepped away.

And He had sent Pero to torment and frighten us.

The sun had already set and night had fallen when we reached Segovia. After Belo greeted the city guards and gave them a purse, we passed through the city gate. Once inside, we hastened to Don Solomon's house.

Our host was already asleep, but his nosy daughter greeted us and turned from me to Papá. "This one is still traveling? She isn't betrothed yet?"

Belo said he was tired.

She led Belo and Papá away and then returned to take me to a bedroom and a bed shared by her three grand-daughters. I stretched out on the edge, taking as little space as I could. I prayed to be surrounded by God and His angels, counted my many worries, and finally slept.

Early in the morning, in the dining room, Belo told Don Solomon what had befallen Pero. A warm breeze wafted through the windows. The long trestle table was laid with bread and white cheese.

"Please—" Don Solomon gestured at the food and helped himself to a wedge of cheese. Then he sat on the bench that was drawn up to the table, with his back to it.

We served ourselves. Belo sat next to Don Solomon, and I sat next to Belo. Papá took a folding chair by the fireplace.

After we thanked God for the food, Don Solomon said, "Your grandson picked a bad time. I doubt you'll get His Excellency's help." He told us that the bishop's parents and his grandmother, who were dead, had been determined to have Judaized. The Inquisition wanted to burn their bones to punish them.

I shuddered.

"His Excellency is treading carefully in hopes that Their Majesties will keep that from happening." Don Solomon flecked a speck of cheese off his scarlet robe. "You'd have done better if you'd gone to Ávila."

Belo said, "Torquemada is there?"

The grand inquisitor.

Don Solomon nodded. "He's directing the questioning from the priory there, but your grandson is here."

Belo turned to me. "Loma, the inquisitors will find Pero innocent if Torquemada tells them to."

Belo and Papá decided not to rush to Ávila in hopes of seeing Fra Torquemada before sunset, when the Sabbath would begin.

"Once we see Pero," Belo said, "we may know what to say in Ávila."

Don Solomon said he'd take us to the house where Pero was being held. "I know the inquisitors."

Papá put his bowl on the table. "Let's see what they've done to him."

My chest tightened.

The Inquisition was being conducted in a private house that had been rented to the inquisitors. In silence, Papá and I walked side by side through the city. Ahead of us, Belo strolled with Don Solomon, setting a slow pace that irritated me. They talked, and once—I could hardly believe it—Belo laughed. I began to count steps.

Why did the Inquisition care that Pero had gambled, which was probably his offense? Gambling was a crime, not heresy.

One hundred and thirty-two steps. Why had he been brought here and not tried in Alcalá de Henares?

My worries revolved from fears for Pero to fears for us to fears of the sights I would soon see and the screams I would hear.

We left the judería. Ahead, bells clanged from a church, announcing nine in the morning. Soon we reached it, with a horseshoe-arch entryway and long porch lined with more arches, each of them reminding me of gaping mouths waiting to swallow Jews.

I reached for Papá's hand. He clasped mine, but his was hot and sweaty and brought little comfort. I hung on, though, not wanting to hurt his feelings.

Finally, we reached a sad little triangular plaza—no fountain, no trees.

Don Solomon stopped and gestured across the plaza at a long house, three stories at one end, tapering to one story at the other. The doorway arched, reminding me of the church we'd just passed. The door knocker was a foot-long iron lizard.

An omen! I touched Bela's amulet.

Don Solomon raised the knocker and let go, producing a *clank*.

26

A friar answered the door. When he saw Don Solomon, he smiled, revealing two missing lower teeth. We were ushered in.

The domed vestibule ceiling made me feel like we really had entered a mouth. The air was hot and still, as it would be inside a leviathan. I heard no screams.

Archways to the left and right led to seemingly endless corridors of arches. Across from us and against the wall on our right rose a stone staircase with sixteen steps that ended in a second-story balcony. On the wall next to the stairs hung a tapestry of a blue beast with a horse's head.

The friar welcomed us with a long paragraph of words, like *honored, occasion, delight, extraordinary.* I caught a whiff of incense.

Don Solomon introduced us and explained why we'd come.

The friar said we couldn't see Pero. "The questioning is at a delicate phase. Regrettably, no one may see him. Perhaps in a week. Can you forgive us?"

Pero would stop expecting us in a week! My breath felt shallow. This very friar could be examining us soon. He was tall and appeared strong. Would he flog us and apologize while he was applying the lash?

"No forgiveness is necessary." Belo held out both hands, palms up. "We respect the Holy Office."

That was what the Inquisition was called.

Don Solomon stroked his beard. "Don Joseph and I were talking earlier about the beauty of your monastery. I told him that last year I was allowed to contribute a silver candelabrum. He—"

Belo broke in. "I said I wished for such an honor. I've added to the majesty of the cathedral in Alcalá de Henares."

The friar said nothing.

"I share my father's wish," Papá said, "for myself and for my daughter from her dowry."

Which I was unlikely to need.

The friar stroked his shaved chin. "I'll ask my superior if an exception may be made." He began to turn away from us.

Belo held up a hand. "I hope you'll also allow a physician

to visit my grandson at our expense if we believe one is required."

"I'll see." The friar climbed the stairs, the keys at his waist tinkling. His sandals slapped the steps.

We waited without speaking. The floor was tiled in brown- and rose-colored squares. I started to count, but I had only reached twenty when the friar returned.

"I'm so very pleased to be allowed to oblige you. A physician will be permitted as well, if you think that necessary. Come."

He led us into the corridor to the right of the entrance. On our right, the arches were inset with windows that looked out on the plaza. On the left, a pattern repeated itself: below every third arch was a closed wooden door.

At the fourth door, he stopped and chose a key from nine others on his belt. "We haven't prepared him for visitors."

The stink! I raised my sleeve to my nose, which failed to block the smell. Pero had soiled himself. There was also the acrid odor of vomit.

The friar bustled in and raised the two windows, which looked out on the courtyard, where a fountain spouted glittering water.

Papá rushed to Pero, who drooped on a bench against the wall to our left, and embraced him despite the stench, blocking him from view. "Son, are you all right?"

Belo and I waited just inside the door. Don Solomon left entirely, murmuring that he'd be in the corridor.

Papá straightened and went to the window. Pero wore only his shirt and hose. His left arm rested naturally on his knee, but his right arm twisted at the elbow, and his hand stuck out unnaturally.

Tears ran steadily down his cheeks. His face was pasty, grayish, with dark smudges under his eyes. They must have taken his jewelry. Of everything, that awakened my pity.

"You came, Loma." He beckoned me with his left hand.

Holding my breath, I went to him, and he whispered, "Lizard, I gambled that you'd bring Belo to save me, but if luck hadn't gone my way . . ."

He hadn't betrayed us so far, but he still would if we didn't get him released.

I whispered back, "We'll bring you home as soon as we can." Please understand it won't be today. I stepped away.

In an ordinary voice, he said, "I can't move my right hand and I can't feel it. My elbow is in agony." On a rising note, he added, "They left me like this."

Papá said, "We'll come back with a physician. Be brave."

Belo opened his hands again. "Father, is there a message we can carry for you to Fra Torquemada? We're calling on him after the Sabbath."

Belo was so clever! The inquisitors wouldn't dare

torture or interrogate Pero again until they knew how the wind blew from the grand inquisitor. Pero would also understand what we were up to.

The friar said, "Wish him good health and say we're toiling to do Christ's work."

We returned in an hour with clean clothes from Don Solomon and a converso physician known to Don Solomon, because Christians weren't allowed to be treated by Jewish doctors.

Hamdun came, too, to wash Pero before the physician examined him. I waited outside the chamber while he was cleaned and examined, because I couldn't see my brother's nakedness.

How kind Hamdun was. I heard him say, "There. Ah, I see that must hurt. There. You'll feel better when you're clean. Almost finished."

Hamdun came out with dirty washcloths and soiled clothing, and the physician went in.

After a minute or two, Pero screamed. I winced. My heart-hatred, seemingly, didn't keep me from feeling along with him.

I learned later that he'd been flogged, and his shirt had stuck to the drying blood. The scream had come when the shirt was removed.

Papá came to the door and waved me in. The air was better already.

The doctor probed Pero's elbow, producing squeals from the patient and fresh winces from me. I caught Belo watching me.

"I have to move your elbow back to where it should be. It will hurt."

Pero shrieked, moaned, then fell silent.

The physician waited.

In a surprised voice, Pero said, "It feels better."

A few minutes later, we left. We spent the Sabbath with Don Solomon and his family, and not even Papá returned to Pero before we left for Ávila.

We sat in the meeting room of the monastery of Santo Tomás, four of us clustered on leather folding armchairs. I was between Belo and Papá. Across from us, the grand inquisitor pressed his fingertips together close to his chest. Behind him stood a marble statue of a monk. Above the statue's head hung a painting of a haloed Christ floating in the air, flanked by two other haloed figures. Below them, a skeleton extended its arms and legs over a jumble of naked people, seemingly suffering in hell.

Belo had explained why we'd come and had ended by protesting Pero's innocence. "I'm sure his conversion was sincere. His worldly future would have been more promising if he'd remained a Jew."

The grand inquisitor said nothing.

On the journey here, Belo had told me that Fra Torquemada was known for refusing bribes. I wondered why he'd need money anyway, since the Inquisition took everything that belonged to an accused. He'd have an endless supply.

If he didn't want money, what could we offer him?

He didn't look rich. His robe was brown wool, which must have been horrible in this heat. The cross that hung around his neck was wood and the chain brass.

We waited. My heart thumped.

He was older than Belo, with furrows between his eyebrows, a pushed-in nose, and fleshy cheeks. The hair in his tonsure was curly. His power, I thought, emanated from his small, sharp eyes.

Finally, he spoke—to me. "Are you wed, child?"

Even the grand inquisitor wanted to know! I fought hysterical laughter, swallowed, and said I wasn't.

"Betrothed?"

"No, Your Excellency."

"I am *Fra* Torquemada, not *Excellency.*" He turned to Papá. "Why not?"

"She's devoted to her grandfather."

"Is this true?"

I nodded.

"You're to be commended, child." He fell silent again.

I tried to think how I could use his approval for Pero's sake.

"We're a virtuous family." I breathed shallowly and wished my heart would settle. "Pero tried to persuade me to convert, too."

I sensed Belo's focus shift to me.

"What did he say?" Fra Torquemada asked.

"That the Almighty has turned His favor to the Christians, which God proved by sending His Son."

He nodded. "You disagreed?"

I couldn't argue with the grand inquisitor! Or tell him I hated Christians for their cruelty at Málaga and for making Belo have spells and for thinking we would poison their wells and for kidnapping me when I was a little girl.

I opened and closed my mouth like a fish. At last, words came. "I wasn't sure."

He raised bushy eyebrows. "Your brother may yet teach you to believe."

I nodded. Let him think so.

"When he was named in this case," Fra Torquemada said, "I suspected malice."

Who had named him?

Fra Torquemada turned to Belo. "Your aid to the Church has been noticed."

Belo thanked him and turned his palms up in his lap. "I intend to continue, and my son will as well."

The grand inquisitor did take bribes!

Papá said he would. "And Loma will exert the influence she has."

"As the Lord wills," Fra Torquemada said. "I might have traveled to you if you hadn't come here. I'm involved in a secular matter."

"Just tell me," Belo said, "and I'll do what I can."

"Torquemada in Palencia—you know it?"

Belo nodded. "Charming town. Your namesake. The beautiful river, the old church, the new church."

"But suffering. Taxes are suffocating the good Chris—"

Belo raised his upturned palm. "No more. They mustn't struggle."

"We are righting wrongs today. I will give you a letter saying that I've concluded your grandson is innocent of heresy." He turned to me. "Instead of a dowry, I gave my sister a home in a cloister. She lives a pure life. I wish you a pure life, too, and when you die, heaven with Christ. Spend time with your virtuous brother."

The hysterical laughter threatened me again.

Papá leaned forward. "May I ask: Of what was Pero accused?"

"There was a conspiracy. That's all I may say."

"May *I* ask a favor?" Belo said.

"I'll grant it if I can."

"Expunge Pero's name and all in our family from the

records of the trial. I would not have the shame follow him."

The grand inquisitor nodded. "It will be in the letter."

After reading Fra Torquemada's letter, the friar in Segovia returned Pero's jewelry and released him, saying, "I'm happy you've been proven innocent."

I wondered how innocence or guilt would be discovered in any accused who didn't have someone like Belo to help them.

Pero said piously, "By God's grace." His health was much improved. Though his arm was swollen, he could open and close his hand and wiggle his fingers.

We rode out of Segovia in a blanket of silence as heavy as the summer heat.

A flock of sheep passed us, driven by their shepherd. I counted as many as I could see and wondered how they could bear their own wool during the summer.

Few people were on the road. I asked myself how often my brother would need rescuing in the future, since he'd certainly keep gambling. If he were pulled in again by the Inquisition, we had nothing else the grand inquisitor wanted, and I doubted he'd be convinced twice of Pero's innocence.

Papá broke the silence, speaking in Latin, which the four of us knew and which the guards and any passersby probably wouldn't. "What were you accused of, son?"

He answered in Latin, too. "They don't tell you. If I knew, I could have defended myself." His tone was resentful.

"Who accused you?" I said.

"I don't know that, either."

"Someone you gambled with?" I asked.

"Belo paid my gambling debt."

"*I* paid it," Papá said.

Belo spurred his horse to Pero's side. "You're safe. We're your family." He was using his velvet tax-farming voice. "If we don't know everything, we can't protect you. Was there more debt? Did you owe someone else when you converted?"

Pero looked a question at me: Had I told Belo or Papá about his threat?

I shook my head.

"Yuce Franco."

Papá frowned. "Who?"

"From Tembleque. He came to the judería for his cousin's wedding and then left again. I saw him in the corridor in Segovia."

Belo said, "Yuce is a Jew?"

"He is. I was a Jew then."

I understood. The inquisitors must have asked Señor Yuce if he'd had help committing whatever he was accused of, and he'd named my brother—taking revenge on Pero for not paying his gambling debt.

Belo must have understood, too. "Anyone else? We'll pay."

Pero named the judería's late candlemaker, who'd died of a stomach ailment around the time Pero had declared his decision to convert.

In a shocked voice, Papá said, "Did you poison him?"

Pero cried, "No!" sounding just as shocked.

I said, "But his death was lucky for you."

"Loma," Belo said, "I haven't heard your promised anger at Pero—to be angry once he's safe."

In a voice I didn't recognize—hoarse and deep—I said, "I'll be angry and I'll love him again when he's a corpse and we have nothing more to fear from him."

27

Pero cried, "Ai!" Then: "Fire salamander!"

Poisonous lizard.

"You speak that way to your sister?" Papá said. "Your abuelo wouldn't have helped you if not for her." He turned to Belo. "Thank you." He turned to me. "You speak that way to your brother?"

"I apologize, Pero." But it was true. We wouldn't be safe while he was alive—if a Jew was ever safe.

Pero apologized back and then thanked me.

Belo looked at me, his face expressionless. "How were we endangered by Pero?" It was his tax-farmer voice again. "How will we be endangered in the future?"

My heart thumped as hard as it had in the presence of

the grand inquisitor. What might Belo do to shield us from harm? He could be ruthless.

Pero's eyes were big, staring at me.

If Belo abandoned Pero in the road for bandits to rob and kill, we all would be safer. Marina would be happier eventually.

"Loma?" Belo said.

I still didn't want to reveal Pero's threat, which would doom him. "The Inquisition! No one wants to be near its tentacles. Pero gambles! And he's a converso! And we're Jews! Four risks! Too many!"

Papá came to ride next to me and reached across our horses' backs to clasp my hand. "We can always protect our family."

Could we? I thought of the littles, especially Beatriz, who worried about everything; Clara; and Jento with his hidden drawers. Could we protect them?

Belo rode to the guards ahead of us. After a short conversation, he returned. When we reached the fork in the road north of the village of Hontoria, the guards led us onto the right-hand track, going southwest, rather than southeast toward home.

"Asher, Loma," Belo said, "don't argue. This will benefit you, Pero. You've escaped the Inquisition. I mean for you to escape it permanently. We're going to Cádiz to put you on a ship to Tangier."

Pero cried, "A boat! Have pity!"

Belo continued. "From Tangier, you will wait to join a caravan to Fez. You won't have to wait long. They set out often. I send goods that way. In Fez, you'll find many goldsmiths and silversmiths. I'll give you a letter of introduction to my friend and enough money to set up a workshop—unless you gamble it away. There won't be more from me, and if your papá and sister are wise, there won't be more from them, either."

"He'll lose his family," Papá said.

Belo ignored this. "The crossing is short. You can start over. Not many get such a chance."

Papá said, "In Fez, you can be a Jew again if you want to be."

"Or you may follow Islam," I said, "if that suits your purpose."

He sent me a venomous look, then put back his placid camel's face, behind which any wicked ideas could be forming.

"Marina must have a get!" I cried, remembering her. The writ of divorce.

"Conditional," Pero said. "She may want to join me. I'll write to her."

Papá nodded. "Conditional."

"Can't I just go to a different city in Spain? I won't trouble you again, no matter what."

No, I thought.

"No," Belo said.

"Then Fez will be my home. I'll do my best there." Pero took a deep breath. "Papá, I'll be a Jew again there."

And there, he'd be able to win the protection of the Muslim religion if he needed it.

Or, perhaps he really would reform.

We stood on a quay in Cádiz. Earlier, in the plaza outside the cathedral, we'd visited a moneylender's stall, where Belo was known from his many trips to the city. Documents were signed, and we left with enough ducats to make Pero's future come true. Belo had also written a letter of introduction to his friend in Fez, asking him to help Pero establish himself. And we had Marina's conditional get.

The harbor was discord in noise and motion. Ships' officers barked orders at sailors high in the sails. Masters shouted at laborers, who bore freight out of the warehouses that fronted the wharf. Shipwrights scolded apprentices. Saws rasped and whined. Hammering rang out, louder than a thousand woodpeckers. Fishing boats bobbed. Masts swayed. Clouds scudded across the sky. The sea frothed. The only constants were the blue of the seamen's clothing and the red of their caps.

I smelled dampness, salt, and sardines.

A man in a blue taffeta cape and a red cap approached

us, arms outstretched, walking with a rolling gait, as if the wharf were rocking. "My friend!"

Belo introduced us to shipmaster Señor Carlos Calvo, whom he called the most trustworthy seaman ever to ride the waves. I scrutinized the man's face to decide if Belo was telling the truth.

Master Calvo's face was long, but his nose was short. Deep lines framed his smile and creases divided his rounded eyebrows. He had such dark eyes I could hardly see the pupils, which made their expression unreadable.

He bowed to us and told Belo that I was an "incomparable" beauty. He spoke with an accent, adding an *uh* after words that didn't end in a vowel.

Belo took the master's elbow and walked him several yards from us. Pero went to join them, but Belo waved him away. The two spoke for several minutes. Master Calvo leaned his head toward Belo and nodded and nodded. Finally, Belo pressed a purse into his hand and folded his fingers over it. Then they returned to us.

"Master Calvo tells me his ship leaves with the tide. Pero, be guided by him on the voyage, and I wish you success in Fez." He didn't embrace him.

Papá folded him into a long hug. At the end, he patted Pero's cheek. "Be well. Be safe. Don't gamble. We'll miss you."

God forgive me, I wouldn't miss him.

He held his arms out to me. I went to him for a hug and

a kiss on my cheek. He whispered, "You should convert, Lizard, if you want safety." He let me go and added, loud enough for everyone to hear, "Please persuade Marina to come when I write."

Master Calvo put his arm around Pero's shoulders. "On my ship, gentle folk live in comfort." He walked Pero away, his voice diminishing, talking about the food, the wine, the conversation.

Back home, while Fatima massaged his feet, Belo said, "Loma, don't tell your papá. I instructed Master Calvo that if Pero gambles away all his money and more during the crossing, he's to pay his debt and put him in the galley."

A slave.

I swallowed, not sure what I was feeling. "He isn't strong enough to row all day."

"He may not gamble," Belo said drily, "or he may not lose."

"Will he starve?" He loved his meals so much.

"They'll feed him adequately. They want their oarsmen to keep their strength."

He would gamble and lose again, but maybe not on the voyage.

"Having to work hard," Belo said, "is the only thing that may change him, and people don't always stay slaves."

If he were to die, would his death be on my head for

announcing that I wished him a corpse?

"In any event, we're done with him. You can love him again."

The best I could feel was relief.

Pero's property and possessions were returned to Marina, although Belo had to explain to the bishop why he'd left Spain. He said Pero's reputation wouldn't recover from being suspected by the Inquisition, which the bishop accepted.

A few weeks later, Belo received a letter from Don Solomon that said the trial Pero had been involved in had been moved from Segovia to Ávila. After that, we heard nothing for a long time. I continued to think of Pero and where he might be, whether rowing in a galley or making jewelry, but the trial dropped out of my mind.

Marina couldn't return to Judaism unless she moved to a Muslim kingdom. She stayed in her house, supported by her parents and Papá. I visited her when I could, and she seemed not much changed from when Pero had been downstairs working in his studio: glad to see me, a little bored, still interested in her cooking.

Six months passed without word from Pero. Marina took her get from him to the cathedral, and a priest declared her free to remarry—

—which she did a month later, in February 1491, to a young converso widower from a wealthy family. By May, she was pregnant. I no longer visited her, but I heard the news from Belo.

Though I missed having a friend, I was happy for her. I imagined that in time Pero would become a hazy dream, but she'd remember me fondly.

Two months before Marina's marriage, in December 1490, both Vellida and Ledicia had had healthy babies and recovered well. To the delight of everyone, Vellida had twins, a boy and a girl, Amram and Orovida. Ledicia named her son David. David and Orovida each had a thatch of brown hair, but Amram emerged bald. All of them had gray eyes.

Belo and Papá continued to farm taxes. A special tax, which they had to collect, too, was levied on every Jewish family to pay for the war against Granada. In our judería, Belo and Papá paid the tax for the poor.

They both called it a blessing to be able to do so.

Papá said, "The Jews of Spain are being bled dry."

Belo remained well. We traveled and were away more often than we were home. Missing the littles was a stone in my stomach. I missed the birth of Samuel and Josefina's first baby, a daughter named Esther, after Bela.

I thought this would be the design of the coming years: absent when littles were born or when they passed their important milestones; present for meals and audiences with people who meant nothing to me—until everyone ceased asking about my marriage prospects and my youth was spent.

The first hint of change, though I didn't recognize it, came on a Sunday night in November 1491, when we happened to be in Toledo. A Christian mob tried to open the judería gate. From the rabbi's house, we heard banging and shouting. My hand found Bela's pendant. I remembered the night when I'd been kidnapped. I was too old to be kidnapped, but a Jew of any age could be killed.

Belo and the rabbi went out into the night. I was tempted to go after them. Belo might have one of his spells—but then what would I do?

They returned in a few minutes. The constables of the hermandad were protecting the gate.

In the morning, Belo took me with him to thank the chief constable, whom he knew, as he knew everyone of consequence. The hermandad's building was called an inn, though it had no paying guests. The constables lived there, and so did their prisoners.

The building didn't look frightening: three stories tall, brick, with a clay roof. The door, flanked by columns that rose to the roof, was big enough to admit horses.

The two constables who guarded the entrance wore pointed steel helmets and the hermandad's white overgown with the big scarlet cross on the chest. The cross seemed to shout, *I am a Christian. Be afraid.*

A constable led us up a narrow flight of wooden stairs and down a corridor. A scream echoed up from the stairs behind us and was abruptly cut off. I clenched my teeth to keep from screaming, too.

The constable turned. "Just a thief." He opened a wooden door and had to duck to enter.

Belo and I went in without having to stoop. We were on a courtyard balcony. Next to the door was a wooden bench.

"Señor Cruz will see you soon." The constable left.

Belo sat. I looked over the wrought-iron railing. The courtyard was bleak: no plants, no fountain, just a diagonal pattern of rusty bricks. While Belo prayed softly, I counted bricks, but I couldn't see the ones right below us. The sky was gray, the air chilly. I kept listening for more screams, but I heard none.

Belo said, "This rudeness is odd."

At last, a large man came in, the red cross curving over his belly. He faced us, leaning his back against the railing, which I feared might not support his weight. The balcony was narrow. Only about two feet separated the man from us.

Belo stood to bow, and I curtsied, but this fellow merely nodded.

"I am glad to see you well, my friend," Belo said, smiling, and holding out a purse. "Señor Cruz, thank you for your steadfastness last night. Please reward your men, too."

Señor Cruz's hand closed over the purse, but his leathery face didn't relax. "We did our duty, though many of my men wanted to join the mob, and I half wanted to, too."

"My friend! I'm amazed," Belo said. "If you please, tell me what—"

"You already know." He stared over our heads. "All the Jews and Judaizers know. You laugh over it."

Belo protested that he didn't know. "I'm mystified. People banged on the gate. We heard the clamor." He put his arm around my shoulder. "My granddaughter was terrified."

I probably already looked frightened, because I was, but I made my eyes big.

"The Jewess puts on a good show." He shrugged his plump shoulders. "All right. At Sunday Mass, the priests read a message from the inquisitors in Ávila. A gaggle of Jews and conversos were found guilty of crucifying a boy from La Guardia and cutting out his heart—"

My hand pressed against my own heart. No Jew would do that!

"—and using it in sorcery to destroy all Christians by

giving them rabies, and then to take our property, as if"—
he leaned across the space that separated us and jabbed
his index finger into Belo's chest with each word—"you . . .
didn't . . . have . . . enough . . . already."

28

Belo tried to draw back, but the wall was right behind him.

I pushed words out. "He's an old man!"

Señor Cruz dropped his hand. "By Christ's grace, the spell failed, and the guilty were burned in an auto-da-fé."

I was panting in horror.

Belo cried, "No Jew . . . The commandments . . . We never—"

"Enough." Señor Cruz held up his hand. "We did our duty. You may go."

Belo held himself erect until we were beyond the inn of the hermandad, but then he stumbled and would have fallen if I hadn't caught his elbow. "It's not an attack. I'm only shocked, which I thought impossible."

It wasn't until we turned into the next street that I realized: the trial Pero had been in had been moved to Ávila.

But that was more than a year ago. "Belo, could that be the trial Pero was caught up in?"

He said it probably was. "They take their time, the inquisitors. It's a slow business, extracting the answers they want."

Another dreadful thought struck me. "Do you think Christians attacked the judería at home?"

"It's possible. We must go."

The littles!

We left Toledo an hour later. Soon, a band of gray-gold smoke throbbed along the horizon ahead. When we drew close, we saw that smoke wreathed the walled city of Ocaña. Belo said that the judería was probably aflame, but we didn't stop. We could have done nothing.

Riding every inch with me was the memory of the time eight years earlier when the hermandad at home had failed to keep out the mob.

We spent the night on the side of the road. Hamdun built a fire and served us a meal of dried beef and flatbread. We sat on a rug before the fire to eat.

While we ate, Belo mused, "A chief constable, a man of that station, doesn't usually heed the rabble's nonsense, even the priests' nonsense. Why did he listen this time?"

Why would anyone believe Jews could murder a child? Christians and Jews met daily at the marketplace. We bought their goods. They bought ours. Why would they trade with us, if they thought we were evil and wanted to destroy them?

I took another strip of beef and asked Belo.

"You know the answer to that. You've seen it again and again."

Seen what?

Oh. "Money," I said. "They sell, we buy; we sell, they buy. It makes everyone nice. If they kill us, they lose, too. Why don't they remember that?"

He said three words I'd never heard from him before: "I don't know."

At home, our chief constable had done his job. Everyone was fine. I spent half an hour hugging and petting Jento. At nearly seven, he felt himself too old for cuddling, but he had to endure it anyway. Then I ran in turn to my sisters' houses and Samuel's.

I didn't want to frighten them, but I made all the littles show me that they were wearing the amulets I'd given them.

Clara, the animal lover, had hung her necklace around the neck of the family cat. "Yowl is old, Tía Loma. She needs it more than I do."

I took it off the cat and clasped it around Clara's neck. "The pendant will protect you so you can protect Yowl. Yes?"

She nodded.

The others were wearing theirs, even confident Todros. I was both sorry and glad they understood that Jews needed a safeguard.

In January 1492, in the cathedral plaza, heralds announced the monarchs' victory in Granada. All of Spain was free of Muslim rule.

In the judería, we were foolish enough to rejoice.

At dinner, Belo said, "No more war taxes for a while. The poor will be less poor. Peace will be good for the Jews." He poured himself more wine.

"Can Loma stay home now?" Jento speared a chunk of lamb with his knife. "She's teaching me to be better at backgammon. I need her."

I paused with my knife halfway to my mouth.

"We still have to make money," Papá said. "Do you like studying with Señor Osua?"

Jento nodded. "He says I have a gift for numbers."

Like me.

Belo sipped his wine. "He has to be paid, so we still have to travel."

I resumed eating. "Will the Jews of Granada have to be

ransomed?" Those of Málaga had been prisoners for two years before they were set free.

"More Jews live there," Papa said. "Let's hope the monarchs are merciful."

They were, A week later, Belo received a letter from Don Solomon, who wrote that the Jews of Granada could stay in their homes and live as they had under the Moors. Two days after that, royal notices were delivered to Belo and Papá, declaring that their tax-farming commissions had been renewed.

Later, I wondered if these two events—the Jews of Granada and the renewals—were planned to keep people calm, to stop us from suspecting and preparing, and then to create panic when the monarchs loosed their lightning bolt.

At the beginning of February, Beatriz turned eleven and Papá teased her about her betrothal prospects. She fluffed her hair, just as Vellida used to. Belo teased her, too, which pained me.

On March 26, a royal messenger knocked on our door and presented Fatima with a scroll tied with a red ribbon.

The scroll was a summons to Belo to attend the king and queen at their camp outside the new city of Santa Fe, near Granada. I was to come, too. "'Your presence, kind friend, is required, and the attendance of your granddaughter Paloma Cantala is needed as well. Do not tarry.'"

There was my name, with King Ferdinand's signature below. I touched the signature. Belo would keep the scroll, and my name would live there forever. I'd joined the annals of the Jews of Spain.

A flurry of packing followed. Granada was far to the south. We'd be traveling for more than a week, and who knew how long we'd have to stay.

As we set out, Belo wondered if the monarchs had decided to levy a new tax on the Jews. "For a cathedral or some such. No doubt they'll try again to convert you. Don't frighten me the way you did in Málaga, Loma."

"I was a child!"

We reached the monarchs' camp in the evening of Wednesday, April 4. The Spanish court was arrayed in tents on a hill north of Santa Fe. While Hamdun pitched our tent on the outskirts, Belo sent a messenger to let a secretary know that we had arrived. The messenger returned in an hour with tidings that Don Solomon was expected, too, and our audience would await his coming.

In the morning, since Don Solomon still hadn't arrived, Belo and I strolled through the camp, which bustled with servants, slaves, courtiers, priests, and monks. Belo greeted the courtiers and clerics he knew and invited them to our tent. In the afternoon, he entertained fifteen guests. I sat on a cushion and embroidered a tablecloth

I'd brought with me to work on.

No one paid attention to me until the Duke of Medina-celi came. He lowered himself creakily onto the cushion next to me. "Lately, my knees hate me."

I smiled. In this crowd of strangers, he seemed, slight acquaintance though he was, like an old friend. "Belo's feet have hated him for years."

He smiled back and then sobered. "More and more, the queen wraps herself in a cloak of Christ. When she was young, she danced. You should have seen her lift her skirts above her ankles and throw back her head. She had a beautiful neck!"

I hadn't noticed her neck. Feeling I had to say something, I told him that I liked to dance.

He went on. "Everyone eavesdrops on anything I say to Don Joseph, but no one pays attention when I speak to you." He raised his hands in mock protest. "I would speak with you anyway! Between us, you are my favorite Cantala!"

Belo was his favorite, but I didn't contradict him. "What would you tell my abuelo?"

"The grand inquisitor is here. Tell Don Joseph to prepare himself."

"For what?"

He shrugged. "I don't know. Something is coming, but people are aware I'm a friend of the Jews. They don't confide in me."

* * *

Don Solomon arrived in the evening. When he'd settled on a cushion next to Belo, and sugar candies were brought and prayers said, I told him and Belo about the duke's warning.

Both thought it rumor of a fresh levy.

Don Solomon smoothed out his silk overgown. "They think they can tax us into the arms of the church."

In the morning, a secretary appeared at our tent flap with Don Solomon already in tow to escort us to the monarchs, and, for once, we were taken directly to them, which made me uneasy.

Their tent was as richly furnished as a room in a castle, with overlapping carpets, four tables, three benches, ten folding leather armchairs, seven cushions, and three pole lamps threatening to set everything ablaze. The secretary who brought us remained, and two slaves stood at the tent flaps. The monarchs sat on their canopied thrones, and the infanta perched on a high-backed chair at her father's side. She wore a white surcoat over a white gown, white for mourning. Her husband had died over the summer.

Next to Queen Isabella stood the grand inquisitor, Fra Torquemada.

Don Solomon and Belo bowed, and I curtsied. King Ferdinand's eyes were on Don Solomon and Belo, but the other three blared smiles at me. Princess Isabella, who began to rise, sank back when the grand inquisitor rushed to me.

He took my hands. His were hot. "Your devotion to your grandfather continues." He turned to the queen. "She is an excellent young woman." He returned to her.

"We are met again!" Princess Isabella glided to me so smoothly she seemed not to have feet. She kissed both my cheeks. "Mamá, she's as plump and pretty as ever." Continuing to smile warmly at me, she backed away to her father.

She was thinner. I had heard her grief was endless, but she seemed happy now.

Queen Isabella herself left her throne to embrace first Don Solomon, then Belo, and then me. My unease grew. King Ferdinand nodded affably at the three of us.

When the queen had returned to her throne, Belo took my hand and gripped it tight. He didn't think this was going to be good, either.

Queen Isabella nodded at the slaves. One brought chairs for each of us. Belo let my hand go.

King Ferdinand said, "We will always be grateful to you, Don Solomon and Don Joseph. You helped Christ give us victory here in Granada."

Don Solomon said that it was his joy to serve them. "We hope to continue as long as we have breath."

Belo nodded. I nodded, too, not that it mattered.

"That is our hope, too," the queen said in her breathy voice.

Why did she have to hope? They could make it so.

King Ferdinand leaned back in his throne. "We have long thought on this—"

"Wait!" Queen Isabella held up her hand. "I can hardly say how much I long for closeness with you three and all your families." She touched the gold cross on her chest. "You are in our hearts, but there is a divide that cuts off embrace."

Conversion again.

She went on. "The Jews of Spain will have to choose, and we—"

Her husband began his set speech. "Our New Christians—"

But the queen broke in again. "We believed separating the Jews in their juderías would be enough to end the Judaizing among converts, but—"

"The Judaizing continues." King Ferdinand's voice was a little louder. "We have concluded there is one remedy—"

"And one inducement," the queen put in.

"Would *you* like to tell them?" the king asked.

"I defer to you, my lord, as we arranged." The queen folded her hands.

"We signed a decree. The Jews of Spain must choose: they may remain Jews—"

Ah. We could choose. They weren't going to force us.

"—or they may remain in Spain—"

"—which is the wish of our hearts," the queen said.

For a moment, I was bewildered.

But King Ferdinand made all clear. "Those who become Christians may stay and keep their possessions. The decree expels all Jews from Spain."

29

I looked at Belo to see if a spell was starting. His face reddened, and he gripped the arms of his chair, knuckles white. No spell. Fury.

What would happen to our littles and all the Jewish children of Spain?

Fra Torquemada was smiling gently, like a snake with its eyes on a frog.

Belo began, "How long—"

Don Solomon raised a hand to stop Belo, who, undoubtedly, was beginning an angry speech. Sounding hoarse, he said, "I'm astonished. Who will do what I do for Your Majesties? I would hate for you to be ill served."

I wanted them to be dreadfully served.

Queen Isabella rushed to Don Solomon, crouched, and embraced him in his chair. With her face inches from his, she said, "Dear friend, we don't want to lose you! We want you closer than ever." She held out an arm toward Belo. "And you!"

Princess Isabella flowed to the back of my chair, where she hugged my shoulders and held me. She brushed my hair aside and kissed my cheek near my ear. "And you!"

I sat stiffly and endured her.

Belo cleared his throat. "When will the decree be announced?"

Queen Isabella said, "Soon."

"Before it is, may Don Solomon and I return to share our thoughts with you?"

"You may," King Ferdinand said.

"We know you're surprised." Queen Isabella rose from her crouch.

Fra Torquemada folded his hands across his belly. "If wolves were harrying the flocks of the Jews, they wouldn't suffer the wolves to stay." He gestured at the king and queen. "We three are the shepherds of Spain."

Queen Isabella opened her arms wide. "Think of the joy of Spain when you convert. Think of our love and our gratitude. But you may argue with us if you must."

* * *

We walked in silence to Don Solomon's tent. I kept thinking of Queen Esther in the Bible. If I were like her, I could use my wiles to win over the king. He'd love me and would save the Jews just so I wouldn't cry.

I had no wiles! And King Ferdinand never looked my way.

As soon as we entered Don Solomon's tent, Belo burst out, "Why? How did we offend the Almighty?"

Don Solomon went to a table and poured wine for himself. "I'd like to know how long they've been planning this." He turned to me, standing just inside the tent flaps. "I feel my age today, Loma."

As soon as we were all seated on cushions, he and Belo began convincing each other that the monarchs' decision wasn't settled and they could be persuaded out of it.

While they marshaled their arguments, I thought of my family—especially the littles—if they failed. Where would we go? What kingdom would take us?

My hands were freezing. I was Belo's helper, nothing besides that, but I was essential to him, and since he protected the family, I was the protector of us all. I was terrified.

I didn't want to be baptized! The queen and the princess might go around Belo to force me, and I didn't think he'd abandon me to be a Christian alone.

I rubbed my hands together, but they wouldn't warm.

* * *

Later in our tent, each of us lay on our pallets with the tent flap open to let in the light of the torch stuck in the ground outside.

"Can you smell the sea, Loma?"

The salt tickled my nose. "Yes. I like it."

"I relish it." He raised himself on one elbow. "You may wonder why Solomon and I are confident."

I did. I rolled onto my side to see him better.

"The monarchs spend and spend and always need money. They think they're poor. Ordinary Jews and Christians *are* poor."

We were wealthy.

Sometimes Belo could read my mind, or so it seemed. "We may be poor eventually. It's worse every year. But for now, we'll find money from somewhere so they can erect another cathedral or conquer the infidel in Africa. When we can, we'll rebuild. We've done it before."

I wouldn't bring discord into the tent by arguing, but I didn't think money would persuade Fra Torquemada.

Belo added, "The Almighty has given us this king and this queen, who could be worse. Their hearts are tender toward me and you and Solomon. My own heart is filled with gratitude."

Their tenderness was all for Belo. I was just a conduit to him.

He began to rehearse his words to the king and queen.

I lay back and concentrated on the rumble of his voice, not the words. I let my many worries go and fell asleep.

The next afternoon, we returned to the monarchs at our allotted time but had to wait for an hour in a small tent.

When we finally were called, we were alone with the king and queen, aside from servants and slaves. No chairs were brought for us.

Don Solomon and Belo took turns speaking, as they had decided. They had prepared three arguments. I gripped Bela's pendant so tightly that there was an imprint on my palm afterward.

Don Solomon began inauspiciously by coughing. Then he said, "We Jews contributed to the war against the Moors. The aljamas are poor now because the war took its toll, but with peace we'll replenish and be ready to contribute to the next endeavor that's close to your great hearts. Spain is richer with us than without us."

While he spoke, Queen Isabella shook her head, but King Ferdinand looked thoughtful. He was believed to always think first of his purse.

The queen leaned forward. "This isn't a matter of money. Those who leave will pay future taxes before they go."

Really?

Ah. Another inducement for people to convert and stay.

"We hope that so many will flock to the font that we won't collect much. We're sure the conversion of you three"—she nodded at me—"will convince almost all."

Don Solomon began the second argument. "This expulsion comes because some conversos Judaize, and some Jews are thought to help them. If this is true, as it may be—"

We all knew it was.

"—we'll reform ourselves. If our converso cousins come to us, wanting to follow our law, we'll send them back to the Church, which they chose."

Or didn't choose, since many had been forced.

He finished: "This will be the practice in every aljama, because the punishment for defiance will be excommunication forever."

That was what the monarchs said they wanted. I held my breath.

King Ferdinand frowned. Queen Isabella tightened her mouth.

The king said, "Why hasn't this already been done? It—"

The queen broke in. "You knew this was dear to our hearts."

Don Solomon nodded. "We'll allow no slips—none—ever again."

There would be slips. I knew that—and so did Queen Isabella.

"If we could be sure . . . ," she said. "But we can't. A year will pass, a decade will go by, and the instruction will resume. We must have a permanent solution."

"I assure you, it won't resume," Don Solomon said.

The king said flatly, "I don't believe you."

Softening his words, his wife said, "We know you intend it to be true."

It was Belo's turn. In Don Solomon's tent, I'd been sure the queen at least wouldn't be able to resist his words.

He cleared his throat. "Yesterday, you called Don Solomon *friend*. I hope Your Highnesses consider me a friend, too."

"We do!" Queen Isabella cried.

"How glad I am for that. Your Majesties, we've seen the nobles, the towns—even the priests—be thorns in your sides with their conflicting demands on your goodness. Your Jews, who have always been yours, have wanted only what you want."

Queen Isabella nodded along with Belo's words.

He went on. "We don't argue against your decrees. We haven't rebelled or caused civil war. Never. When you suffer, we suffer with you. Always. When you rejoice, we rejoice. Always."

The queen's eyes were wet. The king's were dry. His face was expressionless. I thought he might yawn.

Queen Isabella wept openly. "If you don't accept baptism, how I will miss you."

‿❨ 30 ❩‿

Back in Don Solomon's tent, where servants had laid out supper, Belo said, "God hardened the hearts of the king and queen."

Don Solomon sat at the table. "Sit." He helped himself to just a chunk of bread. "I'm not hungry."

We sat. Belo said the prayers, and we ate. I could always eat, but I swallowed each bite over a lump in my throat.

"Loma," Belo said, "what do you think?"

I wiped my mouth on my napkin. "Where are we supposed to go? Have they decided for us? When? What will happen if we won't go and won't be baptized, either?"

Don Solomon frowned. "I hope we can keep it from coming to that, but if it does, the vultures will make sure the Jews leave with little."

He said *the* Jews, not *we* Jews, but I didn't think he meant anything by it.

Belo seemed not to notice. "I wonder if the king and queen both want us expelled, or really just one of them."

Don Solomon said, "The king looked interested when I talked about riches."

"How much can we offer?" Belo asked.

They began to name wealthy families and rich aljamas and how much could be expected from each, and both agreed to contribute most of their own fortunes. I volunteered my dowry.

They finally arrived at 300,000 gold ducats.

"I'll tell them," Don Solomon said. "They can't ask for more."

But how much would they want next year and the year after?

Don Solomon and Belo also agreed to enlist Old Christian friends, like the Duke of Medinaceli and Cardinal de Mendoza, to plead for us. Many were here at the camp, in attendance on the monarchs. Our kind friends, almost as dismayed as we were by the decree, spent what was left of the afternoon and into the evening filing in and out of the royal tent.

But their efforts failed. Our offer of money, made the next day, came closer to success. King Ferdinand looked meaningfully at his wife, but she frowned. He shrugged, and that was the end of it.

Don Solomon and Belo decided to try one more time. Belo would speak to the queen and Don Solomon to the king, who seemed more interested in money; his wife was most moved by emotion and philosophy.

I wondered if I could appeal to the princess. Would Belo mind if I did?

Better not ask.

On Monday, because the monarchs took no appeals on their Sabbath, we waited to learn if an audience would be allowed. In the morning, Belo and Don Solomon talked about how all the Jews might leave the kingdom and where they might go, but they frequently interrupted themselves to say, *if it comes to that.*

After the big meal of the day at noon, Belo and I went to our tent, for him to nap and for me, presumably, to embroider and wait for him to wake up. But as soon as he was solidly asleep on his pallet, I took one of his velvet purses, which he kept in a saddlebag in the middle of the carpet, and left the tent.

Outside, I told Hamdun to come with me, because I couldn't walk through the camp alone. I wondered if he had heard about the decree. He was so kind he would surely pity us. Would he continue to work for us and go wherever we went—*if it came to that?*

We followed the path to the monarchs' tents. My heart began to flutter. The princess's tent, shut tight against the bustle of the camp, was guarded by two slaves.

A parade of secretaries strutted by. I chose one, simply because he was shorter than the others. "Kind sir."

He continued flouncing along.

I jingled the coins in the purse.

"Yes?" He stopped.

"Would you be so good"—I shook the purse again— "to ask the infanta if she has a moment for Paloma?"

"She does not." But he turned and started toward the tent. A yard from the flaps, he held out his hand.

I put two ducats in it. "You are most gracious. Thank you."

He went inside and reemerged quickly, looking as smug as ever. "In point of fact, she happens to be free to entertain you now." He held a flap open for me.

My throat tightened. I knew what she would be thinking.

She met me halfway into the dim tent, lit by four candles, took my hands, and pulled me farther in. I smelled incense. Gracefully, she lowered herself onto a mound of cushions and tugged me down with her.

I almost never cried, but I began to sob. I hadn't meant to—the tears just poured out.

Princess Isabella put her arm around my shoulder and held me close. "Cry, lovely. Cry, sweet."

She used the tone I reserved for the littles when they were in distress. She had no children, and maybe she wanted to be a mother as much as I did.

Finally, my sobs slowed and stopped.

"You wanted to see me. You have something to say?"

I hadn't planned it, but what came out was an accusation. "You care about me only if I'm ready to be baptized."

"Baptism is what I want for you because it's best for you. I've wanted it ever since I sent for you to come to my tent, and there you were, plump and innocent as a satin pillow—smooth and without a mark on you."

Like a sacrificial lamb.

"I was so happy you were the granddaughter of my parents' favorite because I might see you again. I long to make you truly my sister. If you're stubborn and leave Spain, know that you can return to me."

I whispered, "We may not live to return."

By *we* I meant the littles. If I died, I died.

She clasped my hands in hers. "You must not die!"

How could I persuade her to help us?

She went on. "All will be lost for you if you die."

Because I'd be in the Christians' hell. An idea arrived that I thought Belo would approve of. "You want to save our souls, but they'll be lost to you when we leave. If we stay, the priests can continue to come to our synagogues and preach and persuade some of us, like my brother."

She nodded. "That's the part that troubles me—along with the agony that the stubborn will endure. But my good parents say we must help the souls that have already joined the flock, the New Christians. They're in grave danger from Jews. I don't mean you! You haven't tempted them"— she looked mock stern—"have you?"

I shook my head.

My argument had failed, but I tried another branch of it. "There can be more disputations if we stay." The disputations were debates between Jews and Christians about which religion was right. "I think Belo would welcome being part of one, and if the Christian theologians win, he might be one of the prizes."

She looked thoughtful. "I lost my dear husband because God is angry with me. I wasn't devout enough." Her eyes swam. "He was the perfect prince, my Afonso." She patted my leg. "Paloma, I know what it is to suffer. I'll bring your proposal to Mamá."

"Thank you!" I stood.

She stood, too, planted a kiss on my forehead, and held out her cheek to be kissed. "I'll send a secretary with my good parents' answer."

Belo was still asleep. When he awoke and heard what

I'd done, he was jubilant. "Loma, you may have saved the Jews. Like Queen Esther."

I blushed with happiness.

But a secretary came in the evening with two messages. From the princess: alas, my ideas had failed to persuade. From the monarchs: audiences for Don Solomon and Belo would be granted the next day. I would be allowed to go with Belo.

He comforted me. "It was a valiant effort."

The next morning, on inspiration just before entering the queen's tent, I picked up a handful of the soil outside and closed my fist around it.

This was her bedroom tent, and it had an entire bed in it: bed frame, canopy, mattress. Smiling, she rose from her throne chair and held out her hands. She clasped Belo's right hand and my left, the hand that wasn't holding the earth.

"My dears," she said, pulling us in, "sit." She gestured at two cushions. "Speak and I'll listen."

Belo sat, but sprang up as soon as he began. He paced back and forth as if he owned the tent. "Majesty, you want to save us, and we're grateful. We know that toward us, you're moved by love."

Queen Isabella nodded. "And toward all my Jews."

"But they won't be entirely yours if they become

Christians. They'll belong first to the Church and to the towns."

"Christ will reward me for the sacrifice." The queen's tone was dry. A royal joke.

Belo launched his first argument. "Everywhere I go in the juderías, the people ask about you and your children. They believe themselves to be your flock, and they want their shepherdess to be happy and healthy. They are as close to you in spirit as your rings are to your fingers."

The queen shook her head, spraying tears. "It's hard to fast, as you know, Don Joseph—not easy to do without. But Christ asks me to do without your beloved people as long as they persist in error."

Belo stood still. "It's perilous, what you do."

He hadn't rehearsed this in my presence. I was squeezing the soil in my hand to clay.

His voice deepened. "You may discover by a sign, by the coming of the true Messiah, by the end of all, that you've built on the sands of a lie, and the truth has been lost to you."

He was threatening her! She could kill us right now!

But she laughed. "You're suggesting *I* become a Jew?" She laughed harder. "Imagine my husband's face!" Even harder. "Imagine Fra Torquemada's!" She finally controlled herself. "It's always a delight to be with you, Don Joseph."

I smiled uneasily.

Belo smiled, easily. "I have another argument along the same lines, but more serious."

"I'm prepared to hear it."

Belo folded his hands behind his back and swayed a little. "It's futile to try to wipe us out. You know that we're meant to be on earth at the end of days. Pharaoh's reign is over, Caesar is dust. But we remain, stubborn as ever. Why do something that will harm many, hurt Spain, and in the end fail?"

She shook her head. "It *is* the same argument, and by its logic, too, we should all become Jews, but you know that's impossible. We believe that since Christianity came from Judaism, we are the new chosen, who will remain until the end."

"I'll never go to the baptismal font, Majesty, nor will any in my family who has not already done so."

She came and sat on the cushion that Belo had left. "Paloma, you won't?"

"No, Your Majesty. Your Majesty? My abuela of blessed memory told me when I was a little girl that Jews had been in Spain for a thousand years." I opened my hand. "This is Spanish soil, and there are Jewish bones in it." I wondered if that could be true. "Please don't tear us from the earth we belong to."

She was weeping again! She hugged me, let me go, and

looked up at Belo. "Don Joseph, in truth, God has put this thing into the heart of the king. If I wanted to, I couldn't change it."

But she didn't want to.

Outside, a chilly wind blew. April in southern Spain was usually mild, but we were being thrust into the cold, and the Almighty had sent weather to prove it.

Don Solomon's renewed monetary arguments failed, too. In early afternoon, we sat in his tent with a dinner none of us wanted spread before us. I sat between Don Solomon and Belo, who took up the end of the bench. Hamdun sat on a cushion near the tent flap.

Belo recounted our conversation with the queen. "We'll leave in the morning. There's nothing more to be done."

Don Solomon said he would go, too. "Ferdinand and Isabella must have agreed between them what to say to us. He said Christ had told Isabella the Jews should be expelled." Don Solomon had gained useful information along with his failure. The expulsion would be proclaimed across Spain between April 29 and May 1. All Jews had to depart by July 31.

Just three months!

We couldn't take gold, silver, or horses with us. Anyone who remained would have to convert or would be killed.

"But you, my friend," Don Solomon said, "are permitted

to take two thousand gold ducats, and everyone in your family may take one thousand. You may all take jewelry with you. I should give you the letter now, before I forget." He went to a leather file case that was propped against a pile of cushions near the tent flap. Groaning as he crouched, he picked up the case and brought it to the table. "Here." He took out a paper, folded in half and closed with the royal seal.

Belo put it to the side of our empty bowl. "And they'll keep the rest. You can take more with you, yes? You've been in their service the longest."

Don Solomon helped himself to a ladle of goat stew and said the blessing. Then he stirred and stirred his bowl without eating. "I'm going to convert. I told His Majesty."

A fly buzzed over the stew. I waved it away. Had he said he was going to let the priests baptize him?

Belo put his head down next to our bowl and pounded his fist on the table in a slow rhythm. Don Solomon just stirred his bowl.

Why hadn't he told Belo that he was thinking about converting? Was he thinking about it during all the planning of the appeals? Might he have tried harder if he was going to stay a Jew? Might we have succeeded?

Cowardly old man! Deserter! Traitor!

Belo looked up and stopped pounding. "They didn't win until now. Jews all over Spain will say, 'Don Solomon is our leader. He's setting an example for us. If the wise Don Solomon—'"

"I'm eighty years old. I'm not Moses. I don't want to die in the wilderness."

"Loma? Do you think Solomon is wise?"

I abandoned my fear of discord. "He's foolish or evil. His children's children and their children will be real Christians, even if he won't be. They'll do to the Jews what Christians have always done: imprison us, terrify us, kill us."

Don Solomon blanched. "It won't be that way."

Belo said, "My friend, my dearest friend, think of what you lose—the law. Think of your descent."

"I'm not a Talmud scholar like you. My real love is for my fellow Jews, which will be my loss, which will leave me longing forever. But I'll serve the Jews better by staying in Spain. The exodus won't be easy. I'll help."

Belo took a ladle of stew for himself and me.

He began the prayer. "Blessed are You, Eternal One our God, Univerrrsall Ruuull—" The right side of his face drooped. Before I could save him, he toppled off the end of the bench.

Hamdun ran to him. Between us, we carried him to a chair, where he continued to slump, his left eye closed, his right half open, no expression in it. But he was breathing.

"He'll be better soon," I said. "He always is."

This time, he wasn't.

31

Don Solomon sent Hamdun to find a physician. While we stood over Belo, I began the prayer, since Don Solomon didn't.

> *May the One Who blessed our ancestors—*
> *Abraham, Isaac, and Jacob,*
> *Sarah, Rebecca, Rachel, and Leah—*
> *bless and heal Belo.*

Don Solomon joined in.

> *May the Holy Blessed One*
> *overflow with compassion upon him*
> *to restore him . . .*

When we finished, he said, "I wouldn't have told him if I'd thought . . . I wanted him to hear it in my own words."

I said nothing. We watched Belo in silence. Eventually, Don Solomon sat again.

After half an hour, the Duke of Medinaceli himself and his personal physician, Don Miguel, entered the tent, followed by Hamdun.

The duke embraced Don Solomon. "Your decision delights my heart."

The physician was a tall, middle-aged man in a yellow-and-white silk overgown and a pointed green hat that added almost an extra foot to his great height. He put down a linen satchel and looked thoughtfully at Belo for a minute or two before he touched him. Then, as Don Israel had, he took Belo's pulse, and I approved of how carefully he lifted Belo's wrist. "Thready. How old is he?" He looked at Don Solomon.

"Much younger than I am!"

The duke looked at me, but I said I didn't know, either.

"I'll bleed him." He smiled at the duke. "Bleeding works best in spring." He untied the strings of his satchel. "I have other remedies, too."

Don Miguel spent more than an hour with Belo, bleeding him, applying a mustard plaster to his forehead, and putting herbs on his tongue. Don Solomon sat, but the duke and I stood nearby. Hamdun hovered a yard away. I kept holding my breath, looking for a sign that the treatment was having an effect.

Belo stirred once, opened his left eye, and seemed to see us. He said something I couldn't understand. Saliva stood in the corner of his mouth.

"What, Belo?"

He said more, also incomprehensible.

Finally, the doctor put his things back in his satchel. "The first treatment often fails when later ones sometimes succeed. I'll return tomorrow morning."

Sometimes?

He didn't know that Belo, like me, was stubborn, though he didn't look stubborn now, sagging in the chair, breathing noisily.

The duke thanked the physician and stayed with us after he left. When Don Miguel must have gone far enough not to be able to hear, His Grace said, "The king and queen will know soon—in an hour or two—that Don Joseph has been struck. Queen Isabella will take it as a sign from God and will baptize him. Paloma, if you want him to remain a Jew and want to remain one yourself, flee!"

The breath rushed out of me. How could I take him? Where would we go? Would I ever see the littles again?

"But"—the duke gripped my shoulders—"if you let them baptize him, he'll get the best care, wonderful care, and he'll be safe. He'll be more likely to recover. The monarchs love him." He let me go. "And I'm very fond of you. I hate to think of your uncertain future as a Jew." He stepped back. "What will you do? You mustn't hesitate."

I didn't need to. "If Belo wakes up and finds himself a Christian, he'll have another spell." And die cursing me.

But how would we leave Spain? I fought back tears. Would Belo die anyway?

Don Solomon pushed himself out of his chair. "I can't go with you. I have to organize the departure. I have to send people ahead to Portugal, visit . . ."

Whatever else he said, I didn't hear. I'd never traveled without Belo or Papá.

But we had Hamdun and guards. I started for the tent flaps. "We have to get ready." I needed a cart for Belo, who couldn't sit a horse. Hamdun followed me.

Don Solomon said, "Wait! The road will be watched."

"Queen Isabella," His Grace said, "will think it her holy duty to find him and bring both of you into the fold."

Don Solomon added, "Her people will persist until they succeed."

I turned back. We had to go and couldn't leave.

"I'll hide him." Don Solomon surveyed his tent. "I don't know where."

He'd give us up soon enough. I touched Bela's pendant. She sent the thought, or God did. "Can we be disguised?"

No one answered. I supposed they were thinking.

A sensible, planning part of me took over. "People don't notice the poor."

Both of them were smiling at me.

His Grace said, "Don Joseph's prodigy. I have two donkeys." He chuckled. "The poor ride donkeys."

Belo couldn't sit a donkey. I looked at him to see if anything had changed, but nothing had.

Hamdun coughed.

I nodded at him.

"Don Joseph can ride with me."

Ah. Hamdun would prop him up.

The duke and Don Solomon approved the suggestion. In a few minutes, all was arranged. His Grace would give us two donkeys and three shabby, hooded cloaks from his servants, cloaks without the badges that would mark us as Jews. Don Solomon would send the guards after us with a cart. Beyond the camp, when we came to a deserted spot, we would wait for them to catch up. Then we'd all turn off the road until night.

I sent Hamdun to tell the guards and gather what we needed from our tent.

His Grace took my hands. "May luck travel with you." He kissed Belo's forehead. "I wouldn't have dared do that if he was awake." He left.

I'd found my way home when I was kidnapped. I'd visited Pero without telling anyone. I said to Don Solomon, "We'll go to Málaga."

"When you get there, find a ship for Lisbon. The aljama will welcome you."

I nodded, but I'd already decided to go to Naples, where Bela's sister and her family lived. No need to tell Don Solomon, the traitor, where to find us.

I wasn't thinking clearly and didn't see my mistake.

A short while later, Hamdun returned and gave me the saddlebag full of ducats from our tent. A servant came with the cloaks. He said the donkeys were waiting outside.

Hamdun stood Belo up, and he managed to keep his feet though he teetered. I wrapped a cloak around him.

When we were cloaked and hooded and our finery hidden, Don Solomon hugged me. I stood stiffly, but then I thanked him. Would I ever see him again? Would he be a Christian if I did?

Hamdun draped Belo's arm over his shoulder. "I have you. Never fear."

"The letter!" I took it off the table, glad I remembered.

Don Solomon said, "You won't need it. I'll deliver it to your papá."

He was right. We'd be gone. I was loath to trust him, but I had to.

At a gesture from Don Solomon, a servant opened the

tent flap. Hamdun, Belo, and I exited, followed by Don Solomon, who shouted at us, "I don't pay you to spend my money on wine. Get out of my sight."

I hadn't thought of it, but he was explaining our departure to anyone in earshot: We were tipplers, and Belo was so drunk he couldn't sit a donkey.

Thank you, Don Solomon. I still despise you.

Hamdun hoisted Belo on the donkey's back and climbed up after him. I mounted my donkey and spurred it. Hamdun spurred his.

The road out of the camp was cobbled. No one seemed to notice us. The flow of people and carts was mostly against us: nobles on horses; mule-drawn carts bearing provisions; burdened mules and donkeys; clusters of Christians on their way to settle in Granada.

Belo might be jounced by the donkey's gait. I prayed he wasn't in pain. Could he feel pain?

Did the monarchs know yet? Were they sending for Don Solomon? Would he betray us again? I wished I hadn't told him we were going to Málaga.

I almost giggled. The secretaries who'd made us wait endlessly might be delaying the physician from passing along his news. The search for us may not have begun.

Any bushes and trees that had once lined the road had been razed for the siege. There was nowhere for us to hide.

Even though the air was cool, the sun shone in the

late-afternoon sky. The river Genil, which the road fol-lowed, *shooshed* as it streamed by.

After half an hour, a fan palm rose along the edge of the road. If no one had been about, we could have con-cealed ourselves behind it, so long as we kept the donkeys still and they didn't bray. But we were overtaking a dozen barefoot monks, arguing among themselves about the holiness of ale.

The monks paid us no heed. The cobbles ended, and the road became pale and dusty dirt. A farmhouse stood on our right. Chickens pecked in the yard. Beyond the house, we passed an olive tree with a wide enough trunk to hide us, but now four noblemen rode by. Ahead, more fan palms and olive trees cropped up, along with oleander bushes. If the road ever cleared, we'd have places to go.

A cloud drifted in from the west. The road curved. A shepherd came toward us, driving a flock of geese and raising dust. Belo's head sagged back against Hamdun's shoulder. Anyone going by would see his face.

I said, "Please keep his face down."

Hamdun palmed the back of Belo's scalp, as a mother might a baby's, and lowered his head.

Merciful One, thank You for Hamdun. Now, how much trouble would it be to hold people back to give us three minutes to hide? Help me save Belo, who loves You. I love You, too.

The cart and our guards should reach us soon. Had Don Solomon told them not to speak to us if others were near? I turned to look. A party of nobles cantered toward us. I didn't see our people.

The nobles passed us. A few more clouds sailed out of the west.

Hamdun said, "Oh, oh, oh, oh."

Belo was sliding sideways, but Hamdun managed to straighten him again.

About twenty minutes later, God gave us our miracle: the nearest travelers were just dots, and the road was lined with fan palms and olive trees. I turned my donkey, and Hamdun followed.

Behind our screen of fronds and leaves, I dismounted. Hamdun did the same, while lifting Belo to the ground, where he set him against the trunk of an olive tree. Hamdun held the donkeys' reins loosely and let them nuzzle him. Then he led them down the riverbank to drink. I crouched to tip Belo's head back so I could dribble the watery wine from my flask into his mouth. He took the draft and swallowed, which I considered a good sign. His left eye, the alert one, I thought, watched me with what I hoped was recognition.

He said, loudly, "Lo . . . ," and trailed off.

My name, or almost! But too loud. I put my finger over my lips, and he didn't try again. I patted his cheek, walked to the fan palm, and peeked between the fronds.

Alas, I could see only a swath in front of me, five yards or so of dirt, and, across the road, an oleander bush next to another olive tree. I'd hear travelers, but I wouldn't be able to distinguish our guards until I could see them, and then we'd still have to wait to see if anyone else came along. Emerging would be a moment of great danger.

The day waned, and the fronds took on a dusky glow. My stomach grumbled. Our provisions were in the cart. For a while, no one had crossed my range of road. People were probably setting up camp for the night or finding lodging.

I thought of the littles at home and the adults, who didn't yet know what was about to befall them. Would I ever see them again?

I hoped they were happy at this moment. I imagined them: Jento and Todros playing tag with the other boys in the street outside the synagogue; energetic Jamila, jumping up and down in Ledicia's house; Clara, petting her cat, Yowl; Beatriz, wondering where I was and worrying.

Belo was watching me. I didn't want him to see me weep, so I blinked the tears away. What was he thinking? Did he have thoughts?

I heard hooves and clinking. The leader of our guards, Señor Menahem, Belo's favorite, trotted into view on a piebald horse. He was followed by three more guards, the cart, and two donkeys, loaded with provisions.

The timing was perfect. The road ahead and behind was probably empty. Still, I waited, counting in a measured way to a thousand. I didn't want our party to get too far from us, because I didn't know what lay ahead.

I held my hand up, which by now was dim in the fading light. I pointed to the road, and Hamdun nodded. But as I began to part the fronds, I heard clinking and hooves coming from the direction of Granada. I straightened and gestured in a downward motion to Hamdun.

A party of ten trotted by. The final rider wore a high, pointed hat that, despite the failing daylight, I could still tell was green. The physician Don Miguel!

32

We had to let them go by. I shook my head violently at Hamdun, hoping he'd see. He seemed to, because the shadow he had become didn't move.

Had the Christians sensed us?

People may have been watching Don Solomon's tent and our tent, and this party may have followed Señor Menahem and the others ever since they left the camp.

Did Señor Menahem realize what the party clinging to them was? Did he understand we couldn't show ourselves? What might he do?

How long would the Christians stay with them?

When I finally thought we wouldn't be heard, I whispered, "The doctor who treated Belo rode by with others."

What if Hamdun ran out? Would he be rewarded with a fat purse?

He whispered, "Then we must stay here."

We each had a flask of watery wine but no food. Did Belo need food to get better? I was ravenous. I regretted not eating in Don Solomon's tent.

Belo began to speak softly—not words, just sounds, but I recognized the cadence of prayer. I said the Shema, hoping it would bring him comfort, and he fell silent.

I was afraid to continue traveling. We'd be lone wayfarers at night. If Don Miguel and his company turned back, they'd see us and be suspicious. I told Hamdun we'd remain here. "In the morning, more people will be on the road."

He helped me lay Belo flat. I wrapped his cloak around him against the night air and folded my cloak to make him a pillow, though I began to shiver. I'd survive.

The clouds on the horizon were still rosy from the sunset. I settled myself on Belo's left and thanked God for food, whenever we would get it. I closed my eyes. Belo's hand found mine. I leaned over him. Half his mouth smiled at me.

I lay back. He continued to hold my hand. I closed my eyes again, ignored my stomach and the chill, and fell asleep—

—and woke to a rustling sound, which turned out to be rain on the canopy of olive leaves. If the rain stopped soon, we'd be all right.

It came down harder.

God! We're not Pharaoh. Why are You sending us plagues?

Drops, cold and stinging, broke through the leaves. I feared a chill would finish Belo off. I could deprive him of his pillow and spread my cloak over him as a blanket, but that would soon be soaked and colder than no cloak. He needed a barrier and warmth, so I lay on top of him, spreading myself as much as I could, my head to the side of his head.

If only I weren't so hungry. And cold. And wet.

He murmured something that, by its tone, didn't sound like a complaint.

"We'll get you to safety. I'll make sure you stay a Jew." If I could. I pushed my myriad worries aside and began to count by eighteens, my falling-asleep trick. Remarkably, it worked even here.

I woke myself by sneezing. Rain still fell. Nearby, Hamdun sneezed in the middle of his Muslim prayers. A donkey sneezed. Under me, Belo sneezed what sounded like an ordinary sneeze. Was he better? I propped myself up to see.

Maybe a little. Both eyes were open, and his pupils followed me, although the right eyelid drooped, and he still couldn't say words.

Morning had come. Somewhere, the sun had risen, but without seeing it I couldn't guess how early or late the hour was. We were safely hidden, and we could safely die here of starvation.

Hamdun stood over us and held out a hand to help me up. I took the hand and stood. His fingers were as cold as mine.

We didn't have to waste time cooking (ha!), but I crouched to tip the last of my watery wine into Belo's mouth. If I was thirsty, I could just tilt back my head. Belo drank and then began his nonsense words, which I believed to be an attempt at prayer.

I hissed, "Softly!"

He stopped, which made me hope he'd understood. I whispered the morning prayer. He moved his lips.

When we finished, Hamdun lifted Belo onto a donkey and climbed up behind him; I mounted, too. Belo sat straighter on the donkey today, a promising sign.

Leaving our hiding spot wasn't as dangerous as entering it had been. Many travelers would have spent the night on the side of the road, concealed from marauders, and they would have to emerge, too. I doubted the three of us were an appealing target for brigands, who wouldn't guess that I had a saddlebag full of ducats and fourteen silver reales in the purse at my waist.

It was lucky that I didn't know the truth, and, seemingly, neither did Hamdun. Brigands would have seen us as valuable—as slaves. He and I could have been taken and sold, and no one the wiser. Belo probably would have been left to die.

But the road was deserted. Not even highwaymen were out in this downpour.

Señor Menahem, please don't be far ahead. Don Miguel, please have returned to the monarchs' camp.

My belly sent me memories of fried stuffed partridges. I could taste the gizzards, eggs, cinnamon, and cilantro in the stuffing.

We passed a farmhouse on the left: two stories, white stone, tile roof. A mulberry tree stood in the yard. Smoke streamed from the chimney. Its owners would be warm and not starving. For a ducat, they might feed us and let us dry off, but they'd question us. As soon as we left, they'd tell a priest. Maybe they'd earn another ducat.

Hamdun's donkey coughed. A few minutes later, mine did. I patted her neck and tried to comfort her. "I know. This is terrible." The coughs became frequent.

Belo coughed, too, so hard his shoulders shook. Hamdun and I exchanged worried looks. With his left arm he pulled Belo close while his right hand held the reins. In all our bad luck, God had sent this sweet man to us. I touched Bela's pendant.

We plodded on. Between humans and donkeys, we made a quintet of coughs, wheezes, and sneezes. The rain continued. I wondered if we'd gone even ten miles from the camp.

Imagining the best, I pictured entering Málaga. We'd go straight to the wharf.

Oh no! I realized the mistake I'd made. Don Solomon would tell Papá that we were going to Lisbon! And that's where he'd take the family.

Belo and I had to go to Lisbon, where we had no relatives, if we were to be reunited, if I were to see the littles again.

I had to see them!

"Loma, your abuelo feels very hot. I think he has a fever."

God forgive me! I was a terrible granddaughter, because the worst thought I'd ever had came to me: If Belo died, I could go home and be with the littles.

I turned my donkey. We had to beg for shelter at the farmhouse we'd passed if Belo was going to get well.

In half an hour, we reached it and dismounted in the yard. Hamdun cradled Belo in his arms. I knocked on the door, which creaked open. A bearded young man stood on the threshold. Bearded! A Jew? Couldn't be.

The man's wife, plump like me, wearing trousers and a short jacket, came to the door, too. Moors.

Hamdun spoke to them in Arabic. He gestured at Belo and me and the donkeys. The couple smiled. The man opened the door wide. The woman took my hands and tugged me in. Her hands were warm. Hamdun carried Belo in behind me. We dripped on a stone slab. I smelled lamb roasting with cilantro and oranges. My mouth filled with saliva.

A wooden staircase rose in front of us. The man gestured to Hamdun, who carried Belo up. The woman let go of my hands and led me upstairs.

To our right, a fire blazed in the fireplace. A girl of three or four stood with her fist in her mouth in the middle of a large room. I wanted to go to her, pick her up, and press my cheek against her silky hair.

The man pulled cushions close to the fire. Hamdun laid Belo down on them.

"Do you think we can take off his wet clothes?" I said. "Can they spare a blanket?"

"Certainly," the woman said in Castilian. Her *r* was more from her throat than on her tongue, but I understood. "I'll bring blankets." She left through an arch across the room from the fireplace.

The man said something in Arabic to Hamdun, who

told me, "We're going to see to the donkeys." The two went down the stairs.

I knelt by Belo. Dots of pink bloomed in his cheeks. His forehead was burning.

"Please be stubborn, Belo."

He blinked his left eye.

The woman bustled back, her arms filled with blankets and linen cloth. Between us, we stripped him down to his drawers. She didn't comment on his silks or his jewels. We rubbed him dry and wrapped him in a blanket. He said his nonsense sounds. I touched Bela's pendant and prayed.

"You're wet, too."

"I'll dry." I was almost warm by now, and I hadn't sneezed since we came indoors.

But she insisted. "Come with me. Your abuelo will be fine for a few minutes."

He couldn't go anywhere. "I'll be right back, Belo."

She scooped up her daughter and led me through the archway into a corridor. The child stared at me over her mamá's shoulder. I smiled and wiggled my fingers at her. She looked dubious. If we were here long enough, I hoped to be able to hold her.

Her mamá entered a bedroom through another archway. I shivered. At home, we would have kept a coal brazier sizzling.

She set her daughter down on a long sleeping cushion.

The child stood and put her fist back in her mouth. I crouched and waved my finger in a figure eight in front of her. Her whole head followed my finger.

"Here."

I turned.

The woman knelt over a carved oak chest. "My things should fit you." She lifted out white trousers that were baggy above the knee, tight below; a shift, like the one I was wearing; a brown shirt that seemed more correct for a man; a short white jacket edged with silver thread; and a red-and-white pleated head scarf over which went a green-and-blue padded band. The folds of the head scarf fell like a curtain with a gap for my face. Everything was linen.

"Try them on."

I undressed and removed my jewelry. Goose bumps stood out on my arms. The woman gave me a length of muslin to dry myself with and helped, rubbing me vigorously until I felt warm. She was beyond kind. I squeezed back tears. Everyone wasn't our enemy.

I donned the apparel and put the jewelry back on. "Thank you!"

"It becomes you."

Belo coughed from the other room. When we got to him, he seemed no worse and no better. I stroked his forehead. Still hot.

"Are you hungry?" the woman asked.

"I am." I blushed. "My abuelo hasn't had any food since he fell ill yesterday." Like Jews, Muslims didn't eat pork, though many of their dietary rules were different from ours.

"When the men return, we'll eat."

I looked up from Belo. "Why are you so kind to us?" We were strangers at a dangerous time, so soon after the war.

"Your servant says you're an angel, the way you care for your abuelo. He said you covered him all night with your whole self to keep him dry and didn't marry for his sake, and you mother your family's children even though they aren't your own."

That was how Hamdun saw me? I waved away the catalog of my virtues. An angel who had—for a moment—wished her belo dead.

Hamdun and the husband returned, both soaking wet. They retired to the bedroom to dry off.

I said, "I'm Loma from Alcalá de Henares. My abuelo is Don Joseph Cantala. We're Jews. Our servant is called Hamdun."

She didn't recognize Belo's name. Her husband's name was Qays, and hers was Yasmina. The child's name was Kanza. The three of them were the angels.

33

On the morning of April 19, a Thursday, we rode our donkeys into Málaga. Belo had survived, but he'd been slow to shed his fever and be well enough to travel. When he was, I had explained about the threat of conversion, since I wasn't sure if he knew the reason for our flight. At the end, I asked him if he'd understood. He'd nodded and said, "Lo."

By the time we left, we'd all, including the donkeys, stopped coughing. Although Belo's spell hadn't passed, he'd improved. He could feed himself with his left hand and could stumble along if either Hamdun or I supported his weak right side. On the donkey, he could sit upright. He could also nod or shake his head. He still couldn't speak sensibly, but he repeated "Lo" often and querulously, until

I thought he'd turned into a grumpy parrot.

I'd asked Hamdun to accompany us to Lisbon, because I didn't think I could manage without him. "The aljama there will pay your passage back to Spain if you don't want to stay." I was confident that the Jews in Lisbon would trust that they'd be repaid.

He'd promised he would go with us.

Generous Señora Yasmina had sent us off with full flasks and food for a day and had insisted we keep the apparel, which would protect us more than our finery. She and her good husband had refused payment for any of it.

As we rode, I imagined the worst for the littles as they left Spain. Beatriz, starving; Todros, waylaid on the road; Clara, separated from the rest of the family; Jamila, sold into slavery.

While I, if all went well, was safe in Lisbon.

When we sailed out of Málaga, only a bit of my heart would be in the boat. The rest would fly home. How could I be kind to Belo with almost no heart? How could I live without my littles, if they didn't survive to join us?

In Lisbon, I wouldn't be helping Belo protect the Jews of Spain.

Almighty, this is unfair!

If not for Hamdun, I doubt we'd have reached our destination, because we never caught up with Señor Menahem and the others. I hoped they were safe.

After our supplies ran out, Hamdun found food and lodging for us with other Muslim families. He passed me off as his niece and Belo as his father, though he couldn't resist turning away and grinning at me after he'd made us his family.

Three days before we reached Málaga, our view of the road ahead became hidden by a cloud of dust that drummed and chimed and jingled and finally resolved into a seemingly endless caravan—I lost count of donkeys and mules when I reached 137, and many more followed, carrying goods from Málaga's port to the rest of Spain. The drums were hooves, and the music was harness bells.

At dawn on our last day of travel, to the astonishment of our hosts, I shed my Moorish garb and put on my jewelry and my silks, which Señora Yasmina had steamed dry at her fireplace. Between us, Hamdun and I dressed Belo and bejeweled him, too, while he helped as much as he could.

I reasoned that a shipmaster would be more likely to do business with a wealthy Spanish woman and a rich, though sick, man than with Muslim peasants. The day was warm, so our drab cloaks were draped in front of us on our donkeys, atop our Muslim apparel.

In late morning, we trotted downhill on a wide avenue,

Calle Alcazabilla, between grand brown-and-pink stone buildings. An open-air market filled the cathedral square, where eleven donkeys waited while their owners bargained for victuals. One of them bellowed, "No! I have a hundred hungry men!"

Ahead, between a break in the buildings, the sea shimmered. We didn't rush, though I wanted to. At last, we crossed the final avenue before the wharf, where inns and taverns stood shoulder to shoulder with warehouses. Goods would be brought to this side and carried out to the docks on the other side for loading on ships—and vice versa for cargo that had come from distant lands.

There was no bustle. The warehouse doors were shut tight. The street was as still as noon in July, when even the flies went to sleep.

But on the wharf, all was busyness. Five large ships and many small fishing boats were in the harbor, and one big ship was entering by oar. A line of men along a rope labored to tug a seventh ship to land. I looked for Pero among the men at the rope, but he wasn't there.

If I'd known anything about sailing, I'd have noticed how still the day was, without even a light breeze.

A crowd of Muslim men and women, abducted in a raid or taken in a skirmish in North Africa, were roped together, waiting to be sold. Poor people! If you lived near the coast, either in Spain or North Africa, just enjoying your ordinary life, not fighting with anyone, you were at risk.

Here and there, collections of goods waited: sawed logs in a miraculously balanced mound; barrels; piles of sheets of leather. A mountain of wineskins rose higher and wider than we were, even on our donkeys, and blocked part of our view of the warehouses, but, happily, not of the ships.

We weren't the only ones riding beasts. Some rode horses. Some *galloped* horses, and then people on foot or on donkeys had to scatter. A man hawking fish pies on a tray jumped out of the way and lost a pie. He cursed the brindle cat that pounced on the treat.

How would I find a trustworthy shipmaster?

Hands from the other side of the wineskins took several away.

No one seemed to notice us, but I felt conspicuous—Hamdun and I gawking, and Belo with his head sunk into his chest. We couldn't stay here.

A secretary sort of gentleman rushed by. A man and a woman stood together, seemingly waiting. She had a kind face—but I wanted indifference. A kind person might question us in order to give us aid.

Idly, I noticed that more wineskins were taken away. A young man, eating an onion, wearing sailors' blue, strolled not far from us, heading for the boats.

I touched Bela's amulet. Bela, help us find a ship.

The young man looked straight ahead, apparently concentrating on chewing.

"Señor?"

He turned, blinked, and seemed to wake up. Not hurrying, he angled toward us. "Yes, pretty lady?" His voice was husky, and he spoke with an accent, an *uh* between *yes* and *lady*, the same accent I'd heard from Master Calvo. He smiled at me, our eyes almost level though I was on the donkey.

"If you please, do you know where the ships are heading when they sail?"

"Yes, lovely lady." But he didn't say.

Families had refused payment for their hospitality, but this fellow wanted money for a sentence or two. We could wait and ask someone else.

"Thank you."

"Lo." Belo's mouth curled in a half smile.

The man decided to grant us his knowledge for free. "For such a beautiful lady as you—" He came close to me and pointed from ship to ship. I smelled his onion. "Genoa, Barcelona, Tangier, Bilbao, Naples. That's my ship, the one to Naples. Palma, Tunis."

"Not Lisbon?"

"Unfortunately, no, if that's where you would like."

Papá would take the family to Lisbon because of what Don Solomon thought. I would lose them all.

But we had to go somewhere. The ship to Naples was smaller than the one next to it. I wondered if it could really make the voyage.

"If you please, who is the master of the one to Naples?" This young man had called it *his ship*, but he seemed too young to be its master.

He just smiled. His teeth were white and straight, and his smile was gay.

Happy shouts broke out from the direction of the docks, over our fellow's shoulder. The men who had been tugging their ship in had succeeded and were cheering. To my left, the wineskin pile continued to diminish. Yet another grandee galloped by.

I produced a silver reale from my purse and held it so he could see it.

"I sail under Master Ambrosio de Miedes." He put out his hand.

I dropped the coin into it, and his fist closed.

"Thank you," I said. Belo always thanked the people he'd bribed. "Where might we find him?"

The fist opened and received another reale, but the answer wasn't worth the coin.

"Somewhere. Eating and mostly drinking. He'll eat and drink and drink and drink until a wind blows."

Oh. The ships were becalmed. That was why the warehouses had been so quiet.

"Then they'll roll—"

"Lo!"

Was I doing something wrong? I shouldn't have asked where the master was?

"Lo!!"

I turned to Belo and saw, no longer hidden by wineskins, a man in a pointed green hat, luckily facing away from us. Don Miguel, the physician!

We had to hide!

". . . him to the ship in a wheelbarrow, and we'll— What's amiss, fair lady?"

"Can you distract the man in the tall green hat?" I reached into my saddlebag and produced a ducat.

He snatched the ducat and ran, the scoundrel. We were about to be caught.

But our fellow barreled into Don Miguel, knocking him down. I signaled to Hamdun, just by pointing my chin. We kicked our donkeys.

Behind us, Don Miguel cried out, and our fellow apologized. How long would he be able to hold off pursuit?

We walked the donkeys away, because trotting would draw eyes. Why hadn't we kept on our Moorish clothes? He wouldn't recognize us in them.

I headed back toward Calle Alcazabilla. With the ships becalmed, we could wait.

"Don Joseph!"

34

We galloped the donkeys to the street.

Where to go?

People stared as we pelted along. We reached the market in the cathedral plaza, where I slowed my donkey, then dismounted. Hamdun followed my lead and lifted Belo off, too. I reasoned we'd be less noticeable on the ground with everyone else.

A faint breeze tickled my cheek, but I didn't think about it.

We stood by a Moorish fruit seller, whose table supported a pyramid of oranges and another of onions, and a basket of dried figs. I saw nothing big enough to hide behind, not even the butcher's stall, with its sheep carcass hanging from a hook on a wooden frame and drawing flies.

I heard shouts. "Make way!"

An alley ran next to the cathedral, but we'd be seen entering it.

"King's business!"

Could I bribe someone here?

Don Miguel shouted, "Don Joseph!"

Who? We had no time.

Could I bribe them all?

Not hurrying, I led my donkey toward the alley. Hamdun and Belo followed with their donkey.

The cries grew louder, close now. "Stand aside!"

Closer, but not yet at the alley, I reached into my saddlebag and filled my fist. "Ai!" I cried. "My ducats! Ai!" I scattered them.

God, let us have enough left for our passage.

Silence fell on the market—followed by an uproar. "Coins!" "Watch out!" "You oaf!"

Madness broke out, through which we surged steadily toward the alley, reached it—

—and discovered it was too narrow for the donkeys.

Hamdun and I exchanged glances. Before I could say anything, he whispered in the ear of one of the donkeys, then slapped both of their rumps. The donkeys cantered away—with our Muslim clothing and Belo's ducats.

I touched Bela's pendant. God, we are in Your hands. As we always were.

We entered the alley.

If we didn't get the ducats back, maybe our jewelry would be enough to pay our way.

Behind us, the uproar grew louder. We progressed through the alley, passing, on the cathedral side, a niche with a statue of Mary holding Jesus as a baby on her lap.

At the end of the alley, I asked Belo, "Do you need to rest?"

He shook his head and half-smiled again.

We emerged into another avenue. I no longer heard our pursuers. Where to go? We had to hide, and we had to have water and food. Toward the docks or away?

Toward. We had to try to reach the ship to Naples.

We couldn't wait on the quay again, because Don Miguel would return there. Belo, how I wish you could tell me what to do!

Two mules trotted past us, pulling a covered wagon. The driver rode the gray mule; the white was unencumbered.

Hamdun supported Belo's right side, as if they shared three legs between them, and he held tight to Belo's right arm around his shoulder.

A warehouse would be the perfect hiding place, but all of them would be locked.

We were in God's hands, and it would be no trouble for Him to open a door.

The late-afternoon sun shone obliquely into the avenue of the warehouses, which was still deserted. The buildings seemed to continue forever. A white cat arched its back and hissed at us. Ai!

We started up the street. A drinking song drifted from a tavern, but no one emerged or went in. The scent of fried fish mingled with the salty air. Belo panted with the effort of walking so far. Hamdun picked him up and ignored his garbled protests.

The warehouse doors were wide and tall enough to allow in wagons and horses. The first four were locked, but God was with us, and the fifth hung ajar.

It might be unlocked because people were inside.

I heard nothing. We slipped in. Slowly, I drew the door shut and eased home the bolt, hoping the door hadn't been cracked on purpose and someone was returning soon.

The only light came from narrow windows high above us. From where we stood, an aisle divided rows of canvas sacks on our right from rows of amphoras on our left that stood as high as my chest. Curious, I put my nose to a sack and smelled coriander, to the stopper of a jug and smelled olive oil. My stomach roared.

We glided down the aisle and continued to the door on the wharf side, which I tugged open a few inches. Harbor noise poured in. We could see only a stripe of the world: a small cloud motionless in a blue sky above the masts of a single ship: not our ship—this one had four masts, and ours had three. I couldn't see the ship itself, because of a parade of people, beasts, and wagons. Our stripe was so narrow that a horse's head and neck would fill it, followed, bit by bit, by the rest of the animal. I didn't see Don Miguel, but he could be an inch to the left or right of our vision. Hamdun and I pulled three sacks to the door to serve us as cushions.

We sat. Belo leaned against me. Minutes ticked by.

I couldn't bear our ignorance, and we had to eat.

Had Don Miguel noticed Hamdun enough to recognize him?

I waited, lost in indecision, until my stomach convinced me. "Hamdun," I whispered, pulling a reale from my purse, "we need to know if Don Miguel is there—"

"Lo!" Belo shook his head energetically.

I understood. Belo thought Hamdun might betray us for a reward.

But I trusted him, and we needed a spy. "Make sure he doesn't spot you. And buy us food. Don't let anyone observe you coming back in here. Wait if you have to." I gave him the coin.

He slipped out the door and was gone.

Softly, I recited the prayer asking God and His angels

to protect us. Belo's voice, though his words were garbled, rose and fell with mine.

When we finished, we waited. Nothing outside seemed to change.

At best, we'd sail to Naples, and I might never be reunited with my family. If Belo died, I would be entirely bereft. Did he think of this? He *could* think—that much was clear. But he couldn't say what he thought.

He snored.

My thoughts rolled on. What would I be without the littles?

A sad and angry husk.

This was more sacrifice than a person should have to make.

If we could have a conversation . . . If I could share my agony—yes, agony!—what would he say?

That his feet needed to be massaged?

Was he thinking of me at all?

He reached over with his good hand and patted my knee. A minute later, he snored again. I called the littles' faces to mind.

In the stripe beyond the warehouse, the colors took on the intensity of dusk.

Outside, people shouted. Figures ran by. A cloud flew across the stripe.

Wind!

The sails on the masts I could see were hoisted and billowed. Soon the ships would sail, and we'd be stranded.

Hamdun wormed inside, bearing something in a cloth.

I jumped up.

"Don Miguel was watching; I couldn't come sooner. But now, he's run to the ship that's most ready to sail." Hamdun opened the cloth to reveal three fish pies. "I'm sorry they aren't hot anymore."

"Thank you!"

We made short work of the pies. When I finished, I wished for three more.

Night fell. Torches lit the ships. Hamdun went out again and came back in a few minutes to say that Don Miguel was marching from ship to ship as they were loaded.

After an hour or two, the ships began to sail, according to Hamdun, who kept slipping out and returning. Finally, all but ours were gone. Except for it, the sea was dark. What was it waiting for?

A shape filled our slice of the outdoors. Don Miguel? The breath rushed out of me. We had no time to get away.

The shape—a man—entered. Tall, but not tall enough to be Don Miguel.

"Beautiful lady, I'm back."

Our fellow!

"I've known where you are ever since your man went

out. The one you fear has given up for the night. I saw him depart."

Hamdun slipped outside. Belo shifted away from me and slumped back. No one spoke.

In a few minutes, Hamdun returned. "I don't see him."

"Why is your ship still in the harbor?" I said.

"Master Ambrosio de Miedes hasn't yet been found, but he will be soon. You want to sail on her?"

"Will Master Ambrosio de Miedes take our jewels for passage?"

"He would, but I've already paid the steward. You'd give away too much, and I'm feeling generous."

I stared at him.

Belo gurgled, which frightened me until I realized he was laughing.

"I've become wealthy."

The scoundrel! "The donkeys and the ducats belong to us, not you!"

"They're mine now. We should go to the ship. The master will be along."

We were in God's hands. I let the donkeys and the ducats go.

But not the littles. I couldn't let them go.

"Come!"

Though there was no moon, the stars were sharp, and

the ship's torches flared in a brisk wind. The wharf was deserted, except for a figure on the pier by the ship. We made our way to him.

In a few minutes, we'd leave Spain. Almighty, let me sprout wings to fly back!

There would be no such miracle.

The figure identified himself as the steward. A ramp ran from the dock to the ship.

I formed a desperate resolution that tore my heart in half. With trembling fingers, I untied Bela's pendant, pulled off my ruby ring, and squeezed both in my fist.

A rumbling sound grew.

"That's Master Ambrosio de Miedes," our fellow said. "We'll be away in a moment."

I tugged on the fellow's sleeve and he stepped away with me.

"Yes?"

I found his hand and folded my ring into it. "It has a ruby. Watch over my abuelo."

"Pretty lady, you're—"

"Don't let anything bad come to him."

I heard him breathe deeply. "I won't. But I hoped to sail with the beautiful young lady."

I ignored that. "Belo has relatives in Naples. The family's name is Furillo." I hoped the name didn't tell him Belo was a Jew. "Please help Hamdun find them."

"I will, lovely lady."

"Massage his feet." If you think I'm so pretty.

He looked startled. "That's a lot to ask for a ruby."

We went back to Belo and Hamdun. I tied Bela's amulet around Belo's neck. "Bela will protect you. I have to go home to the chil—"

Belo cried out. He grabbed my arm with his good hand. I broke away. "The children need me. I need them."

As I ran toward the warehouse, Belo shouted and wailed.

Merciful One, forgive me!

35

On the wharf outside the warehouse, I touched the hollow in my throat where the amulet had nestled. The ship's sails were going up. The steward remained on the pier. I could change my mind, join him, and board when he did.

Alone, how would I get home?

The sails filled. I wondered why the steward remained. The ship glided away from the docks. My choice would last forever.

Bela, do you despise me for what I did?

Through tears I saw the steward—really a dark shape in the night—head toward me. Didn't stewards go with their ships? Terror stopped my tears. I dashed into the warehouse and raced for the far door.

I crashed into a pile of sacks, caromed off it, and raced on.

"Loma! It's only me."

Hamdun! I stopped and called, "Why didn't you go with Belo? He needed you!" He needed me.

"Where are you?" he said.

"Here I am."

"Your abuelo told me to stay with you." He held up his hand to stop my objection that Belo couldn't speak. "He told me with his eyes and his hand that kept shooing me after you."

My tears returned in a flood. I crouched on the stone floor and sobbed. Would he live? Would he find a haven in Naples? Would I ever see him again? Would he speak to me if I did?

Hamdun patted my shoulder.

I got out, "I'm not an angel."

"I don't know what an angel would do."

When I finally stopped weeping, I sat on a sack, and Hamdun lowered himself next to me. Even through the door, I heard the rush of the wind.

"Thank you." That was inadequate. Without him, we would be dead or baptized. "I don't know how to thank you."

"Your belo and especially your papá have always treated

me kindly. I don't have a family of my own." He breathed in deeply. "This is my confession: I didn't want anything bad to happen to either of you, but when misfortune came, I rejoiced to be able to make it less terrible."

I wept again, more softly this time. Trouble still lay ahead, but Hamdun, as much as he could, would continue to make it less terrible. I thanked him again and thanked the Almighty for him, too.

After a few minutes, we became practical and decided that we should leave the wharf now, while it was still dark. On the avenue that led out of the city, we faced into the wind. When we reached the cathedral square, I stopped to look around, wishing that God would send a flash of light to reveal a scrap of food or a few overlooked ducats.

Neither was revealed.

We kept walking. The blocky shape of the fortress above the city interrupted the starry sky. If we were lucky, we'd overtake a caravan we could join. If we weren't, our best strategy would be to hide during daylight and walk at night until we reached Señor Qays and Señora Yasmina, who would help us.

But just beyond the north gate to the city, a caravan slept. We picked our way along its edge, passing men on the ground wrapped in their cloaks, hugging their belongings and lying near their sleeping beasts.

A campfire flared somewhere in the middle of the

caravan. I heard a drinking song and, when it ended, a burst of fury: "You dirty cheat!" Sounds of a scuffle followed.

Gambling. I thought of Pero.

Eventually, we sat on dry, spiky grass a few yards from a mule, lying on its side.

"Sleep," Hamdun whispered. "I'll watch."

"Thank you." I couldn't wrap myself in my cloak, because our cloaks had been with our donkeys. I lay back.

But I couldn't sleep, because my crime against Belo and my worries tormented me. Even counting brought no relief. Hoping to distract myself, I whispered, "Hamdun?"

His shape, indistinct in the dark, stirred. "Yes?"

"Why don't you have a family?"

"I'm poor, and I wouldn't want my children to starve as I did. When I can, I put a little aside from my wages." He chuckled. "By the time I'm as old as Don Solomon, I'll have enough, and I'll find a widow with grandchildren." He paused. "For now, I have you and your brother Jento. Sleep."

I was comforted by an idea, which allowed me to drift off.

My nose woke me. Hamdun crouched, holding close to my face a thick slice of bread mounded with farmer cheese. I sat up and extended my hand. "How?"

He gave me the bread. "There are other servants and also slaves. They're generous."

"Thank you!"

Last night's wind had diminished to a breeze. The caravan had awakened and become a twitchy mass of energy: beasts stamping; men feeding their animals or leading them to drink in the river that accompanied the road.

People passed by us, leaving or entering Málaga on foot, on beasts, driving carts, the stream of them squeezed to an urgent trickle by the caravan, which took up half the road and the field beyond it.

Hamdun said the caravan was waiting to be joined by more people and beasts. The leader was already here: Señor Gonzalo.

"They say he's shrewd, greedy, pitiless—"

My hand went for Bela's pendant, then dropped to my side.

"—and very brave. They say it could be worse." Hamdun grinned. "They say he could be a coward."

"Do you know where the caravan is going?"

"Toledo."

Toledo was good.

"By way of Granada."

Near where the monarchs were and where Don Miguel would return to.

I tugged off my rings, unclasped my bracelet, and buried them in my purse. If the purse had been big enough to accommodate it, I would have added my necklace. "Where is Señor Gonzalo?"

"I think he's behind that horse." Hamdun pointed.

We threaded our way through the throng, and I was terrifyingly noticed. Men made kissing noises and said things they should have said only to their wives. I blushed from my forehead all the way down my neck.

Finally, we reached the horse and went around it.

Señor Gonzalo, a stocky man who reeked of sweat, was tying a saddlebag. From his girth, he liked to eat, which I hoped meant the people in the caravan would eat, too.

I offered him my golden belt. In exchange, he agreed to let us travel with them, to feed us, and to protect us from bandits and from the men in the caravan.

When he agreed to all that, he said in a gravelly voice, "Give me the necklace, too, and your purse."

My face reddened again, this time out of fury. "We had a bargain!"

"We do. Now give me the rest."

Hamdun and I could leave, though I didn't know what the other men would do. We needed this bully. My fingers trembled with rage as I unclasped my necklace. I filled his hand with my purse.

"And I'll take your slave."

I sensed Hamdun stiffen.

I managed to keep my voice level. "He's a servant."

"Not anymore. I'll take him."

36

God help me! My breath stuck in my throat. He could do it. If I found a constable to complain to, the constable would investigate me as well as Hamdun and Señor Gonzalo, and the villain had guessed that.

Still, he couldn't take Hamdun. "No," I got out, sounding hoarse. "I'm sorry, Señor Gonzalo, but you can't have him."

He glared at me and waited. What would Belo do if he were here?

The silence stretched. I thought my heart would explode. To calm myself, I began to count, and my heart slowed. My breaths deepened.

When I reached thirty, he said, "Leave. If you follow us to steal my protection, I'll let these wolves loose on you."

He gestured broadly.

I began to turn.

"On second thought, I can just take him. Who would stop me?"

What would Belo do?

Even now, he'd bribe. I turned slowly. I had nothing.

I had a mind that Belo admired.

"Señor Gonzalo . . ." I faced him and raised my hands, palms up. "You may have noticed I'm wearing silk." Of course he had. If I gave him Hamdun, he'd have my gown, too. "You frightened me, and my wits fled, but I'm not a peasant. My family has friends who are my friends."

"Where is your family? Grand ladies don't travel alone."

I could tell him we'd been attacked, which was believable enough, but then I'd be explaining to a man I hoped to make my inferior.

I swallowed. "My affairs are none of your concern." Truth strengthened my voice. "I've dined more than once with Cardinal de Mendoza and my grandfather. In Toledo, I can commend you to him. He needs courageous men. But you must return my necklace and my purse and stop threatening me."

His expression turned calculating. Would a recommendation to the cardinal be worth more than my jewels and a slave, or—ai!—two slaves?

Finally, he said, "I keep the belt?"

"Yes. That was our bargain."

"Tell the cardinal I go all over Spain. I'm true. I'd never betray him."

"I'll say those precise words."

He returned my things.

I didn't want to stay near him, so we started back across the caravan.

When the men started their calls again, Señor Gonzalo shouted, "Let her be!"

The men quieted, as if the Almighty had closed their throats.

Hamdun murmured, "Your abuelo would be proud of you."

I thought so, too. Would I ever be able to tell him?

As we walked away, I thought of our other danger: Don Miguel, who would likely be among the travelers streaming past the caravan. We had to lose ourselves in the caravan, but the men! And Señor Gonzalo!

I told Hamdun the problem.

"We'll stay with the servants and slaves. They won't betray us."

But Belo spoke in my mind: You mustn't stay with them. That will look weak. Establish yourself near Señor Gonzalo—

Me: Oh, no.

Belo: —but not so close that you seem weak. Create a space around your person that no one will invade without your permission.

Me: How will I do that?

Belo: You're my grandchild. Do it.

I told Hamdun what Belo had said and what I thought we might do.

He smiled. "That's what he'd say."

We made our way back toward Señor Gonzalo, who now reclined on the ground, leaning against a mound of satchels. About three yards from him, I stopped.

Hamdun approached the largest man nearby, with a chest as wide as a cupboard. The man lay on the ground, too, propped up on his elbow, watching us.

"My mistress, Paloma, requires a respectful distance. Please move back."

The man's eyes went to Señor Gonzalo. Mine did, too. Señor Gonzalo said nothing. Merciful One, help me! Belo, help me!

The idea that arrived was sent by neither. I dropped to my knees, put my palms together, and began the prayer I'd heard a hundred times from the priests who invaded our synagogue. "Hail Mary, full of grace . . ." At the end, I crossed myself.

The man had stood and backed away. The others nearby followed suit.

In my mind, Belo approved: You did what you had to, Loma.

But what did the Almighty think?

We left Málaga the next morning, on Saturday, April 21, the Sabbath, less than three and a half months before the Jews, most still unknowing, would have to begin their exile.

I didn't have a view of the whole caravan to make an exact count, but we had well over a hundred mules, many donkeys, and a dozen or more horses. Señor Gonzalo rode a horse, and he found one for me, too.

Hamdun refused to share it with me. "It will make you less safe; I can walk. Caravans don't travel fast."

Ours traveled at the pace of a worm. When we finally neared Santa Fe, the caravan skirted the camp where Belo and I had stayed. Next, we proceeded to Granada, and I deduced from the galloping of secretaries up and down the avenue that the monarchs had relocated there, undoubtedly to the enormous palace, all sharp corners and staring windows, called the Alhambra. In my imagination, every window watched me.

Though I knew I was being silly, I dismounted to make myself less noticeable.

Granada's market filled the square outside the enormous white-stone mosque—now a cathedral. Priests' plainsong drifted from the four open doors. We stopped while Señor Gonzalo bargained for supplies to continue our journey.

When we were about to set off again, a party of a dozen priests hurried out of the cathedral and joined us. Fortunately, they weren't traveling far and would be with us for just a day. I prayed to the Almighty that they would keep to themselves.

They didn't. They found me, because God was punishing me for the many reasons I had given Him.

They were kind! I shouldn't have been astonished—they thought me a Christian. Kind, yes, but worried for me.

Father Davalos, the talkative one, took the lead in asking how I came to be traveling alone. "Marina"—I had borrowed my sister-in-law's name—"what befell you?"

Señor Gonzalo slowed his horse to eavesdrop.

I reached for Bela's pendant. Was it strange that I didn't wear a cross? Had I drawn attention to the fact?

Father Davalos touched my shoulder in a gesture that I knew he meant to be reassuring. He was a short, stooped man, hardly taller than I was. "You may tell me."

My mind flew to all I couldn't tell him.

Belo was a practiced liar and even Papá could lie convincingly if he had to. I swallowed. "My abuelo was struck with a paroxysm." Belo and Papá always told as much of the truth as they could. "He had spells before, but in the past he recovered quickly. This time, he didn't." I swallowed again, grief catching up with my fear. "I was his constant companion after plague took my abuela."

"The Lord took her."

"Yes." I didn't say more, hoping he would respect my sadness.

But he pressed on. "Where was he struck?"

I misunderstood the question. "On the right side. He had no strength there. And in his tongue. He could speak only nonsense."

"I meant, where were you when he fell ill? In Granada?"

"In Málaga." The rest of my story took shape. "My abuelo and my papá and I, along with a servant and three slaves, traveled there from our home in Alcalá de Henares." Where we lived didn't seem dangerous to tell. "At night, when we traveled, I massaged his feet." Tears threatened.

"He was lucky to have such a good grandchild."

Until I left him. "The trip was to buy five large vases for a customer of my abuelo's, but he was struck before we could do it." I'd been along on such missions. "The physician in Málaga said there's a doctor in Naples who can cure such attacks."

Belo prodded me. Don't forget you're a Christian!

I added, "Papá swore to go to Rome with Belo if he recovered."

"To Pilate's stairs?"

I nodded, hoping I wasn't stepping into a trap.

"You didn't go with them?"

"My mamá is all alone. One of us had to go home and one had to take Belo. Papá didn't want me to be unprotected in a foreign city, and we had the servant and the slaves to accompany me, so I was to join a caravan, as I've done." I shrugged. "The slaves slipped away in the night, leaving me with only the servant." I gestured toward Hamdun, trudging several paces behind us. "The Lord watched over me."

"He's our shepherd."

I was about to mount my horse and get away, but he spoke first.

"I suppose you aren't married."

I shook my head.

"Betrothed?"

"My grandfather kept me at his side."

"You're a good child. You'll be rewarded."

Probably not.

The cook rang her bell. The caravan came to a slow halt.

"Will you eat with us, Marina?"

For a moment, I didn't realize he was speaking to me. "I'll be honored."

Señor Gonzalo had issued me a blanket along with the horse. Hamdun spread it for me to sit on.

"Hamdun brings me my meals." God forgive me. "Hamdun, don't forget the pork sausage. Sometimes he fetches only food for Muslims."

Father Davalos sat with me. "They'll bring me something." He waved a hand at his fellow priests. "I don't care what I eat."

He'd care what I didn't eat.

While we waited, he regaled me with a tale of a son who reminded me of Pero, who left home and wasted his inheritance. When the son came back, his father welcomed him. It was a sweet story, revealing again that Christians could be nice to each other.

I wondered what would happen if I couldn't eat the sausage. Father Davalos would work out the reason. At best, Hamdun and I would be left on the side of the road.

The priests returned and gave Father Davalos his dinner in a tin bowl. When the priest prayed over his food, I pretended to pray, too.

Hamdun presented me with my bowl and a wooden spoon: lentils, cheese, cucumbers, bread, and a glistening sausage. "May it go down well, mistress."

I took a spoonful of lentils and had trouble getting even them down.

Don't leave the sausage for last.

I ate a bite of bread, took my knife out of my purse,

and cut a slice of the sausage and stared at it. Mottled with clots of fat, it looked hardly different from beef sausage.

I could never tell anyone about this crime.

Eat it.

I put the slice in my mouth, which filled with saliva. Tears streamed down my face. God forgive me, I began to chew.

I managed not to throw up. I got the sausage down, though without tasting it. Father Davalos patted my arm and asked why I wept. I gulped out that it was because my abuelo loved sausage. "And because you're here. He was devout."

The priest beamed at me.

We reached Toledo on the afternoon of Wednesday, May 2, the day after the expulsion decree had been proclaimed in all churches and synagogues, and three months minus two days before we all had to depart from Spain. I promised Señor Gonzalo that I'd meet him in the morning in the cathedral square to introduce him to the cardinal. May he wait there forever.

A rabbi took us in, and his first question was about Belo. I recounted his pleas to the monarchs and then his paroxysm. The rabbi wept.

"We had hopes he could change their minds." He

wiped a tear away. "The Jews are leaving Egypt again. God willing, the sea will part."

God willing.

On Sunday, accompanied by six Jewish guards from Toledo, Hamdun and I reached home.

Fatima cried out when she opened the door. "Loma!"

Mamá came running. "Where's your abuelo?" Without hugging me or waiting for answers, she ran upstairs, crying, "Asher! Asher!"

I followed her. Hamdun headed toward the kitchen. I felt his absence.

Papá emerged from his study, tears streaming.

No! "Belo didn't die, Papá."

Don Solomon had been here, so Papá already knew we'd had to flee.

"Thank God!" He hugged me. "Where is he? He wasn't baptized? You're not both Christians?" He searched my face.

"We're not." I took a deep breath and told him.

He let go of me. "You abandoned him?"

37

I nodded.

Papá walked away in the direction of his study.

"Loma!" Jento barreled at me and hugged me around my waist.

When I smelled him, when I heard his light voice, and, most of all, when I hugged him back—I was truly home.

Belo, I had to have this.

After a minute or two, Señor Osua, his teacher, came and pulled him away to return to his studies.

Samuel, Josefina, and baby Esther, fourteen months old by now, were expected for dinner. I went to the kitchen, but Mamá shooed me out. "You might poison us all."

God forgive me, I didn't care much what she said. I

went upstairs to the living room.

Mamá or Papá must have sent someone to tell Samuel, because, when dinnertime came, he and Josefina weren't surprised to see me and to not see Belo.

Josefina didn't offer Esther for me to kiss.

When we were all seated, Mamá told everyone not to share a bowl with me. "She's a jezebel."

Bravely, Jento, on my right, pushed his bowl my way.

I left the table, not wanting Mamá's fury to fall on him. As I descended the stairs, she called after me that I was heartless, hateful, ungrateful, and, worst of all, selfish.

Me: Belo, are you glad they hate me?

Belo: Yes.

Me: Is the fellow taking care of you? Are you alive?

No answer.

In the kitchen, I scraped the stew pot and licked the spoon. Then I served myself flatbread and garlic snacks. I carried the bowl to the courtyard, where I sat on a bench. I could always eat.

Papá, why were you kinder to Pero than you're being to me?

Samuel didn't come, though this was our place. Eventually, I went upstairs to my room. I didn't look toward the dining room, so I didn't know if anyone saw me. I took out my backgammon set and played against myself.

God had let me reach home so I could be punished by the people who could hurt me the most.

Esther wailed from the direction of the dining room. I jumped up.

Her cry was cut off, probably with a morsel of food. I sat again.

I heard Samuel's and Josefina's goodbyes.

How strange it was, to be idle.

How wrong it was, when I could help. Papá was certainly preparing for our departure, and he'd have Belo's affairs as well as his own to settle.

That got me out of my room and into Papá's study.

He looked up from writing. "We have to change our plans and go to Naples." From his tone, this was my fault, too.

I said, "I know who owes Belo money and who will pay quickly."

But didn't he want to hear what had happened to me? Didn't he care that I might have died? That Belo and I both could have died?

"You've helped enough." He added, "We have to marry you off, and who will have your hard heart?"

I whirled. He couldn't have said what I thought he had. "Excuse me, Papá. I didn't hear."

"The rabbi is marrying every female over twelve, for

their protection. We'll find someone. Another thing I have to do now."

A wave of laughter rose in me. My whole body shook. I had to lean on Papá's desk to keep from collapsing. My chest hurt, but I kept laughing.

Papá's expression shifted gradually from stony to perplexed and, finally, to alarm. He came around his desk and put a hand on my arm—

—which I shook off. Cleanly, like a knife through butter, my laughter stopped, and fury possessed me.

Not caring if I created discord, I said, "You sacrificed me, though the Almighty didn't tell you to as He told Abraham." My voice sounded like spikes. "You knew I wanted more than anything to have children, and you knew Belo wouldn't let me. You allowed him to not let me. I reminded him of Bela, and you wanted him to have the comfort. You never asked me if I preferred being an angel to being a mother. You could have traveled with him more. Fatima could have gone, too, and massaged his feet." My voice rose. "I would have children by now."

Papá made a sound in his throat.

"So I'm being married to *protect* me? When no one in my own family ever did before? After I crossed Spain alone, with just Hamdun?"

"Loma—" Papá's voice was soft.

"I came home because I couldn't bear being separated forever from the children. Maybe that was selfish." I wept. When I could speak, I said, "I love Belo as much as you do. I brought him safely to Málaga, even though we were followed. I put him on a ship, and I thought Hamdun would stay with him, but Belo sent him to me. I didn't know Hamdun was still on land until after the ship sailed."

Papá hugged me. "I was cruel, God forgive me." He sat me on the cushion by his desk. "I'll talk to Samuel and the others, and I'll try to make your mamá stop. Tell me what happened."

I recounted almost everything, including our meetings with the monarchs. At the end, I gathered my courage and said what I'd promised myself never to reveal: "Papá, I ate pork." Would he throw me out of the house?

He frowned. "Why?"

I told him about the priests. "I had managed not to until then."

"God is merciful." He touched my cheek. "How did it taste?"

My shoulders slumped with relief. "Fatty, I guess. My mouth was so full of saliva I couldn't taste it."

He changed the subject. "We've been arranging marriages ever since Don Solomon came with news of Belo and the expulsion. Most of the pairings have been made.

Would you rather have a husband who is too old or too young?"

"Young." Preferably a baby. Only the Almighty would really be able to protect us.

I was reconciled with my family. The littles were allowed to be with me again. In the time I'd been gone, Clara had grown an inch and promised to be the tallest Cantala eventually.

The next day, my husband was chosen, the marriage contract written, my dowry pledged—a process that, before, would have taken months.

I was laughing often. So many ordinary things became funny when you turned them upside down.

It was funny that my husband-to-be, Hasdai Rosillo, had had his bar mitzvah only a week earlier, and I would turn sixteen on July 7, twenty-four days before we went into exile. Accentuating the difference between us, he was tiny, hardly bigger than seven-year-old Jento, and he was so thin that sunlight seemed to shine through him.

His mother had chosen to convert, and no one had to tell me that I would be his new mother. He would live with us and be taught with Jento. I insisted that he sleep with Jento, too.

I would be kind to him, as I always was to children.

He was the only child of a wool merchant. Papá said it could have been worse.

I chuckled.

While Papá was arranging my mismatched marriage, I had an interlude of happiness. In the morning, I went to Belo's study, which still smelled of his foot salve.

Belo, I thought, I will pack your books. They will be perfect when we reach Naples. Please be alive to read them. Almighty, please let him be alive.

I opened his strongbox and filled a velvet sack with ducats.

Hamdun was in the courtyard, pruning the lemon tree. He didn't hear my footsteps, so I watched his care, his economy of movement, the thoughtful way he paused before he cut.

When he finished, he turned. "Loma! You surprised me."

"I didn't want to interrupt you." I sat on a bench and patted the place next to me.

He laid his shears in the soil at the base of the tree and sat.

"You shouldn't have to wait so long to have a family." I put the velvet sack of ducats in his lap. "Open it."

His breath caught when he saw. "So much!"

I said solemnly, "It is inadequate recompense for your

service to Belo and me." I abandoned formality. "I thought of this when we left Málaga. Hoping to be able to do it made me happy during the journey." The only thing.

His eyes were wet.

"What will you do with the money?"

"First I'll buy a little land and a few goats." He grinned. "Then I'll look for a younger widow than I said before. Someone sweet and kind."

"The goats will be lucky."

He laughed.

Hastily, I added, "And so will she!" Then I asked him if he'd continue as our servant until we left Spain.

"With joy and gratitude, and after you leave, I'll miss you forever."

The next morning, Tuesday, May 8, 1492, I became a wife, along with six other young women, none older than fourteen. I wore my blue gown embroidered with gold thread. On my head sat my turban hat, a band of red around my forehead and over my ears, and, above the band, folds of blue silk. Around my neck hung three gold necklaces, one of them made by Pero when he was still Yuda. But my neck felt bare without Bela's pendant. Two silver bracelets circled each arm.

No one was to feel sad for me, as richly appareled as I was.

The weddings took place in the street outside the synagogue. My nieces and nephews and Jento closed around me while we waited for the hazan.

Hasdai was in the middle of his own family where I couldn't see him.

Vellida, eyes brimming, stood on the edge of the littles. Her twins clung to her skirts.

"Don't cry," I said. "It's funny."

She wiped her eyes. "You're the bravest in the family."

"No credit to me. Anyway, the mettle of all of us is about to be tested."

Clara said, "You don't look very old, Tía Loma."

I laughed. "Thank you."

"You have only one wrinkle." She pointed. "Between your eyebrows."

Todros said, "Hasdai is a good boy, even if he always hums."

The hazan and the rabbi bustled out of the synagogue. The couples were to take turns being married. Because Papá was wealthy, Hasdai and I were first. Papá accompanied me, and Hasdai's father, Señor Judah, accompanied his son.

The son of a wool merchant couldn't dress as we did. Hasdai wore a wool tabard, blue, like my gown, possibly the only auspicious sign. Not propitious that his eyes were red because he was marrying me.

Hasdai's head just reached my shoulder. He hummed, high-pitched and tuneless. His voice hadn't changed yet.

He held out his hand and opened his small fist. I always loved children's hands. On his palm rested a gold ring, which turned out to be too small for my plump finger. I pushed it on as far as it would go. Don Ziza, the goldsmith, would make it bigger.

Señor Judah spread a tallit across our shoulders. The hazan intoned the seven blessings and pronounced us wed. I had a husband at last.

38

There was a meal after the wedding, meager compared with the usual feast, but I plied my husband with hazelnut nougats, butter cookies, and pastry crescents. He needed to be plumper. And when he chewed he didn't hum.

Bringing him the best of everything became a game among the littles.

Todros pulled his shoulders back. "I'm your cousin now. We'll all take care of you."

Thank you, my darling.

After the celebration, late in the night, I led Hasdai to Jento's bedroom and carried with me a plate of sugar cookies. "In case you wake up and are hungry."

I kissed both my brother and my husband on the

forehead. When my lips touched Hasdai's skin, his humming rose to the pitch of a shriek.

I wouldn't be able to spend much time with him during the day, because I had to help Papá settle our affairs. I asked Aljohar to protect him as much as she could from Mamá, and to bring him snacks.

Hamdun accompanied me wherever I went: to taverns for meals with Old Christians or to houses for meals with conversos. Before we left Spain, we had to pay our debts and we had to collect what was owed us. Each of us could take only one thousand ducats with us, but we could also take bills of exchange that banks would honor. If we were going to be able to continue to help the aljama and other Jews who fled to Naples, we would need funds.

But the people who owed us money offered excuses: the harvest was bad; their own debtors weren't paying; they were low on cash. They wanted to delay until we were gone and couldn't collect. But the ones we owed money to pressed for payment.

Everyone wanted to become rich by making us poor. Papá wrote to the monarchs, asking for aid, and paid a messenger to carry the letter, but an answer didn't come. The days marched on.

In the evenings, I devoted myself to getting to know my husband. I played backgammon with him and Jento on their bed, challenging each in turn, or watching while they played each other. After a few nights, Hasdai's age gave him the advantage over Jento, who bit back tears whenever he lost two or more games in a row. Hasdai never teased. He was a nice boy—man. If only he didn't hum!

I brought snacks to munch on during the games: bread slices lathered with roasted garlic and onions or cheese-and-honey sweets or rosewater pastries. In just a week, Hasdai grew a little less thin, and Jento and I began to resemble stew pots.

One night, Jento asked Hasdai why he hummed.

He shrugged. His eyes shifted to me and away, an appeal for rescue.

I reached across the backgammon board for a sweet. "I often count. I know how many tiles there are in every room in the house, because I've counted them."

"How many are there in here?" Jento said.

"There are one hundred and eighty-eight."

"Why do you do it, Wife?"

Wife sounded strange whenever he said it.

Before I could answer, Jento said, "Todros and Beatriz look older than you. It's funny you're her husband."

Hasdai just said, "My papá didn't get tall until he was seventeen."

His papá was a foot taller than mine. When Hasdai was seventeen and I was twenty and he'd gotten his growth, the difference in our ages might not seem important.

Jento repeated Hasdai's question: "Why do you count?"

"It calms me."

"That's why I hum!" Hasdai sounded livelier than I'd ever heard him.

I smiled. "We're alike that way." But if he didn't stop eventually, I'd be counting out loud to defend myself. We'd be the crazy couple of Naples.

When I was out with Hamdun, we often saw workmen at the synagogue, pacing the length of the walls and using their surveyors' tools to measure their height. As soon as the aljama left, the synagogue would be refitted as a church.

I wondered what God thought of this. Was He angry at the priests? Angry at us for failing to prevent our expulsion?

On June 2, Papá told me about a priest's announcement in synagogue that Don Solomon would be baptized on Friday, June 15, in Guadalupe, a month and a half before the Jews' last day to be in Spain.

I thought he would already have been baptized, but Papá said, "The monarchs needed time. They think that if the ceremony is grand enough, more of us will decide to convert, too."

A few families in our aljama were persuaded, but most weren't.

In the judería, sorrow rang from every house. Wherever I was—in the kitchen, the courtyard, Papá's study—I heard wails.

Once, on our way to an inn to try to collect a debt, Hamdun and I followed Señor Ezmel, a locksmith, toward the judería gate. He was walking a donkey loaded with satchels. His son, a boy of about nine, sat atop the pile.

Behind me, a moan rose to a howl. The locksmith's wife heaved past me and snatched her son. Clutching him tight, she turned and started back. But her husband wrested the child away from her.

I understood. Señor Ezmel was converting, but his wife wasn't. He was taking their son, and she wouldn't be able to stop him.

Alcalá de Henares was just a little north of the middle of Spain. Portugal to the west and the sea to the east were equally distant. For a fee, the king of Portugal was willing to admit Spanish Jews for eight months.

Closest of all was the kingdom of Navarre, where the king agreed to take us in forever, if we chose to stay. North of Navarre lay France, where we were unwanted for even long enough to set down one foot.

The southern coast was farthest, and Málaga was the likeliest departure port for North Africa.

Of the 207 families in the aljama, 40 converted; another 40 chose to go to Portugal, hoping the king there would relent and let them stay—or that the Spanish monarchs would change their minds and allow them back in; 12 families set their sights on Navarre and 11 on North Africa. The rest, 104 families, 524 Jews—some elderly, some ill, some children, some pregnant—no doubt influenced by Belo's possible presence there, decided on the kingdom of Naples.

Our number swelled to 532, counting the Moorish servants who chose to go with their families. Of our servants, only Aljohar elected to come. More might have, if not for Mamá. Hamdun wanted to stay and buy his land and goats and find a wife.

I hugged Aljohar when I found out. "You're the best comfort this family has."

She sniffed. "If pirates eat us for dinner, so be it."

I couldn't help laughing. "I don't think pirates are cannibals."

She said darkly, "They may be."

The town council decided that everyone would leave together for the port of Valencia on July 1, which would give us thirty days to get there, buy provisions, pay our departure tax (really, there was such a tax!), and meet our shipmasters. Papá had written to a ships' agent to arrange transport for everyone.

On Wednesday, June 27, Papá and I stopped settling our business affairs and joined the servants and the rest of the family in packing. I wrapped Belo's books in layers of linen.

On June 30, after we'd sat down with the whole family to our Sabbath dinner, someone pounded on the door. Papá went to answer it himself.

He returned alone. His face frightened me—eyes wide, with the whites showing all around. "Loma, Don Rodrigo is here. He says you have to go with him to the inn of the hermandad."

The prison!

39

Hasdai hummed loudly. I stood.

Samuel stood, too. "I'll come with you."

Hasdai didn't stand.

Ledicia said, "Why does she have to go?"

"Don Rodrigo didn't say."

Papá said he'd go with me and Samuel should stay.

Don Rodrigo bowed when I came out. "I'm sorry, Paloma."

I curtsied. "You've always been kind."

He had three guards with him, but no one touched me.

Who had ordered this? Would I be tortured, like Pero had been?

My steps lagged, so Papá held out his hand for me,

meaning I had to keep up. In the hermandad, the small room I was conducted to was furnished with a table, a bench, a bed, and a chamber pot. No windows.

A bed! They were going to keep me here? "Don Rodrigo, the aljama is leaving tomorrow."

"I'm sorry."

The room's walls were white stucco. A crucifix hung next to the door. The floor was large paving stones. The smell: vomit, sweat, excrement. I remembered Pero's cell.

"I'll stay with her." Papá's Adam's apple bobbed in and out as he swallowed again and again.

Don Rodrigo repeated his apologies. "She is to be left alone."

"I can have a lawyer, can't I?"

"Don Martín has offered to represent you," Don Rodrigo said.

A converso attorney who owed us money and hadn't paid.

He didn't visit me that day. I wasn't tortured, either. No inquisitors came. What was this about? Not knowing, not even being able to guess, was its own torment. Did they imagine *I* had crucified a Christian child?

I walked around and around my cell, counting my steps, listening to my heart *clip-clop* and my stomach grumble. They might have let me eat dinner before taking me.

In the evening, Papá brought me Sabbath dinner leftovers. He hadn't been able to discover why I'd been imprisoned. "No one will talk to me. I'm a ghost, already gone."

Belo would have made them talk.

Papá said that he and Samuel had persuaded the families to delay departure for a day in hopes that I'd be released, but I didn't expect that I would be. The Christians wouldn't do anything on their Sabbath, and they didn't.

Early on Monday morning, I had visitors. I heard Hasdai humming before the door opened and he and his father, Judah Rosillo, came in.

Hasdai produced a paper, rolled and tied with twine, from the folds of his robe. "Papá says I have to do this. He says you and I can get married again."

A get, a writ of divorce, and not a conditional one.

Hasdai and I had been married for less than eight weeks. Our lips had never met.

Papá Judah, now Señor Judah, said, "We hope you agree."

I nodded.

"You were a good wife." Hasdai became more talkative than I'd ever heard him. "I'd like you to be my wife again. You are"—he hummed—"sweet and pretty. Please be well. Please do whatever you have to do to be safe."

Convert? Was that what he meant?

"Thank you. I wish you a safe journey. Please eat a lot whenever you can."

He smiled. "I'll try to get fat."

They left. I tugged off my wedding ring and buried it in my purse. A moment later, all the adults in my family entered. The children, who were being protected from seeing me here, had been told that I was traveling and would join the caravan later. Wise, but I was deprived of saying farewell and hugging them and breathing them in.

Everyone wept, even Mamá.

My sisters and Samuel had spouses and children, so they had to leave. I didn't want Mamá to stay with me, but Papá might have remained for a while and then caught up with the caravan.

He said, "Your mamá needs me."

Your daughter doesn't?

Mamá said, "Your papá paid Don Rodrigo a fortune."

Papá put a hand on Mamá's shoulder. "He'll see that you're comfortable and well fed."

"If—" I gulped. "*When* I'm released, how"—my voice rose—"how will I get to you? There won't be anyone to travel with."

"I've spoken with Don Martín and—"

Mamá broke in. "He's been paid well, too."

Papá put his hands on my cheeks. "He's promised to arrange an escort for you."

My lawyer who hadn't visited me yet.

Samuel said, "We won't set sail until the last day if you haven't come."

What do you say to your family when you may never see them again? Nothing is right; nothing is enough.

"Asher," Mamá said, "they're going to leave without us." She started for the door.

Everyone else hugged me and followed her out.

An hour later, even through the hermandad's stone walls, I heard singing and tambourines shaking. The aljama was leaving the city and taking my joy with it—the littles.

A week passed. No inquisitors. Don Rodrigo's men were polite, and I was fed food a Jew could eat.

Don Martín didn't come. No one told me the charges against me.

I had one faithful visitor: Hamdun, who came every morning and every evening. He had found work at a livery stable at the edge of the city.

On the morning after my family's departure, he came with three perfect black figs. "Two for you, one for me."

I protested the unequal division but he insisted.

"I thought you were going to buy land and goats."

"I can buy them anytime."

"And find a widow to marry."

"I can find her later, too."

I hugged him.

"You don't deserve this."

I gestured around my cell. "It's not so bad. It isn't raining."

We both chuckled. He asked if I was getting enough food. I said I was. A few minutes later, he left. In the evening, he brought his backgammon set, and we played by smoky lamplight. He won more games than I did. I hoped I wouldn't be here long enough to learn his tactics. As a great kindness, he let me keep the set.

"You can return it when you leave."

Two weeks passed from the day my family left. No inquisitors. No Don Martín. No charges. Only faithful Hamdun. In seventeen days, I'd have to convert or be executed.

40

I spent most of my days praying, pacing, counting, playing backgammon with Hamdun, and missing the littles.

Once, Hamdun asked if I had decided against accepting baptism.

"I don't know. Since God made me, which do you think He'd like better, that I usurp His power and unmake myself or that I convert and worship false gods?"

"Or pretend to worship them. I don't want you to die. There are enough martyrs."

By Monday, July 23, eight days remained until the final one. If the charges against me were miraculously dropped, there still might not be time for me to reach the coast. But despite Samuel's promise to wait until the last day, our ship might already be underway. Masters, as I had learned, sailed by the winds.

In the afternoon, I had visitors: a handsome, serious-looking young man, whose expression and apparel were too somber for him to be a secretary, and Don Solomon, or the converso who used to be Don Solomon, whose name had become the grand eight-syllable *Alonso López Salazar.* The young man held a bulging linen sack. When they entered, the guard closed the door, but the lock didn't click.

My heart pounded. Had Don Alonso won my release?

"Loma!" Don Alonso's eyes were merry, as if we were in our living room with Belo before any of this had happened.

I curtsied.

He held his arms out, and I went into them. No need to say how much I hated him until I knew his purpose. He smelled of garlic, onions, and saffron. I remembered how the room stank and how, by now, I must reek, too. He murmured, "I miss your abuelo," and let me go.

I stepped back.

The young man bowed, straightened, and smiled, revealing perfect white teeth. He was more than handsome: clean-shaven with cheeks like satin, a firm chin, full lips, clear brown eyes, a straight stance, and—God forgive me!—shapely legs in blue hose. After he smiled, his expression became gloomy again.

I was wearing my rose-colored gown with the gray pleated sleeves. It was one of my best, a Sabbath favorite, but I'd been wearing it for twenty-four days.

"May I introduce my great-grandson, Fernán Pérez Salazar?"

Was this the great-grandson he'd mentioned five years ago as a possible husband for me, whose Jewish name had been Nattan?

"Isn't she lovely, Fernán?"

"Very lovely," he said, holding the sack out to me. "For your enjoyment."

I took it. Why were they here?

"Please open it," Don Fernán said.

I untied the velvet string, but I knew its contents by weight and softness. When I emptied the sack on my table, there were, as I expected, figs, six of them, nice, but not perfect, like the ones Hamdun brought me every day.

"Thank you. You're very kind."

"We're happy to present them." Don Alonso widened his stance. "We guessed you haven't tasted figs in a while."

"Please share them with me." I gave one to each.

We were silent while we ate.

"Delicious!" Overripe. "Please sit." I gestured at my bench. "I regret not having a chair with a back."

"This is fine." Don Alonso lowered himself stiffly.

Don Fernán sat easily.

I sat on my bed and leaned toward them. "Don Alonso, no one has told me the charges I face." I couldn't help sounding resentful. "My lawyer hasn't visited me."

"Don Joseph is charged with usury fraud. The court considers you his agent."

Usury fraud meant charging someone too much for a loan and hiding the extra charges. The accusation was nonsense.

"He never committed fraud! You know that. Who's accusing him?" I calmed a little. Usury fraud had to be a lesser crime than crucifying a child. "On what loan?"

"For a house and an olive orchard near Mérida."

I remembered. The borrower was Señor Mejía, an Old Christian, who hadn't paid Belo back—along with all the others who also hadn't paid us.

The accusation may have reached royal ears and set my imprisonment in motion.

"Señor Mejía is lying."

I thought Don Fernán would think me unwomanly for saying it so baldly, but he smiled briefly before his face became grave again.

"No doubt," Don Alonso said. "We came when I heard of your trouble. Fernán accompanied me as you used to go with Don Joseph. I hope the journey lightened his grief."

I turned to him. "I'm sorry for your sorrow." Whatever it was.

"His wife died giving birth to their daughter, who is healthy."

Mention of the baby captured me. "How old is she?"

Don Fernán said, "Six months. She's with my good sister, who has a son her age."

They were so sweet at six months! "What's the baby's name?"

"Regina."

A Christian and Jewish name. "Pretty."

If I converted and married this handsome man, as I believed Don Alonso (and possibly his great-grandson) wanted, I would have a baby instantly. And I would certainly be released. A lump formed in my throat.

The littles would be lost to me, but they probably were anyway.

Don Fernán might never care for me. He may have doted on his dead wife, but that didn't matter. I might never care for him, either. I'd love his child.

"She needs a mother," he said.

Ah, he did want it.

Don Alonso added, "She needs the kind of mother you'd be. Fernán needs your kind of wife."

An educated converso woman who adored children and knew Jewish law.

"I'm divorced."

Don Alonso chuckled. "We're told your husband was just past childhood, and he was supposed to protect you."

Don Fernán opened his hands the way Belo did when he was about to bribe someone. His voice was soft. "I'd protect you."

No one could protect anyone. Only God could, and He hadn't so far.

Don Fernán sprang up. "I'll be back in a moment."

I saw the queen and the princess behind all this. But how important could I—just a woman—be in their plans? Did they think Belo would return to Spain and convert if I stayed?

Don Alonso may have put that idea in their heads.

It made sense, especially if they believed that boatloads of Jews would follow him.

No one knew if he was still alive!

Don Alonso loved him. The queen seemed to, too. They hoped he was alive—but not nearly as much as I did.

While Don Fernán was gone, Don Alonso said, "Your children with Fernán will be, if not kings and queens, the powers behind kings and queens, the wealth that keeps Spain rising. Our blood will have its revenge for what was done to us."

Us, the Jews? Revenge by strengthening our enemies? By *becoming* our enemies?

Don Fernán returned with a scroll tied with a silk ribbon. My writ of divorce had been tied with plain twine.

He gave it to me with another bow. "Please read it."

The document proved to be a bill of exchange for 17,600 maravedis.

I looked in wonderment at Don Fernán. "What does it mean?"

"I bought Señor Mejía's debt. There was no usury fraud. Señor Mejía just wanted to avoid paying. The money is yours."

They wouldn't have called it buying me, but they were trying to.

41

I recited the Shema. The two New Christians joined me—softly.

If they were heard, would Don Rodrigo run in, take them to another cell, and summon the inquisitors?

Would my converso children, the future powers of Spain, have to whisper in corners what they believed most deeply? Would I have to teach them to?

Belo spoke in my mind: Don't convert! Think, Loma! You can live and remain a Jew. Think!

The door to my cell hadn't been locked, because the charge against me had been dropped. Don Alonso and Don Fernán, whether they realized or not, had given me freedom and the means to reach my family in time—with luck and God's help.

Belo would give them something in return.

What? Not my jewels. They had plenty of jewels.

What?

In all Belo's and my visits to New Christians, our hosts longed most to be treated as if they were still Jews.

"Thank you." I felt obliged to curtsey. "God willing, when I'm reunited with Belo—"

"Loma!" Don Alonso cried.

I held up my hand and stopped the words, whatever they were going to be. "I'll tell him what you did for me. I'll tell him that righteousness still lives in Spain, and that you'll do whatever you can to help the fleeing families. And, later, as you can, you'll aid the ones in exile."

Don Alonso looked thoughtful.

God forgive the lie I was spinning. "Your conversion was good for the Jews, because now we have a powerful ally in you and the descendants Don Fernán will surely have. You'll keep alive our traditions."

Don Alonso nodded, his eyes moist. He would tell the monarchs something about me that would satisfy them.

His grandson was looking sad again. I wanted to give him a gift, too.

Belo or God sent me inspiration. I wet my lips. "Don Fernán, the sort of man you are, your offer of protection . . ." I forced myself to say the next words, because they were true, and he would like them. "... your person—" His handsomeness that lit up the room.

He blushed.

"—I'll treasure the memory forever." I touched his hand. "If I live to be old, I'll think of you and how happy we might have been together."

He bowed.

I curtsied and turned to Don Alonso. "Will you help me again?" I held out the bill of exchange and asked him to use it to pay for an escort for me to Valencia. I doubted that my lawyer, who had done nothing, would come forward with the money he'd been given for this.

He waved away the paper and promised that horses and guards would be at the judería gate in the morning.

Maybe I would see the littles again!

After they left me, I hastened to Don Rodrigo to confirm that I could leave and to thank him for making my stay no worse than it had to be. In parting, I gave him my garnet ring. I might need him again—I hadn't left the city yet!

In fact, I needed him immediately. Thinking more clearly than I was, he assigned a constable to accompany me home.

But I had an errand first. The constable hurried to keep up with me as my feet flew to Hamdun's livery stable, where I found Hamdun gentling an elderly man onto a horse. I smiled, watching his care.

When the old man had set off, he rushed to me. "They let you go?" He didn't ask the next question though I saw it on his face.

"I'm still a Jew." I gave him his backgammon set. "There will be an escort tomorrow morning to take me to Valencia. Can you see me off?"

"I will."

Papá had sold our house to a converso family, friends who hadn't turned against us and had paid almost its worth. When they knew that my presence wouldn't endanger them, they were happy to let me spend the night in my old room and share the bed—after I'd bathed—with their four-year-old daughter. The child's mother, who was more or less my size, gave me a clean gown and shift.

Because of the daughter, I slept more deeply than I had in weeks.

In the morning, Hamdun and I embraced at the judería gate, which hadn't been closed overnight, which I assumed would never be closed again. We both wept. I told him that when I thought of the blessings God had given me, he'd be among the highest.

He said he'd remember me and our adventure forever. "I'm filling my eyes with you to hold in my heart."

Don Rodrigo, who'd decided to come with us, coughed.

We set off at a trot, Don Rodrigo, seven constables, me, and—ominously—a priest. But I turned my thoughts to joy and imagined my reunion with the littles.

We made better time than I thought possible, trotting through most of every day despite the relentless sun. The uniform of the Santa Hermandad warned off bandits. Though the priest rode next to me and regaled me with parables of Christ, he never hectored me.

In towns or villages, we slept in the local monastery or church, with the priest smoothing the way for my presence. In the mornings, we changed horses, so our mounts always started out fresh.

Almighty, please don't bring me all this way just to discover that every ship bearing Jews has sailed.

As the sun set behind us on July 30, ahead, across the plain, Valencia's spires pricked the sky. A pulse hammered in my throat.

We reached the wide Turia River, spanned by a wooden bridge, but we didn't cross. Instead, we galloped on a sandy road along the river. Reeds waved in a marsh to our left. A seagull soared overhead. I smelled salt.

Warehouses rose ahead, their coral-colored bricks deepening in the dusk. The buildings blocked the port, but a ship peeked out at the end of the line of them.

We reached the bay. Five tall ships and a swarm of fishing boats clogged the harbor. On the wharf, the scene was as busy as it had been in Málaga—seafaring folk running errands, climbing sails; laborers bearing chests, cabinets, and bedsteads.

Clusters of people stood, facing the sea, surrounded by sacks of belongings. A baby cried. A child ran circles around a woman.

I dismounted and gave my reins to a constable. Crying "Jento, Todros, Beatriz"—naming all the littles—I ran.

A voice I didn't recognize called, "Don Asher! Your daughter!"

Papá emerged from the farthest group, followed by the rest of my family.

Beatriz reached me first and hugged me. In a month, she'd grown taller than I was. "I told God I wasn't going if you didn't come."

I kissed her cheek. "Here I am."

"I didn't tell Mamá, though."

Todros, usually too old for hugs, hugged me. "Beatriz and I were going to stay together. We had a plan."

Everyone else—my sisters and brothers, but also aunts, uncles, cousins—engulfed me. I was passed from person to person for hugs and kisses.

Even Mamá embraced me. "I had resigned myself to the loss of you, too."

Too?

Vellida squeezed me. "I don't know what I would have done if you didn't come."

Papá held me longest. "Thank God we have you back. We've suffered enough."

Finally, they let me go, and we all looked at each other, smiling.

I remembered Don Rodrigo. "Papá, we have the chief constable to thank for getting me here in time."

Papá took the hint, untied his purse strings, and hurried to Don Rodrigo. Whatever he gave the chief constable must have satisfied him, because he bowed from his saddle and turned his horse. The others followed, their hooves swishing in the sand.

The hermandad was a part of Spain I'd never see again.

I turned back. "Where's Clara? Where are you, my love?"

42

Clara, the shyest child, the one least expecting attention, wouldn't come forward with everyone else. I expected her soft *Here I am.*

Vellida started weeping. Her husband held her.

The littles surrounded me. Papá, Ledicia, and Samuel took turns telling me about the disaster, while tears streamed down my face. The aljama had spent two days outside the town of Motilla del Palancar, because Yose Serrano's wife had begun to give birth—slowly, and the community had agreed to stay together—so everyone waited.

Tragically, both she and the baby had died. Another day was lost holding the funeral and burying her.

Meanwhile, on the day of the burial, Clara, the animal

lover, seemed to have made friends with a shepherd and his flock of sheep and goats. Vellida had been occupied with the twins, and her husband had been sitting with Yose, so neither had paid much attention. It wasn't until dusk that my sister looked for Clara and failed to find her. The shepherd and his flock were gone, too.

They'd spent the next two days searching and had finally found her body, stripped of her silk gown, silver rings, gold necklace, and the amulet I'd given her.

Vellida sobbed. "God forgive me! I didn't watch my child!"

I rubbed her back while my tears continued to flow. If I'd been with them, this wouldn't have happened, because I wouldn't have had children of my own to look after.

Gentle Clara. Had she cried out when the shepherd hurt her? Had he been quick?

After my tears lessened, I thought of Yose Serrano—shame on me. He'd remarry. Maybe he'd remarry me.

Night fell while my family and I were sad together. The wharf activity dropped off, though some sailors continued to work by the light of a full moon.

I asked when they'd reached Valencia, and the answer was three days before today. Papá had paid our departure duties and had organized the purchase of provisions, because we would bring everything with us, including water. An impressive accumulation of sacks, barrels, and jugs stood to the side of all of us, to be carried on board in the morning. We had water; vinegar; wine; hard cheese; honey; dried raisins, figs, and dates; almonds; matzo, because leavened bread would spoil; salted sardines and cod; and beef sausages. There seemed enough to take us to distant Constantinople—or the moon!—if God willed it.

We also had fresh fruit, bread, soft cheese, boiled eggs, cucumbers, onions—to be eaten before they rotted.

"We're spending tonight on the wharf so the ships don't sail off with our belongings, Tía Loma," Beatriz said.

Silly. If the masters decided to leave, none of us could stop them.

"Which is our ship?"

"That one!" Todros pointed. "Isn't she pretty? Ships are girls."

I smiled. We'd have to keep him from climbing the sail ropes.

"Her name is the *Santa Flora*," Jento said. "Papá knows the master."

The *Santa Flora* was bigger than the ship that had taken Belo.

"Will we all go on it?" I said. "The whole aljama?"

"No. We have two ships." Todros pointed to another ship, smaller than ours.

Beatriz said, "Our whole family will go on the *Santa Flora*, and some others will, too. There will be two hundred and eighty-five people on our ship, counting you."

It should have been 286, with Clara.

How would we all fit inside? "We'll be so close, we'll tickle each other."

Hasdai's humming preceded him. He bowed, and I curtsied.

"I'm very glad the Inquisition didn't get you. I've eaten a lot. I eat all the time."

He could have been one of the littles, telling me this triumph.

"I'm happy to hear it." God forgive me, I hoped he wasn't going to be on the same ship with us.

"We're going to be on the same ship. Will you—"

Don't say it!

"—play backgammon with me?"

I smiled. "With pleasure." If the backgammon sets weren't packed away.

"And will you marry me again when we reach Naples?"

He'd said it.

"Let's get there first, God willing, before our parents decide anything."

He nodded and left us.

Bearing a torch, Papá came and took me by the elbow.

The littles tried to follow, but he held up his hand. "You'll have her back soon."

I followed him a few yards down the wharf, away from everyone.

He said, "I think I did everything Belo would have, but he'll tell me if I made mistakes."

He would, if he was alive and in Naples—and if we got there.

"Please hold the torch, Loma."

It wavered in a light wind. "Do you want me to marry Hasdai again?"

He was untying his purse strings. "What? No. Samuel and I can protect you on the ship. You don't need a husband now that the journey is over." He chuckled. "He asked you?"

"Yes. He isn't unkind or foolish, but I don't want to."

"He had you once." Papá kissed my forehead. "He should count himself lucky. Here." He removed a paper from his purse and held it out. "Give me back the torch."

I did and took the paper. "What is it?"

"A letter from your abuelo."

Everything went dark and silent. Then light and noise returned—brighter, more harmonious than before. "He's alive!"

Papá said, "The messenger met us on the road two days after we left home. Read it." He lowered the torch, because moonlight wasn't bright enough to read by.

The paper seemed to unfold itself in my trembling hands. The handwriting wasn't Belo's.

Dear Loma,

Your cousin, Bela's nephew, is writing this, because my fingers cannot yet form letters that anyone can read. These are my words, however. The All Merciful has returned speech to me though my tongue lacks its old nimbleness.

You were wrong and cruel to leave me.

There it was. He hated me.

No explanation excuses it. If the Almighty had taken me, I'd have died cursing you, but now I forgive you and pray you are safe. I remember the night you shielded me from the rain and kept breath in my body. You gave me your pendant, which, perhaps, kept evil away. I haven't yet decided whether or not to give it back to you.

I smiled.

I hope you are not fearing my wrath so much that you have turned the family away from Naples. We must be reunited, because our Messiah is coming soon. It is to

his coming that I attribute my recovery—so that I may
proclaim him with a voice as clear as a golden bell.

King Ferrante has ruled that the Jews of Spain may
settle in his kingdom, for a price, of course. The sum isn't
onerous, and I'll help pay, along with the community here.
If you are not married, though I think you must be, I have
a husband for you: our sailor from Málaga, who has been
studying day and night to become a Jew and has repaid
me a thousand times in good deeds for his theft of our
belongings.

That fellow?
I wished I could tell Hamdun.

He speaks often of your beauty. I believe he began his
conversion for you, and now our law has captured him.
He is a lover of travel. We'll cross the kingdom of Naples
together. Hasten to us!

Devotion to him again, this time with a husband of his
choosing. It would have been of his choosing before, but a
lot had happened since then. I didn't know if I wanted the
fellow, who still had no name.

Commend me to your papá and mamá and your sisters
and brothers. Tell them to be strong, as I know you will be.

Be good as well, and obey your papá.

Belo

Papá said, "A convert with no money?" Of course he'd read the letter. "We can do better." He kissed my forehead again and left me.

Everyone made bedding out of their satchels. My things had been brought in hopes that I would come, but they were already on the ship. Ledicia spared me two of her family's bundles, and I established myself near her. The littles circled me.

Jamila said, "We'll catch you if you try to get away."

I promised not to attempt it.

Ledicia hummed in her high, sweet voice, and I harmonized from my lower, huskier range. The littles piped in. Then voices rose from everywhere on the wharf, adding words, so hum became hymn. We sang for half an hour, until one voice after another fell off, Ledicia's and mine dying last.

Papá woke me at dawn and gave me three chunks of bread and three of cheese, more than I usually ate in the morning. "You may not want to eat once we sail."

I said a hurried blessing and wolfed down my last meal in Spain. My sisters and Samuel were busy with their youngest ones, so I fetched bread and cheese from Aljohar and woke Jento and my older nieces and nephews.

Half an hour later, a man called from the dock, "Come, Jews! Hasten away!"

People hoisted their sacks. The old and the infirm leaned on the healthy. Yose Serrano, carrying his son on his shoulder, stuck out above the rest. Would he be on the same ship as ours?

I kept the littles with our family, though Jamila tried to tug me toward a girl she'd befriended. We wound up in the middle of everyone with our view blocked. I could see only the tops of the three sails.

Finally, we neared the ramp to the ship, and I had a view again. On board, people spread across the ship's deck. Yose Serrano was crossing the ramp to the other ship.

I insisted on escorting each little across ours. "I won't have you falling in and being eaten by a fish."

As soon as we had all boarded, a *thunk* came from behind us, the ramp being returned to wherever it went. The sails flew up, and there was the latest drollery: the center of each sail was embroidered with an enormous scarlet cross, like the uniform of the hermandad's constables.

The deck dipped and rolled. The sails filled. My stomach lurched. The *Santa Flora* was underway.

Without looking back at the shore, I cried, "Farewell, Spain! I won't regret the loss of you."

* * *

The tribulations of the Jews of our aljama didn't end with our departure. Yose Serrano's ship was taken by pirates. Ours was blown north then becalmed. Our food, which I had thought to be more than we could ever eat, ran low. When the winds picked up again, we made for the nearest port and were denied not only entry but also supplies, a villainy that was repeated as we sailed down the coast.

The one great blessing was our ship's master, who was unfailingly kind and made his crew be kind, too. When they had time to fish, the sailors shared their catch with the aljama children. If there had been enough, I don't doubt they would have shared with the adults, too. Unless the seas were very rough, the captain let us be on the deck, rather than crammed together in the hold.

Now, eighteen days later, I sat on a tall coil of rope watching the littles in a game of tag. If I hadn't been exhausted by hunger, I would have joined the chase.

Beatriz left the game and sat by me. "Tía Loma, I'm cold."

The sun was glaring down. A bead of sweat trembled on the tip of my nose. How could she be cold?

Her face was flushed. Fever? Merciful One, where is Your mercy?

The master shouted that we'd dock in Naples in the next hour.

I scrambled up and pulled her up, too. There would be physicians in Naples.

The littles ran to the bow, and we followed them. I stood next to Papá, who was next to the master. Mamá arrived at Beatriz's side and, blessedly, said nothing.

We rounded a mountainous island, near which seven fishing boats bobbed. Jento and Todros wormed their way to me.

Beyond the island, the coast was a thick and wavy green line. The ship angled in. My knees felt spongy, either from fear or weakness.

Jento cried, "Let me see. Can I, Loma?"

"I have no strength to lift you."

Papá managed it and set Jento on his shoulders. Vellida's husband placed Jamila on his shoulders.

The coast grew into a succession of green and rocky low hills. Palm trees sprouted near the water. I saw the straight lines of a city far ahead.

We drew closer, and the shapes sharpened. The city grew and grew. A tiered watchtower made of rose-colored bricks stood in the harbor on a small island.

The master said, "See the New Castle?" He pointed and chuckled. "Not so new anymore."

The castle—cream-colored walls, three towers in the front—was the city's defense against invaders. A crenelated wall faced the sea.

Almighty, let the defense not be against us!

Houses crowded a low hill, their walls creamy, too,

their roofs an orangey brown. I saw cathedrals, but there were always cathedrals. The lines of the buildings were less graceful than at home.

Not home!

"Loma!" Jento extended his hand down to me.

I reached up to clasp it.

A stone pier projected into the bay and made a ninety-degree turn to the left. Steps led down to the water for the convenience of travelers. People stood waiting. In a minute, we'd be able to make them out.

Sounding hoarse, Beatriz said, "You're crying, Tía Loma."

Was I?

Oh! There was Belo on the dock, in gray silk, legs spread, standing without assistance, smiling his most benevolent smile. I kept my eyes on only him and didn't look for the fellow. He was there or he wasn't. I would marry him or I wouldn't. But I would be with Belo again, and I would marry someone.

Bela spoke in my mind: Little fritter, that long-ago Loma had such a happy life in Naples. She had many healthy children, who were her reward for always doing her best.

AUTHOR'S NOTE

The Jews who came from the Iberian Peninsula, which is shared by Spain and Portugal, are called Sephardic. My father's ancestors (and half of mine) were among them. My father was born David Carasso in 1912 in Salonika, Turkey, and was still a baby when the city was annexed by Greece. His family had lived in Salonika for about four hundred years, but his first language was Spanish, or possibly a Jewish variant called Ladino. If my grandfather hadn't emigrated to the United States when my father was very young, he probably would have learned Turkish and other languages, too. The Carassos were all polyglots— speakers of many tongues.

He had a sad childhood. His mother died when he was just a few months old; his father died a few years later; and he was sent to live and grow up at the Hebrew Orphan Asylum in New York City, which is the background for my first historical novel, *Dave at Night*. The orphanage was Jewish, obviously, but not Sephardic, and he lost both his Spanish and a direct connection to his roots, though he knew about them. And he changed his name from Carasso to Carson, to be more American.

Here's a strange anecdote, though: When he was in his sixties, he vacationed with my mother in Spain, where, at a restaurant, my father, who thought he spoke no Spanish, told a waiter, flawlessly in that language, "This gentleman dropped his fork. Please give him another one." My mother's jaw dropped. My father snapped back into the present as if from a dream and had no idea what he'd just said.

I'm an example of the lingering connection that many Sephardic Jews feel to Spain. An uncle knew that our ancestors had gone from Spain to a city in Italy that starts with a *T*. The city was probably either Taranto or Otranto, both of which were at the time in the kingdom of Naples, where Jews were allowed for a while, until they were again forced to leave, in a series of departures that spanned almost fifty years. Loma would have been uprooted again. I predict she weathered this, too, and continued to have her happy ending.

My ancestors went next to Turkey in the Ottoman Empire, where they were welcomed. The immigrants stayed together and built synagogues named after the communities they'd left, which is why my uncle had an inkling. I have no information about their ancestral home in Spain. If any Carassos are reading this and have an idea, I'd love to know!

From childhood on, I've been fascinated by this family history, especially, maybe, because my father never talked about it, out of ignorance or pain. Salonika had been very much a Jewish city until the Holocaust, when its Jews were wiped out.

One of the notions that stayed with me as I wrote this book is that Loma is my own ancestor, a girl with the grit and perseverance to get through terrible times. I believe that all of us, Jewish or not, in ancient or more recent history, have forebears whose survival was uncertain and who struggled and made it against all odds.

On to more general history!

In the Middle Ages, Jewish girls and boys married when they were very young by modern standards. After the expulsion decree was proclaimed, many young women were hastily married off, in hopes of giving them a little protection.

Jewish girls in Spain were more educated than they generally were in the rest of Europe at the time. In well-to-do families that had only daughters, a teacher would be employed to instruct them, but if there were sons—fair or not—they would have the teacher, and the girls would learn from their brothers.

There were slaves in the Middle Ages, and rich Christians, Jews, and Muslims had them. The slave trade in sub-Saharan Africa was just starting in the fifteenth century, so few slaves were black. In Europe, most were Muslims from North Africa, and in North Africa, most were white Christians. Often, slavery was the result of battle, because the defeated were enslaved. Sometimes people were captured in raids along the coast of Spain and North Africa. Occasionally, people actually sold themselves into temporary slavery to pay off a debt. Jews were enslaved, too, but if there was a local Jewish community, the community would buy their freedom if it could afford to. The ransoming of the Jews of Málaga really happened.

Some believe that fewer Jews than Christians caught the plague during the Middle Ages. If that is true, it may have been because the Jews had to live apart, and because washing and bathing were part of Jewish ritual. But no one at the time understood what caused most diseases, including plague, so Christians came up with the explanation that Jews were poisoning their wells and causing the plague on purpose.

Loma's abuelo Joseph Cantala is very loosely based on the historical figure Isaac Abravanel, courtier, financier, and philosopher, who is still renowned for his accomplishments. When he refused to convert, a plot was hatched to steal and forcibly convert his one-year-old grandson. Luckily, the family was warned and the grandson made it out of the country to Portugal.

Belo's great friend, Don Solomon Bohor, is loosely based on Abraham Seneor, who was even closer to the Spanish monarchs than Isaac Abravanel was. Abraham Seneor, who was eighty years old at the time of the expulsion, did convert to Christianity and took the name Fernando Nuñez Coronel.

Historically, Christopher Columbus was in Málaga at the same time as Isaac Abravanel, so I thought it would be cool to have him make an appearance. He did have Jewish financial backers, and he did use Abraham Zacuto's *Almanach Perpetuum* on his voyages.

Gambling was considered a serious crime in the Middle Ages, although many committed it. Sadly, the Spanish Inquisition trial that Pero got caught up in because of his gambling really took place. Several New Christians and Jews were accused of crucifying a Christian boy, known as the Holy Child of La Guardia, and cutting out his heart to use, along with a Communion wafer, in sorcery to kill all Christians by giving them *rabies!* The accused were tortured into confessions, but the confessions, naturally, didn't match up. For example, there were as many confessed locations of the boy's body as there were confessors, and a search for a body was never made. And no child was ever declared missing!

I chose the route to Naples for Loma and her family because that's the way my ancestors went. When the fleeing Jews arrived there, many were sick with plague, as I hint with Beatriz's fever at the end. The refugees infected the local population—which didn't enhance their popularity!

Each of the limited options open to the expelled Jews was perilous. France and England had already expelled their Jews, expulsions that were less significant than the Spanish one only because the Jewish population of those kingdoms was smaller. The Jews who entered landlocked Navarre from Spain were safe for only six years before they were all forced to convert. Those Jews who didn't leave Portugal quickly weren't allowed to leave at all and were forcibly converted. In the next century, however, restrictions were loosened and some left, and many of those returned to Judaism. The people who sailed to North Africa were at risk of piracy and were at the mercy of their ships' masters, some of whom were murderously anti-Semitic. If they reached their destination, they were vulnerable to attack by local tribes. Those who got to the city of Fez were denied entrance for a while because of a famine, but eventually they were allowed in and were permitted to stay.

I read many learned books and articles for *A Ceiling Made of Eggshells*, and you can find a bibliography on my website, www.gailcarsonlevine.com. I'll mention just two here that may interest readers:

Authentic Everyday Dress of the Renaissance: All 154 Plates from the "Trachtenbuch," illustrated by Christoph Weiditz (in the sixteenth century). This may be the first-ever costume book and is certainly one of the earliest. Most of the fashions come from Spain. The drawings are in black and white, but notes tell the colors.

A Drizzle of Honey: The Lives and Recipes of Spain's Secret Jews by David M. Gitlitz and Linda Kay Davidson. The clerks of the Spanish Inquisition recorded everything! The recipes in this cookbook, which I was told about by my cousin Joe Carasso are drawn from ingredients mentioned in Inquisition annals. So far, I've made the vermilioned eggs, though, following family tradition, I cooked the eggs many hours longer than the recipe in the book calls for. The flavor is subtle and interesting.

Here's my cousin's recipe:

COUSIN JOE'S SEPHARDIC EGGS

INGREDIENTS

12 eggs

1 tablespoon of olive oil

3 tablespoons of white vinegar

1 teaspoon of salt

2 teaspoons of white pepper or 1 teaspoon of black
pepper

small bag's worth of onion skins and onion tops
(as many as possible that will fit in the pot) from
brown onions

1 tea bag

1 tablespoon of coffee grinds

Put all the ingredients in a pan that will allow the eggs
to be covered (or nearly covered) with water. Cook on a very
low fire so that the water is simmering for 12 to 24 hours.

Note: Traditionally, this dish was made with just onion
skins. My family added one of either pepper, tea, or coffee.
I use all of them for a richer flavor, but they can be made
with any of them to good effect.

GLOSSARY

abuela: grandmother

abuelo: grandfather

aljama: the Jewish community in a town or village in Spain

bisabuelo: great-grandfather

converso: a convert from Judaism to Christianity after 1391, when many forced baptisms took place

Don: Sir, a title of respect

Doña: Lady, a title of respect

ducat: a gold coin

get: a writ of divorce, the document that finalizes a divorce

hazan: cantor, or singer in Jewish services

hermandad: the local police force

infanta: the daughter of Spanish monarchs

Judaize: to practice Judaism in secret, while pretending to be Christian

judería: the neighborhood where Jews were required to live; the Jewish ghetto

maravedi: silver coins of little value, used mostly in paper transfers of money

New Christian: a converso

Old Christian: someone from a family that was Christian before 1391

reale: a silver coin

sanbenito: a tunic worn by people who had been condemned by the Inquisition

tallit: a prayer shawl worn by men

tevah: the lectern members speak from in the synagogue

tía: aunt

Torah: the first five books of the Hebrew Bible

ACKNOWLEDGMENTS

A Ceiling Made of Eggshells owes a great debt to the kindness and generosity of historians, and, first among them, to Jane S. Gerber, professor emerita at the City University of New York, who guided my reading, answered my many questions, read the manuscript when I finished, and gently let me know where I'd gone astray.

Many thanks also to Teofilo Ruiz, distinguished professor and Robert and Dorothy Wellman Chair in Medieval History, University of California, Los Angeles; to David Gitlitz, professor emeritus, University of Rhode Island; to John Vidmar, OP, associate professor, Providence College; and to Karen E. Carr, retired member of the history department of Portland State University.

Marc D. Angel, rabbi emeritus of Congregation Shearith Israel, has my gratitude for commenting on my manuscript from his wealth of knowledge about Judaism, especially in Iberia. Thanks also to Rabbi Laurie Gold for welcoming me to Temple Beth Elohim in Brewster, New York, my hometown, and answering my questions about Jewish practice.

Thanks to the librarians at the Center for Jewish History and to Amanda (Miryem-Khaye) Seigel and Anne-Marie Belinfante, librarians at the Dorot Jewish Division, the New York Public Library.

Between the tenth and the twelfth centuries, Spanish Jews enjoyed a flowering of poetry in Hebrew. The poems in this book were inspired by *The Penguin Book of Hebrew Verse*, edited by T. Carmi, in which the poems were translated into prose in English. I made them poems again and relied on the chapter "Notes on the Systems of Hebrew Versification," in hopes of attaining a little authenticity. You may notice that one poem is an acrostic on the word *hospitality*, because acrostic poems were common, often on the poet's name.

Writing, at least for me, isn't efficient. The pages I wrote about the crossing to Naples are in the belly of my computer, where they will stay, but I still needed help getting them right before I realized I should cut them. Thanks to Richard Dorfman of New York City's South

Street Seaport Museum and to Charles Bendig, doctoral student in naval archaeology at Texas A&M University. For help with pages I did keep in the book, about medieval wharf activity, I don't have a name to thank, only a Reddit Ask-A-Historian handle: Terminus-trantor.

My cousins Joe Carasso and Lucienne Carasso Bulow astonished me with their reach into the past. Many thanks to Joe for help with astrology and for the hints that led me to Naples as Loma's destination. And to Lucienne for the introduction to Rabbi Angel and for Sephardic music.

From Spain, via phone and Google Translate, thanks to Lola Zueco, Fundación Tarazona Monumental, and to staff at the Judería de Sevilla. Many thanks to my friends Melinda Caro Montanaro and Gabriel Montanaro, for their on-the-ground research and the photos and brochures they brought back from Seville.

Much gratitude to discerning reader Amy Ehrlich for looking at the manuscript in its earliest stages. "Be a novelist!" she said, and I gradually became less timid.

Thanks to Charlotte Lang-Bush for her help, also in the early stages.

Eternal thanks, always, to my editor, Rosemary Brosnan, and to the team at HarperCollins, and to my agent, Ginger Knowlton. You are the most constant, stalwart support a writer could have.

However, despite all the wonderful assistance I had, I'm

sure I made mistakes. If time travel to fifteenth-century Spain were possible, readers—and I—would be amazed at all I got wrong. Many apologies! How I wish we could go back (safely, possibly invisibly) and witness events!

Also by
Gail Carson Levine